In shape, it was almost triangular

A smooth front rose up to an almost comically tiny head, set at the apex of the triangle. The back was a long slope that tapered down to the floor. It appeared to be about six feet long. Four legs were set under it, almost as a kickstand might be set beneath a motorcycle. Two tiny red eyes gleamed above a square snout and a mouth full of needle-tipped, alloy-coated teeth.

Tensely, Brigid breathed, "It's not an animal...it's a droid, a robot."

The mechanoid stood silent for another moment, then its head rose on a segmented metal neck, turning this way and that, as if it was smelling a nonexistent breeze. It took one step, halted, took two more and stopped again. The man continued to walk silently, unaware of the machine stalking him. The metal stalk of its neck abruptly lowered, sinking the head between its dull gray shoulders.

Then it sprang.

Other titles in this series:

James Axler
Outlanders

DEVIL
IN THE
MOON

BOOK I

A GOLD EAGLE BOOK FROM
WORLDWIDE.

TORONTO • NEW YORK • LONDON
AMSTERDAM • PARIS • SYDNEY • HAMBURG
STOCKHOLM • ATHENS • TOKYO • MILAN
MADRID • WARSAW • BUDAPEST • AUCKLAND

First edition May 2002
ISBN 0-373-63834-5

DEVIL IN THE MOON

Special thanks to Mark Ellis for his contribution to the Outlanders concept, developed for Gold Eagle.

DEVIL
IN THE
MOON

The Road to Outlands—
From Secret Government Files to the Future

Almost two hundred years after the global holocaust, Kane, a former Magistrate of Cobaltville, often thought the world had been lucky to survive at all after a nuclear device detonated in the Russian embassy in Washington, D.C. The aftermath— forever known as skydark—reshaped continents and turned civilization into ashes.

Nearly depopulated, America became the Deathlands— poisoned by radiation, home to chaos and mutated life forms. Feudal rule reappeared in the form of baronies, while remote outposts clung to a brutish existence.

What eventually helped shape this wasteland were the redoubts, the secret preholocaust military installations with stores of weapons, and the home of gateways, the locational matter-transfer facilities. Some of the redoubts hid clues that had once fed wild theories of government cover-ups and alien visitations.

Rearmed from redoubt stockpiles, the barons consolidated their power and reclaimed technology for the villes. Their power, supported by some invisible authority, extended beyond their fortified walls to what was now called the Outlands. It was here that the rootstock of humanity survived, living with hellzones and chemical storms, hounded by Magistrates.

In the villes, rigid laws were enforced—to atone for the sins of the past and prepare the way for a better future. That was the barons' public credo and their right-to-rule.

Kane, along with friend and fellow Magistrate Grant, had upheld that claim until a fateful Outlands expedition. A displaced piece of technology…a question to a keeper of the archives…a vague clue about alien masters—and their world shifted radically. Suddenly, Brigid Baptiste, the archivist, faced summary execution, and Grant a quick termination. For Kane there was forgiveness if he pledged his unquestioning allegiance to Baron Cobalt and his unknown masters and abandoned his friends.

But that allegiance would make him support a mysterious and alien power and deny loyalty and friends. Then what else was there?

Kane had been brought up solely to serve the ville. Brigid's only link with her family was her mother's red-gold hair, green eyes and supple form. Grant's clues to his lineage were his ebony skin and powerful physique. But Domi, she of the white hair, was an Outlander pressed into sexual servitude in Cobaltville. She at least knew her roots and was a reminder to the exiles that the outcasts belonged in the human family.

Parents, friends, community—the very rootedness of humanity was denied. With no continuity, there was no forward momentum to the future. And that was the crux—when Kane began to wonder if there *was* a future.

For Kane, it wouldn't do. So the only way was out—way, way out.

After their escape, they found shelter at the forgotten Cerberus redoubt headed by Lakesh, a scientist, Cobaltville's head archivist, and secret opponent of the barons.

With their past turned into a lie, their future threatened, only one thing was left to give meaning to the outcasts. The hunger for freedom, the will to resist the hostile influences. And perhaps, by opposing, end them.

Chapter 1

The Day of the Basilisk dawned with wind, a brief flurry of sleet and the stink of blood. Foxcroft Sanatorium was a place of great beauty, with its high whitewashed walls and meticulously manicured lawns. But the cloud-covered sun shed a ghostly, colorless illumination that painted the grounds in stark contrasts of shadow and light.

The assembly was the greatest of the year since it was the last of the three feast days, the Period of Behavioral Mastery. All who lived within proximity of the sanatorium flocked to wait in murmuring excitement for the basilisks to choose which among the Prey Party would face them in the operating arena.

Mina, her limbs aching and leaden with exhaustion, looked down the slope into the Valley of the Divinely Inspired. People milled around the walls of the sanatorium and jostled one another for seats in the bowl-shaped amphitheater. The opening ceremonies had already been completed. Chief of Staff Eljay and his assistant, Dr. Sardonicus, were already allowing the preliminary sacrifices into the arena, offering up their blood and flesh to the basilisks.

Crouched in a clump of underbrush sprouting between two moss-covered outcroppings, Mina could see quite clearly how the stadium was filled by people whose excited shrieks filled the air.

On one side of the amphitheater, ragged people milled uncertainly through a narrow doorway. Men and women, cripples and the elderly were forced out into the open. One hobbled about with the aid of a crutch. All of them were streaked with blood that trickled from superficial cuts on their arms and legs. The preliminary sacrifices were the Chronics, the habituated respondents, diagnosed by Eljay and Sardonicus as being untreatable.

Trumpets blared discordantly. Mina knew the noise signified nothing, but was meant only to agitate the caged basilisks. When a gate on the opposite wall slid aside, the Chronics cried out and tried to escape back through the door, but they were driven back by the lashing whips in the hands of white-coated attendants. The other gate opened completely, and black-winged shapes lunged through it.

Stimulated by the blaring horns and driven to shrieking madness by the scent of blood, the basilisks swarmed toward the humans. A few of the people tried to hold their ground, while others turned and fled. The basilisks pursued them, alighting on the elderly and the crippled first, slashing at their faces with razor-keen teeth and talons. Instinctively, the creatures sought to put out their eyes, knowing blinded prey was the easiest.

The man with the crutch flailed furiously, using it

as a bludgeon. He managed to hold the basilisks at bay for a few moments until one landed on his head. Dropping the crutch, he tried to protect his eyes. An instant later he went down under a pack of the shrieking creatures.

The audience in the arena shrieked like basilisks themselves.

Mina's stomach lurched with nausea as she watched the black-winged creatures flitting over the eviscerated bodies in the center of the arena. From the grounds outside the amphitheater came the brassy blasting of trumpets.

The basilisks crawling over the bodies of the Chronics lifted their heads, like hounds sniffing the wind for a scent. With a piercing, collective shriek, all of the creatures flung themselves into the air. Like an eruption of smoke, the flock rushed up, drawn toward the noise.

Mina's eyes followed them in their swift flight. She saw the pattern of fields and the thatched huts built along the bank of the river, and wondered if any of the Prey Party had been stupid enough to hide there.

The Valley of the Divinely Inspired was broad and deep, with a sweep of level plain and a belt of thick forest bordering the base of the hills. The branches of the trees glistened with moisture. The sight was stirringly beautiful to Mina, even though she had never left the valley and had no knowledge of another place for comparison.

She shivered in the postdawn chill and peered

through the screen of leaves, hoping to sight fellow members of the Prey Party. She saw no one and she didn't know if that was bad or good. She pushed back her explosion of thick black hair from her face. It was an unruly mass of loose curls, as if only the wind had ever combed it. Her eyes were equally black, with a small red *N* branded between them. She wore a ragged crimson tunic, and her bare arms and legs were almost as brown as the winter grass that eked out an uncertain existence on the face of the ridge.

Mina steadily gulped the cold air, despite the way it burned her lungs. She knew she had been lucky so far in eluding the basilisks. Most of the Prey Party had sought concealment in the trees, hoping the tangle of branches and leaves would provide a protective barrier. Climbing toward the Forbidden Waste was something that didn't occur to the valley-bred.

Faintly, from the direction of the forest belt she heard a high, gargling shriek. It rose to a shrill pitch of agony, then ended abruptly as if a hand were clapped over the shrieker's mouth—or the throat had been torn out by razored talons.

Mina shivered again, rubbing her arms briskly. She wondered who among the Prey Party had fallen under the fangs and claws of the basilisks. Whether it was one of the three thieves, the slacker or the daydreamer, she had no way of knowing. The scream was masculine and she was the only female in the party, the only one diagnosed and branded a nymphomaniac.

She didn't necessarily resent the designation since she really didn't know what the word meant. She did know, however than whenever Chief Eljay needed females for the Prey Parties, he would choose women at random, classify them as nymphomaniacs and have them branded as such.

The pain of the branding iron was intense but brief. However, it angered Mina enough that she was determined to survive the hunt. She had already managed to live through the Day of Tilkut and the Day of Bast. But the Day of the Basilisk was the last one in the cycle and always the worst. Outdistancing a half-starved, mangy bear had been childishly easy for her. Evading a hungry cougar was a bit more dicey but she had accomplished it. Successfully escaping the basilisks was less than a fifty-fifty proposition.

Even as the thought registered, Mina heard a flutter of leathery wings overhead. She stopped breathing instantly. A shadow flitted across the uneven ground in front of her hiding place and circled lazily. She watched the dark outline slide away over the terrain. When she no longer heard the flap and rustle of wings, she cautiously began to breathe again. She felt as if she had held her breath for an eternity.

A series of high-pitched whistling shrieks drew her eyes in the direction of the riverside. Near a cottonwood copse she saw a flock of black shapes held aloft by furiously fluttering wings, dipping and diving, trying to flush their quarry. Mina's throat constricted with horror as the half-naked figure of a man sprang from the shadows between the trees. He ran in long-legged bounds toward the river, and she recognized him as Chez, the youth diagnosed as a chronic slacker.

There was nothing lazy in the way he raced toward the water. His arms and legs pumped furiously but the cloud of winged shapes followed him. From that distance, the basilisks reminded Mina of scraps of dirty cloth, unfolding and folding in the air.

The clot of flying creatures circled, swooped and struck. There was a moment in which the leathery wings engulfed Chez like a black, writhing cloak, but he continued running. Wet crimson gleamed briefly between the wriggling bodies. On the ground before her the dark shadow slipped silently over the ridge face, and she watched the basilisk arrowing toward its brethren.

Mina waited a few seconds more, then slowly backed out of the brush, ignoring the thorns scratching her arms and legs. Bent in a crouch, looking up at the sky every few seconds, she began climbing toward the ridgeline. She had no plan except to reach it and find a hiding a place among the tumbles of stone for the rest of the day. She wished she possessed the courage to climb down the far side of the hill and leave the Valley of the Divinely Inspired entirely. But all that lay there was the Forbidden Waste. No one, not even Chief Eljay or Dr. Sardonicus knew for sure if the waste was finite or stretched out to encompass the entire world.

The old legends about brightly lit cities with shiny, cloud-scraping towers at the edge of the waste had been lost in the stream of time, but leaving the valley was still taboo. The primary reason was simple. The Forbidden Waste ringed the valley like a vast zone of death. The indisputable fact was that people who went out into it didn't return. Starvation, thirst, wild animals worse than basilisks or even demons—people didn't come back from the Forbidden Waste.

Besides, the only reason for even considering leaving the valley was the legend of the city of the flaming bird, the phoenix. Mina had never spoken to anyone who had even glimpsed it from afar and the people of the valley long ago lost faith it even existed. For that matter, they lost faith that anything existed beyond the waste.

According to legend, the world had once been green with pure water and air that smelled good. People lived in the shining, sky-scraping towers and never worried about anything. Despite the manifest silliness of those stories, they were still enthralling, particularly to children. Mina had been one of those children, and her mind still replayed the old fables.

Halfway to the crest of the ridge, she heard a sibilant screech and a shadow swooped down from the sun. Mina dropped flat, banging her elbows painfully on the rock-strewed ground. The clawed tip of a wing passed so close to her head it yanked a clump of hair out of her scalp. She bit back a cry, knowing the basilisk would rise to a soaring spiral, pause, then swoop down again.

Mina lunged forward, dragging her way up the slope, scraping her knees raw and bloodying her knuckles against the sharp rocks. Her heart thudded frantically within the cage of her ribs like a terrified bird. She knew she wouldn't make the top of the ridge before a basilisk would alight on her head and tear first into her eyes, then sink its fangs into her jugular.

A gully seemed to appear out of nowhere, a gash through rock and earth like a knife cut. The edges were hidden by scraggly undergrowth. The lip of the bank was rotten with erosion and it crumbled beneath her weight. She plunged headfirst down the steep incline, but she managed to thrust her arms out in front of her as if she were diving into the river. The gully floor was covered by a carpet of soft, damp loam, so she didn't break any bones.

Still, she landed hard enough to jar the air out of her lungs, and she lay on her stomach, gasping and gagging for a long, panicky moment. Her shoulders ached, and her hands and wrists smarted from impact with the ground. Then she wobbled to her feet and began a scrambling run along the narrow channel, not knowing where she was going but dimly aware the path she followed could lead to only one place—the Forbidden Waste.

However, she had no inclination to climb out. The walls of the ravine provided some protection from the basilisks. They couldn't pursue her in a straight course since their wingspans were greater than the width of the gully. It was an eerie place, a labyrinth beneath ground level, a network of nearly identical paths overhung by roots and tufts of dry grass.

Mina threaded her way through a maze of cracks, slamming her knees and scraping her elbows on outcroppings. Nevertheless she kept running, stumbling and lurching from wall to wall. The farther she sprinted, the more rugged the ground became, scattered with rock formations sprouting from the ground. Every bump struck by a bare foot triggered vibrations of pain through her head. She knew she was leaving a trail a blind Chronic could follow, but it couldn't be helped. The pain of a stitch stabbed along her left side, the muscles of her legs felt as if they were caught in a vise and her vision was shot through with gray specks.

Over the rasp and gasp of her own labored breathing, Mina heard the flapping of wings behind her, then a strident screech of triumphant malice. The skin between her shoulder blades crawled in anticipation of a basilisk alighting there. As she realized the basilisks had found her, all the old feelings of terror she had known as a child returned. The only reason she didn't begin screaming in horror was that she had no breath for it.

A stone turned beneath her foot and she lost her balance, staggering for several yards before she fell heavily. Spitting out bits of dirt and loam, she lifted her head, dragging in great lungfuls of air. Blinking grains of sand from her eyes, she saw she lay in an open space, a crossroads of sort where four paths branched off in different directions in the shape of an X.

Mina struggled to her hands and knees, trying to soften the harsh rasp of respiration. Over her gasps, at the periphery of her hearing, she heard a new sound—a faint, high-pitched whine so distant that she couldn't really be certain she heard it.

Mina began to rise when she felt a tingling, pins-and-needle sensation all over her body, as if she were skirting a low-level electrical field. The tingling became a prickle. The fine hairs all over her body seemed to vibrate, to bristle. The air pulsed like the beating of gigantic, invisible heart. At the very center of the crossroads a hazy, blurred shimmer arose, reminding her of a ripple made by a fish just beneath the surface of the river.

She gazed at it, frozen in place. Particles of dirt lifted from the gully floor, whirling and spinning, growing from a dust devil to a swirling, cylindrical tornado. It glittered as if powdered diamonds were caught within its powerful vortex.

Mina was so entranced she didn't move until the basilisk sank its needle-pointed fangs into the calf of her left leg. Screaming, she rolled onto her back, kicking frantically at the black shape hanging on to her leg by tooth and claw. Its whiplike tail coiled around her ankle, and Hell glared out of the obsidian black eyes.

The basilisk was barely six inches long, though the spread of its talon-tipped wings was more than two feet. Its body was covered by a layer of blue-black overlapping scales, its three-toed hind feet tipped with curving claws. The reptilian head appeared to be little more than a maw full of serrated, razor-keen teeth.

Mina reached for the winged monster, and its fangs crunched into her right ankle, grinding at the bone. Her hands swatted out, closing around its neck. The basilisk opened its mouth to voice a thin scream. Mina yanked her torn leg free, then struck with a balled fist at the devil-beast. Bone snapped, and blood spewed from the creature's maw amid a few fangs, like slivers of ivory.

The basilisk spread its wings and sprang into the air, the whiplike tail lashing and laying open Mina's left calf. She cried out, more in fury than fear or pain. She stumbled erect, turning to run again, then lurched to a clumsy halt. Her cry of anger became a wordless call of wonder.

On the ground rested a shape that resembled a very squat, broad-based pyramid made of smooth, gleaming metal. It appeared to be only one foot in overall width, its height not exceeding ten inches. A waxy, glowing funnel of light fanned up from the metal apex of the pyramid. It looked like a diffused veil of backlit fog, with tiny shimmering stars dancing within it.

As Mina stared, the light expanded into a gushing borealis several feet wide, spreading out over the crossroads. A thready pulse of vibration suddenly tickled her skin, and shadows crawled over the gully walls, moving in fitful jerks and leaps. A faint hint of a breeze brushed her face and ruffled her hair.

Then a yellow nova brilliance erupted from the tip of the pyramid. Mina felt the shock wave slapping her breath painfully back into her lungs, tumbling her off her feet. Her eyes stung fiercely.

Mina cleared her vision with a swipe of her hands. Through the blurred afterimage of the flare, she saw three dark, shadowy shapes shifting in the fan of light. The shadow shapes looked distorted, as if they approached from a great distance, elongated and strangely silhouetted by a sun she couldn't see. The edges of the light seemed to peel back and fragment, and a trio of human figures in black stepped out of nowhere and stood in the crossroads. Behind them, the glowing funnel disappeared back into the small pyramid, as if it were liquid and had been sucked down into the tip.

Shocked into paralysis by the sight, her limbs frozen, her mouth gaping wide, Mina lay in a half-prone position and stared unblinkingly at the three shadow people standing before her. From throat to fingertip to heel, they were clad in one-piece black leathery garments that fitted as tightly as doeskin gloves.

Mina couldn't move, not even when one of the shadow people stepped forward, extending a gloved right hand in a gesture of greeting or help.

Mina looked up at the woman, noting her tall, willowy, athletic figure. A curly mane of red-gold hair spilled over her shoulders and draped her upper back, framing a smoothly sculpted face dusted lightly with freckles across her nose and cheeks. The color of polished emeralds glittered in her big, feline-slanted eyes.

"Hi," said the shadow woman, her lips curving in a smile. "My name is Brigid. I hope we didn't scare you."

Chapter 2

Brigid Baptiste maintained the friendly, nonthreatening smile and kept her hand extended as a gesture of help and to show she was unarmed. The raggedly dressed, blood-streaked girl only gazed up at her through a tangled hayrick of dark hair. Her black eyes bulged with astonishment as if she had never seen either a smile or an open hand before.

A cacophony of piercing, whistling shrieks wafted down from above, interwoven with the flapping of many wings. As if the sound were an electrical current, the dark-haired girl's expression of blank, goggle-eyed shock became one of soul-deep terror. She crawled like a crippled crab toward the nearest gully wall, leaving a crimson trail.

Brigid snapped up her head, squinting momentarily against the glare of the midmorning sun. A swarm of black shapes crossed the blue expanse of sky, reminding her of a flight of arrows arcing through the air. The winged creatures wheeled around, circled for an instant in perfect formation, then darted downward. The beating of a multitude of leathery bat wings sounded like a round of applause made by gloved hands.

"Screamwings," she bit out, taking a hasty back-step, sidling between Kane and Grant. From a sheath at the small of her back, she drew a Sykes-Fairbairn combat stiletto with a six-inch, razor-keen blade.

The two men flexed their right wrists, and with a faint whine of tiny electric motors, actuators popped their Sin Eaters from forearm holsters into their waiting hands. Stripped down to skeletal frames, the Sin Eaters were barely fourteen inches long. The extended magazines held twenty rounds of 9 mm ammo. There was no trigger guard, no fripperies, no wasted inch of design. The Sin Eaters looked exactly like what they were supposed to be—the most wickedly efficient blasters ever made.

The index fingers of the two men hovered over the firing studs of the weapons as the screamwings dived and dipped and banked at such a blurring speed, Grant and Kane couldn't draw a bead on them. They had seen screamwings once before, in the ruins of New-york, and not before or since had they encountered creatures that were such stripped-down, bare-essential predators. Kane remembered Brigid theorizing that the screamwing was a species of raptor that had lost its feathers and regressed to its reptilian roots.

A clot of the creatures described a wide circle around the three standing people, wings slapping, fang-filled mouths emitting little piping shrieks. Grant, Kane and Brigid tried to keep them framed within their fields of vision, but the blinding speed and maneuverability of the monsters made it nearly impossible. A screamwing suddenly broke formation and glided directly toward Brigid, drawn toward her red-gold hair. She slashed out with her knife, and its edge sheared through the creature's scaled torso, slicing it in two with a single upward stroke.

Voicing a thin prolonged scream, it fell amid a thrash of wings and a spray of crimson. Drawn by the sound of pain and scent of blood, the circling screamwings banked sharply and fluttered directly toward the three people.

The Sin Eaters roared deafeningly, the slugs racing upward. Brigid caught a glimpse of the girl clapping her hands over her ears in reaction to the booming reports. Shooting from the hip, Kane and Grant seemed to tear a ragged hole in the clot of screamwings. Scarlet sprinkled down in a warm drizzle, and small bodies thudded to earth all around them. The monsters didn't flee. Instead of being frightened by the carnage done to their flock, they grew even more maddened. The dead and injured creatures were set upon by other members of the swarm.

More and more screamwings lanced across the sky and joined the flock. Black wings beat and thundered in the narrow gorge as the creatures flew in a tightening circle around the three people, like a cyclone cloud with a hollow center. Claws struck out and lashing tails whipped at their eyes.

A screamwing landed on Kane's chest, the curving hind claws trying to secure a grip in the black fabric. The talons didn't penetrate, but he felt the pressure nonetheless. He crushed the creature's skull with a swipe of his blaster's barrel and kicked it away from him. He and Grant continued firing short 3-round bursts. With each shot and dying scream, the outraged survivors shrieked all the louder. Some of them turned on one another to vent their frustrated rage, talons raking raw strips from scaled bodies.

For the next minute, the black winged monsters rained down, fairly carpeting the gully floor with an ankle-deep layer of feebly snapping jaws and thrashing tails.

Then, like a cloud of billowing black smoke, the surviving screamwings broke formation and veered away. They hovered a few seconds, shrieking in frustration, then soared into the sky, the flapping of their wings and keening cries fading. Grant, Brigid and Kane released their pent-up breath in profanity-seasoned exhalations. The men thumbed the magazine toggle release of their guns and ejected the empty clips. They inserted fresh ones in the swift, smooth motions that came of long practice.

Kicking a small scaled body out of his way, Grant stepped toward the girl. She cringed against the gully wall, a high-pitched wail of fright starting up her throat.

"Don't go any closer," Brigid said. "You're scaring her."

Grant's face contorted in a frown, but he came to a halt. A down-sweeping mustache showed jet-black against the coffee-brown of his skin. Beneath it, his heavy-jawed face was set in a perpetual scowl. Brigid knew that the more Grant frowned, the more satisfied he felt with circumstances.

The sprinkling of gray in his close-cropped black hair gave him a patrician air, like somebody's curmudgeonly but essentially good-hearted uncle. A very broad-shouldered and thick-chested man, Grant stood four inches over six feet and he realized to the girl cowering in the gully, he had to have seemed like a ferocious giant, a bit of Outland folklore come to life.

"We just rescued her," he said, trying to soften his lion's growl of a voice to a soothing rumble. "She should be grateful, not scared."

"Three people popping out of nowhere is a little more nerve-racking than screamwings," Kane commented. "At least she knew what to expect from screamwings."

"I wonder where she's from?" said Brigid. "She's just a kid."

Kane glanced warily to the sky before he gave the girl a swift visual inspection. She looked very short, smaller even than Domi, which made her very small indeed. She was thin, her dark hair a wild and unruly mass of curls. Her big eyes were black and very bright. She wore only a ragged, threadbare shift of faded red, and her bare arms and legs were scratched and streaked with blood. There was a small red letter *N* emblazoned on her forehead, the result he guessed of a painful application of a branding iron. He couldn't help but wince.

Brigid noticed the reaction and repressed a smile. She had seen Kane stroll through a corpse-littered battlefield with apparently no more concern than if he had been walking into the cafeteria at Cerberus redoubt. But a girl-child bearing the scar of a branding iron made him flinch. She knew, however, that Kane either felt something or he didn't, and in contrast to Grant, his high-planed face always mirrored his emotions.

An inch over six feet, every line of Kane's rangy, flat-muscled body was hard and stripped of excess flesh. His thick, dark hair was tousled, sun-touched highlights showing at the temples and nape. His left hand impatiently pushed through a curving comma that fell over his forehead. He kept his right hand, his gun hand, free.

A faint scar showed like a white thread against the sun-bronzed skin of his left cheek. His piercing eyes were gray with enough blue in them so the color resembled the high sky at sunset. The alert, wary look in them never changed. But Brigid had seen his face transformed into something ugly and terrible by rage, and then changed to the epitome of warm humor when he laughed.

It was difficult for Brigid to keep in mind that Grant and Kane had spent their entire adult lives as killers—superbly trained and conditioned Magistrates, not only bearing the legal license to deal death, but the spiritual sanction, as well. Both men had been through the dehumanizing cruelty of Magistrate training yet had somehow, almost miraculously, managed to retain their humanity. But vestiges of their Mag years still lurked close to the surface, particularly in threatening situations. In those instances, their destructive ruthlessness could be frightening to anyone. Although she owed both men her life, she still occasionally feared them, so she wasn't surprised by the girl's reaction.

Kneeling in front of her, Brigid said softly, "We mean you no harm."

After waiting a moment and receiving only a wild and wide-eyed stare in response, Brigid added, "There's nothing to be afraid of."

Kane snorted in derision. "Oh, yeah. Three people in black long johns appear out of thin air and start blowing the shit out of a screamwing flock. It probably happens every day in these parts."

Brigid cast him an over-the-shoulder glance that glittered with irritation. "Sarcasm isn't going to help us find out where we are."

"I thought we knew," Grant said gruffly. "Around Sedona, about 115 miles north of Phoenix, Arizona."

"If we're going to chart the parallax points," Brigid replied dryly, "we need to be a little more precise than that."

A faint aspirated whisper issued from the girl's lips. "City..."

Brigid returned her attention to the girl, watching as her mouth worked as she tried to form words. "City of...flaming bird?"

Kane started to step closer, caught the flash of fear in the girl's eyes and stayed motionless. "What did she say?"

"I think she's trying to ask us a question," replied Brigid.

She smiled encouragingly. "What do you want to say?"

The girl coughed. "Are you from the city of the flaming bird? The Phoenix?"

Grant muttered, "At least she speaks English, not some Outland dialect."

Kane nodded in agreement. It was always a chancy business communicating with outlanders, particularly in settlements that had been isolated since the nuke-caust of two centuries. He retained vividly unpleasant memories of the Outland settlement known as Boon-town and the debased form of French spoken by its inhabitants. In the Outlands, people were divided into small, regional clans, communications with other groups stifled, education impeded and rivalries bred. The internecine struggles in the Outlands were not only condoned by the baronies but encouraged.

Outlanders, or anyone who chose to live outside ville society or had that fate chosen for them, were of a breed born into a raw, wild world, accustomed to living on the edge of death. Grim necessity had taught them the skills to survive, even thrive in the postnuke environment. They may have been the great-great-great-grandchildren of civilized men and women, but they had no choice but to embrace lives of semibarbarism.

The people who lived outside the direct influence of the villes, who worked the farms, toiled in the fields or simply roamed from place to place, were reviled and hated. No one worried about an outlander or even cared. They were the outcasts of the new feudalism, the cheap, expendable labor force, even the cannon fodder when circumstances warranted. In return, they feared and hated anyone not of their clan. The girl's terror was fueled by generations of conditioning.

"Are you asking if we come from Phoenix?" Brigid asked the girl.

Eyes still wide, she bobbed her head.

"No, we're not from there. We're from much farther away. Where are you from?"

The girl made a vague gesture with one hand, toward the top of the gully.

"That doesn't tell us much," Brigid replied with a smile. "But first things first...do you have a name?"

She bobbed her head again but said nothing more. Brigid waited, then asked, "Will you tell it to me?"

The girl's response was a thready whisper so faint Brigid had to lean forward to hear her. "My name is Mina."

"Mina...that's a pretty name. Short for Wilhelmina?"

Mina's shoulders moved up and down in a shrug, indicating that she didn't know and the subject didn't hold much interest for her. Brigid stood and extended her hand. "You look like you could use some medical attention…maybe even some food and water."

Tentatively, as if she half suspected Brigid's black-gloved fingers were really venomous serpents in disguise, Mina took her hand and allowed the red-haired woman to help her up. Brigid nodded toward the two men. "You already know my name…this is Kane and Grant."

Mina's dark eyes shifted from Kane to Grant and back to Brigid again. "Did you come across the Forbidden Waste?" Her voice was stronger now, a little more sure but still quavering with an undercurrent of fear.

"No," Kane answered. "Like Brigid said, we came from far away."

Brigid glanced toward him. "Let me have the medical kit."

After a second or two of hesitation, Kane pushed his Sin Eater back into its forearm holster where a locking solenoid caught it with a purposeful click. The sensitive wrist actuators ignored all movements except the one that indicated the gun should be unholstered. It was a completely automatic, almost unconscious pattern practiced by both Grant and Kane.

Reaching around behind him, Kane removed a small canvas case from the small of his back. Velcro tabs crackled as they were pulled away. He handed it to Brigid, who opened the flap and swiftly took out a variety of first-aid items. Mina stood stock-still, not even whimpering as she was treated for her injuries. After the blood was swabbed away, Brigid saw most of the girl's wounds were superficial, shallow abrasions and scratches. She sprayed them with disinfectant from a small aerosol can.

Kane silently admired the deft ease with which Brigid Baptiste tended to Mina. Reba DeFore, Cerberus redoubt's resident medic, had done a good job teaching her field medicine. But Brigid's bedside manner was superior to that of her mentor's, which, Kane reminded himself, wouldn't be too difficult. A swampie's bedside manner was probably more sympathetic than DeFore's.

Only the teeth- and claw-inflicted lacerations on Mina's leg required bandaging, and that also came from a can. Brigid used another aerosol spray to apply a liquid bandage. A skinlike thin layer of film formed over the cuts along her leg. The substance contained nutrients and antibiotics, and would be absorbed by the body as the injuries healed.

While she finished treating the girl, Grant and Kane watched the skies warily. They could still hear the whistling shrieks of the screamwing horde, but they were very distant and didn't increase in volume.

Kane glanced down at the front of his one-piece garment where the screamwing had clung. The black fabric showed only a faint series of vertical lines where the winged monster's talons had scored.

"Saved again by this stuff," he observed wryly. "One of the few things we owe Sindri."

Grant grunted. "I still put more faith in our body armor. At least it's bulletproof."

Kane didn't dispute him, but not because he necessarily agreed with him. They'd argued the issue to death over the past couple of months, ever since they absconded with the suits from Sindri's stronghold on Thunder Isle.

Kane had christened the garments shadow suits, and though they didn't appear as if they could offer protection from a mosquito bite, they had learned the suits were impervious to most wavelengths of radiation. The suits were climate controlled for environments up to highs of 150 degrees and as cold as minus ten degrees Fahrenheit. Microfilaments controlled the internal temperature.

The manufacturing technique known in predark days as electrospin lacing electrically charged the polymer particles to form a dense web of formfitting fibers. Composed of a complicated weave of spider silk, Monocrys and Spectra fabrics, the garments were essentially a single crystal metallic microfiber with a very dense molecular structure. The outer Monocrys sheathing went opaque when exposed to radiation, and the Kevlar and Spectra layers provided protection against blunt trauma. The fibers were embedded with enzymes and other catalysts that broke down all toxic and infectious agents on contact. The spider silk allowed flexibility, but it traded protection from firearms for freedom of movement.

Regardless, Kane still felt the shadow suits were

superior to the polycarbonate Magistrate armor if for nothing else than their internal subsystems. Built around nanotechnologies, the microelectromechanical systems combined computers with tiny semiconductor chips. The nanotechnology reduced the size of the electronic components to one-millionth of a meter, roughly ten times the size of an atom. The inner layer was lined by carbon nanotubes only a nanometer wide, rolled up sheets of graphite with a tensile strength greater than steel. The suits were almost impossible to tear, but a heavy enough caliber bullet could penetrate them and, unlike the Mag body armor, wouldn't redistribute the kinetic shock.

Brigid began returning the medical instruments to the case. "You'll heal just fine, Mina. But I'd recommend you stay away from screamwings for the next few days."

Mina didn't smile. She gazed at Brigid with something akin to adoration shining in her dark eyes. Suddenly, she blurted, "Basilisks."

Brigid regarded her curiously. "Basilisks? What about them?"

Mina gestured to the many scaled and winged bodies on the gully floor. "We call them basilisks. Or Chief Eljay does. He's says they're therapeutic."

Brigid's eyebrows rose toward her hairline, then knitted at the bridge of her nose. "We call them screamwings. They're a species of mutant and not a common one. The last thing they are is therapeutic. Basilisks are creatures of mythology, whose eyes could cause plants to wither, trees to die and birds to fall from the air.''

Mina seemed uninterested in the differences between the two monsters. ''Chief Eljay says they do that. That's why the Forbidden Waste is still a waste.''

Brigid started to speak but Kane interjected impatiently, ''She doesn't need a lesson in mythology, Baptiste.''

Brigid gave him a glance of green glittering irritation. She wasn't quite the ambulatory encyclopedia she appeared to be, since most of her seemingly limitless supply of knowledge was due to her eidetic memory, but her apparent familiarity with an astounding variety of topics never failed to impress—and occasionally irritate—Kane.

Addressing Mina, Kane asked, ''Who is Chief Eljay?''

''He's the chief of staff, the head therapist of the sanatorium and the leader of the entire valley.'' Mina paused, nibbled her underlip nervously and added breathlessly, ''The Valley of the Divinely Inspired.''

''The *what* inspired?'' demanded Grant. ''What's so divine about your valley?''

Brigid smiled ruefully. ''Divinely inspired is an old euphemism for insanity.''

Turning to the girl she asked, ''Where's the sanatorium?''

Mina gestured to the top of the gully walls. ''Over that way, but I can't go back until sundown when the

Day of the Basilisk is over. If Chief of Staff Eljay or Dr. Sardonicus sees me, they'll only set the basilisks on me again. And if they see you, they'll put you in the group therapy circle.'' She did a poor job of suppressing a shudder at the concept.

"Should we assume that's something we should avoid?" Kane asked wryly.

Mina nodded vehemently, her curls bouncing. "Oh, yes."

"Tell you what," said Brigid. "Let's sit here for a little while and you can tell us all about the valley, the sanatorium."

She glanced at Grant and Kane. "I need to run a systems diagnostic on the interphaser before we power it up again."

Mina stared searchingly at the little gleaming pyramid on the ground. "Did that machine bring you here? From where? Will you tell me where you come from? Will you tell me what it's like on the other side of the Forbidden Waste? Do you need machines to cross it? Will you tell me?" She spoke in little eager bursts.

Kane smiled at the sudden onslaught of questions. Now that her fears had been allayed, the girl's curiosity consumed her. "Sure, we will. But I don't know if it'll be half as interesting as your story."

Chapter 3

In actuality, Mina's story was not as strange as many the three travelers had heard over the past couple of years. Still and all, it did have the cachet of being unique.

Speaking in breathless, fitful bursts, Mina told them how the little valley had sheltered Foxcroft Sanatorium during the days of doom and the endless night that followed. Therefore, according to Chief of Staff Eljay, it had been spared because it was divine.

Eljay himself was the latest in a long line of chiefs of staff, and when the caduceus stick was passed, so was the oral history of Foxcroft and the valley. In the beforetime, Foxcroft had served as an exclusive sanctuary for those seeking divine enlightenment. The institution was dedicated to helping people find it, either through long immersions in ice-cold water, applications of electrical current or prolonged periods of isolation in darkened, cushioned chambers. Others were encouraged to wear the jackets of clarity, canvas garments with sleeves that could be tied together in the back. Allegedly, wearing the jacket while residing in a cushioned chamber helped facilitate clear and untroubled thought patterns.

The people who lived in and around the sanatorium now were descendants of those touched by the divine spirit. Of course, a caste system that clearly delineated the different degrees of "touchiness" was practiced.

Occupying the top rung of the valley's social ladder was, of course, the chief of staff and his immediate associates, including Dr. Sardonicus. Everyone else was spread out over the lower rungs in no particular order. A person's position could change, either for good or ill, depending on the completion of various therapies or the whims of Eljay.

During the Period of Behavioral Mastery, a person could climb up a rung if he or she was successful in the task facilitation. Essentially that meant the person survived the Day of Tilkut, the Day of Bast and the Day of the Basilisk. That was the main task—to facilitate staying alive while a member of a Prey Party.

Shortly before the three feast days that comprised the Period of Behavioral Mastery, Dr. Sardonicus reviewed the charts in order to identify the incurables, known as the Chronics, the drains on the valley's resources. Curiously, every year Sardonicus managed to find an even dozen.

The males were generally designated as slackers or self-medicators and literally branded as such. Sardonicus was less creative with the female Chronics. Invariably they were classified as nymphomaniacs and branded with a small *N*.

Mina touched the red scar on her forehead. "That's what I am."

Brigid looked up from where she crouched over the metal-walled pyramid. Her eyes glittered with emerald sparks of anger and repugnance. "Do you even know what a nymphomaniac is?"

Mina frowned thoughtfully for a moment, then shook her head. "I don't even know what slacker or self-medicator is."

Brigid cast a questioning glance toward Kane and Grant. When she saw that Kane was trying very hard to repress a grin, she demanded, "You think this is funny?"

He unsuccessfully turned a chuckle into a self-conscious cough. "You've got to admit there's a comical element to her story."

Brigid straightened, saying darkly, "Let yourself be branded—maybe with the letter *A*—and we'll see how long you laugh."

Taking a deep, calming breath, she declared, "It's pretty obvious how a deranged society like hers got started."

Without waiting for anyone to ask, Brigid said matter-of-factly, "Foxcroft was more than likely a private institution that catered to wealthy predarkers with a host of problems—psychological, mental, substance abuse, you name it. Since we're pretty close to Sedona which was something of a New Age Mecca before the nukecaust, this institution was probably only one of many like it in the area.

"The original staff of the sanatorium and the patients had no choice but to band together for common cause. Over the course of the last couple of centuries, a society based on psychological jargon and methodology evolved. It was the only thing the people here had to use as a template. They obviously have no idea of the true meanings of the terminology or the therapies.''

Grant knuckled his chin contemplatively. ''What the hell did they use for food?''

''This valley was apparently isolated enough so it was spared the most acute effects of the nukecaust,'' Brigid answered. ''I wouldn't be a bit surprised to learn the institution was always self-sufficient with its own generators and vegetable gardens.''

Kane looked at the girl. ''That's how it weathered skydark. Does any of that sound familiar to you, Mina?''

She blinked in consternation. ''I don't understand…what is nukecaust and skydark?''

Kane frowned at the girl, but Brigid nodded as if her reply were expected and completely satisfactory. ''That pretty much supports my theory. She and her people have been cut off from the outside world since the nukecaust. They never heard the common terms for the holocaust and the nuclear winter.''

''That's not necessarily a bad thing,'' Grant observed bleakly. ''They probably never heard of the barons or the hybrids or the Mags, either. Sometimes I wish I never heard of those things myself. If you've got nothing for comparison, there never was an ending, only a new beginning.''

The new beginning for humankind occurred on January 20, 2001. The detonation of a nuclear warhead in the basement of the Russian embassy in Washington, D.C., began a chain reaction, like the toppling of a row of dominoes. By the end of that day, the world in general and America in particular had been transformed into the Deathlands, a shockscape of ruined nature, a hell on earth. Massive quantities of pulverized rubble were propelled into the atmosphere, clogging the sky for a generation, blanketing all of Earth in a thick cloud of radioactive dust, ash, debris, smoke and fallout. The entire atmosphere of the planet had been hideously polluted by the nukecaust, producing all manners of deadly side effects in the ecosphere.

In the century following the atomic megacull, what was left of the world was filled with savage beasts and even more savage men. They lived beyond any concept of law or morality, and made pacts to achieve power, regardless of how pointless an exercise it seemed.

Survivors and descendants of survivors tried to build enclaves of civilization around which a new human society could rally, but there were only so many people in the world, and few of these made either good pioneers or settlers.

It was far easier to wander, to lead the lives of nomads and scavengers, digging out Stockpiles, caches of tools, weapons and technology laid down by the predark government as part of the Continuity of Government program and building a power base on what was salvaged. The scavengers knew that true wealth did not lie in property or even the accruing of material possessions. Those were only tools, the means to an end. They knew the true end lay in personal power. In order to gain it, the market value of power was measured in human blood—those who shed it and those who were more than willing to spill it.

Some of the scavengers used what they had found in the Stockpiles and elsewhere to carve out fiefdoms, tiny islands of law and order amid a sea of anarchy and chaos. These people formed ruling hierarchies, and they spread out across the ruined face of America. They profited from the near annihilation of the human race, enjoying benefits and personal power that otherwise would have been denied them if the nukecaust had not happened.

The hierarchies spread out and divided the country into little territories, much like old Europe, which had been ruled by princes and barons. The different hierarchies conquered territories, and claimed them as baronies. Although these territories offered a certain amount of sanctuary from the crazed anarchy of outlying regions, most of them offered little freedom.

After two centuries, the lingering effects of the nukecaust were more subtle, an underlying texture to a world struggling to heal itself, but the side effects of the war still let themselves be known from time to time, like a grim reminder to humanity to never take the permanence of Earth for granted again.

One of the worst and most frequent side effects were chem storms, showers of acid-tainted rain that could scorch the flesh off any mammal caught in the open. They were lingering examples of the freakish weather effects common after the holocaust and the nuclear winter. Chem storms were dangerous partly because of their intensity, but mainly because of the acids, heavy metals and other chemical compounds that fell with the rain, so corrosive it could strip flesh from bone in less than a minute.

Fortunately, chem storms were no longer as frequent as they had been even a century before, but there were still a number of places where the geological or meteorological effects of the nukecaust prevented a full recovery. These regions were called hellzones, areas that not even the passage of time could cleanse of hideous, invisible plagues.

Eyeing Mina closely, Kane again wondered just how many truly human people populated the world, but there was no way to hazard an accurate guess. Even the intelligence-gathering apparatus of the Magistrate Divisions in the villes could not learn with any certainty about what was transpiring beyond the continental boundaries. Radio waves wouldn't reach across the sea because lingering radiation and atmospheric disturbances disrupted shortwave carrier bands.

As far as he was concerned, learning that Mina

came from an isolated settlement with little or no knowledge about the world outside her valley wasn't much of a surprise. There were probably hundreds of similar pockets scattered all over the world with no conception of the nukecaust or skydark or that life was more than a rudimentary struggle for survival.

As if she picked up on his thoughts, Brigid commented, "This valley would make for a pretty interesting sociological study."

"Yeah," Grant rumbled, "if we were on an academic field trip. Which we aren't."

Kane nodded in agreement. "Mapping out the parallax points is our mission objective. We're bench markers this time around, not anthropologists."

Mina murmured something inaudible.

"What was that?" Brigid asked.

Hesitantly, Mina asked, "Is that why you're here? To mark benches? There are a lot of benches at the sanatorium."

"That's good to know," Grant said blandly.

Mina's gaze fastened onto the gleaming pyramid. Her eyes narrowed in suspicion and she said quietly, "No, you're not here for benches."

Grant, Brigid and Kane exchanged swift glances. When neither of the men showed an inclination to respond to the girl's observation, Brigid said, "We're explorers, more or less."

A corner of Kane's mouth quirked in a smile. "Sometimes we're more, sometimes we're less."

Facing Brigid, he said, "We killed a wagload of

screamwings and helped Mina here rise in status in her settlement. That's enough extracurricular activities for one morning. Recalibrate the interphaser and take us home.''

Brigid's back stiffened at the peremptory tone as she returned her attention to the little metal pyramid. Kneeling beside it, she touched a seam on its alloyed skin and from the base a keypad slid out. With an index finger she began tapping in a numerical sequence.

Mina watched the process with undisguised fascination. Haltingly, she asked, ''What is that?''

''You wouldn't understand,'' Grant retorted brusquely. ''I'm not sure if I do.''

''Tell me anyway. Please.''

Distractedly, Brigid replied, ''It's a miniature quantum phase transducer, version two.''

Kane threw the girl a wry smile. ''Is that of any use to you?''

Mina's lips stirred as she silently repeated Brigid's description beneath her breath. Kane was tempted to dismiss the girl's attempt to learn something new as a wasted effort. His many years as a Magistrate had conditioned him to view all outlanders as inferiors, human due only to an accident of biology.

Both he and Grant had come to realize otherwise since joining the group of exiles at the Cerberus redoubt. They had no choice, particularly since a fellow exile and one of their most trusted allies was Domi, a feral Outland girl. Besides, all those at Cerberus were outlanders now in that they could never return to their lives in the villes. So, if living as an outlander made them citizens in the kingdom of the disenfranchised, then Domi and even Mina were heirs to the throne.

At a wordless utterance of irritation from Brigid, Kane turned toward her. "What is it?"

She shook her head in angry frustration, red-gold tresses tumbling. "A glitch in the telemetric software. The satellite uplink is lost. I'm going to have to reboot the entire system."

Grant glanced at the sky, as if he expected to see the Comsat hovering overhead within reach. "Are you sure it's not the satellite?"

"No, I'm not. I'm only sure the uplink is off-line."

It had been a source of wonder to all of them when they learned that the Cerberus redoubt was linked with two of the very few functional satellites still in orbit, a Vela reconnaissance model and a Comsat. They were aware that in predark years the upper reaches of the planet's atmosphere had been clogged with orbiting satellites, many of them designed for spying and surveillance purposes. According to legend, there were settlements of a kind in space, even on the moon itself. They were just as aware that ville doctrines claimed that all satellites were now simply free-floating scrap metal. For a time, in the decades following skydark, pieces of them fell, flaming and disintegrating, once their orbits decayed.

"That means Cerberus isn't receiving our biolink

transponder telemetry, either,'' Brigid continued. ''I hope nobody panics.''

All the Cerberus personnel carried subcutaneous transponders. They were nonharmful radioactive chemicals that fit themselves into the human body and allowed the monitoring of heart rates, brain-wave patterns and blood counts. Based on organic nanotechnology developed by the Totality Concept's Overproject Excalibur, the transponders fed information through the Comsat relay satellite when personnel were out in the field. The computer systems recorded every byte of data sent to the Comsat and directed it to the redoubt's hidden antenna array. Sophisticated scanning filters combed through the telemetry using special human biological encoding.

''How long do you figure this will take?'' Kane asked, trying not to sound either impatient or anxious.

''Hard to say,'' Brigid answered. ''I'll have to run a system diagnostic. If I find any errors, they'll have to be fixed before we can risk phasing back to Cerberus.''

So far, the interphaser hadn't materialized them either in a lake or an ocean or underground, a possibility that Kane privately feared. He knew an analogical computer was built into the interphaser to automatically select a vortex point above solid ground.

Kane, Grant and Brigid had endured weeks of hard training in the use of the interphaser on short hops, selecting vortex points near the redoubt—or at least, near in the sense that if they couldn't make the return trip through a quantum channel they could conceivably walk back to the installation. Only recently had they begun making jumps farther and farther afield from Cerberus.

Grant grunted as if unconcerned. "We've got food and water to last a couple of days...longer if we ration it." He cut his eyes toward Mina. "Unless, of course, your settlement offers us hospitality."

Mina's expression twisted into a mask of horror. She gestured wildly, as if trying to wave away the very concept. "No, *no!* No outsiders have ever come into the valley! There are strict rules about it. No one leaves, no one ever comes in! Chief of staff says we can't risk contamination!"

Not looking up from the keypad, Brigid asked, "Does he mean radiation contamination or cultural contamination?"

Mina replied, "Don't know, don't care. Just contamination."

His curiosity piqued by the girl's extreme reaction, Kane asked nonchalantly, "What'll happen if we just show up at the institute asking to use the toilet?"

Mina didn't answer, but a basso profundo voice wafted down from above. "You'll be flushed."

Chapter 4

Grant, Brigid and Kane reacted with varying degrees of surprise. Brigid didn't shift position, but only looked up toward the overhanging lip of the gully. Her face remained expressionless. During her years as an archivist in Cobaltville's Historical Division, Brigid had perfected a poker face. Because historians were always watched, it didn't do for them to show emotional reaction to a scrap of knowledge that may have escaped the censor's notice.

Grant's and Kane's responses were not so restrained. The tiny electric motors in their power holsters droned faintly, and Sin Eaters slapped into the men's waiting hands. The barrels pointed up at the group of people arrayed in a line on the ravine's edge. There were eight of them, a mixture of men and women. All of them stared down, some whispering among themselves. Their faces registered dismay.

The women wore loose-fitting, sleeveless shifts. Strange little white caps were perched on their heads. Brigid had seen pix of similar headgear in books. They were nurse's caps, or imitations of them.

All of the men were attired in baggy overalls of a material resembling denim. They were uniformly bald, their heads obviously shaved. Three of the men carried long bars of dark iron, filed to a point at one end and hooked at the other. The bars were some four feet long, an inch in diameter, a combination of bludgeon and skewer.

"Sec men," Grant muttered in weary exasperation, employing the old postskydark euphemism for security forces.

Mina bleated in fear and dropped to her knees, head bowed. Kane scanned the men's faces, wondering which one had spoken in such a deep voice. His eyes swept over them, then tracked back to a face that showed an expression the exact opposite of dismay.

Although he was attired in the same baggy denim overalls, his bony frame was stretched at least six and a half feet from the soles of his feet to his bald pate. The overalls fit poorly; they drooped on his skinny body like rags on a wire hanger. He couldn't have topped the scales at more than 150.

His pale blue eyes, however, were alert and intelligent. His nose was hooked, his jaw prominent, almost prognathous. His face bore a design in black paint, meant to represent a pair of scalloped wings sweeping up from the corners of his eyes and almost meeting in the center of his forehead. Kane assumed the artwork had something to do with the Day of the Basilisk.

At the moment, the bottom half of the man's face was split by a wide grin that displayed two rows of exceptionally white, exceptionally pointed teeth. The light glanced off them, and an involuntary shudder went through Kane's body. The man's teeth were made of burnished steel.

For a moment Kane couldn't understand what the man found so amusing that he continued to grin. He came to the realization he couldn't help it—two puckered scars curved up from the corners of his lips, disappearing into the folds of his cheeks. The man's mouth had been sliced, stitched and fixed in a permanent macabre grin. The scars were old, so the disfigurement had happened a long time ago.

Behind him he heard Brigid murmur, "Dr. Sardonicus, I presume."

The grinning man heard her and bowed his head in her direction. "Quite so. I'm happy to learn that our little Mina has filled you in about our valley. Did she also happen to mention that outlanders are not permitted here?"

"She might have made some sort of reference to it," Grant said blandly.

Sardonicus bestowed a slit-eyed stare on the pistol in Grant's hand. "I thought I heard gunfire, and I must admit that's a sound I never thought to hear again." He paused and added genially, "But the spice of new experiences is the sauce in the feast of life, wouldn't you say?"

When he didn't receive an answer, Sardonicus barked, "Mina! To me. Groundskeeper Hogan, give her a lift."

Without hesitation, the girl rose to her feet and

stepped beneath the lip of the gully. A man lowered his iron bar so Mina could grasp the hooked end. He pulled her effortlessly up to the ridge. He was big, his bare arms rippling with overdeveloped muscles. He kept his eyes fixed on Grant's face during the entire process. His mouth twitched in a slight sneer of superiority.

When Mina stood between Sardonicus and Hogan, the grinning man asked, "May I have your names?"

Kane waggled the barrel of his Sin Eater negligently. "No need. We won't be here long enough to establish any kind of familiarity."

"I beg to differ." Sardonicus turned toward Mina. "Do you know who they are, child?"

Obediently, the girl pointed to the three people one at a time, reciting their names in turn. "Grant. Brigid. Kane."

Sardonicus nodded. "Ah. And how did Grant, Brigid and Kane come to be here?"

Mina shook her head. "I don't really know, Doctor. I think it has something to do with that little metal thing on the ground over there."

Sardonicus squinted in Brigid's direction, apparently not in the least interested in the litter of screamwing corpses. "Ah," he said again. "And what is that little metal thing on the ground over there?"

"Brigid called it a quantum interphase transducer, version two." Mina repeated Brigid's words crisply, imitating even her pronunciation.

It was impossible for Dr. Sardonicus to frown, but his arched eyebrows curved down to the bridge of his prominent nose, lending him the resemblance of a hawk in a high state of consternation. "Gibberish."

Brigid slowly climbed to her feet, standing over the pyramid. Kane could faintly hear it ticking through the reboot process. "It's a machine that helps us to travel from place to place," Brigid said with studied calm. "It harnesses vortex points, natural earth energies, to open portals between hyperspatial channels. That's a very oversimplified explanation, but you get the general idea."

Sardonicus stared at her unblinkingly, his grin frozen, his teeth glinting. He seemed to be trying to figure if Brigid was mocking him or just dissembling. Neither Grant nor Kane blamed him for his momentary loss of words. Kane in particular retained vivid memories of the time, nearly two years ago, when the operational theory of the prototype interphaser had been first explained to him by its creator, Mohandas Lakesh Singh.

One of the brilliant minds of the twentieth century, Lakesh was more than 250 years old. He had spent a century and a half of those years in cryogenic stasis, and after his resurrection some fifty years before, he had undergone several operations to further prolong his life. Neither his resuscitation or the reconstructive surgeries had been performed out of Samaritan impulses. His life and health had been prolonged so he could serve the Program of Unification and the continent-spanning network of baronies.

The interphaser was Lakesh's latest creation, actually a newer version that evolved from the Totality Concept's Project Cerberus. Utilizing bits of preexisting technology, the aim of Project Cerberus was essentially converting matter to energy and back again to matter. The entire principle behind matter transmission was that everything organic and inorganic could be reduced to encoded information. The primary stumbling block to actually moving the principle from the theoretical to the practical was the sheer quantity of information that had to be transmitted, received and reconstituted without making any errors in the decoding.

Scientists labored over a way to make this possible for nearly fifty years, financed by black funds funneled from other government projects.

Project Cerberus, like all the other Totality Concept researches, was classified above top secret. A few high government officials knew it existed, as did members of the Joint Chiefs of Staff of the military. The secrecy was believed to be more than important; it was considered to be almost a religion.

The matter transmitter had other, less destructive applications, as well. Given wide use, it could eliminate inefficient transportation systems and be used for space exploration and colonizing planets in the solar system without the time- and money-consuming efforts to build spaceships.

However, matter transmission had been found to be absolutely impossible to achieve by the employment of Einsteinian physics. Only quantum physics, coupled with quantum mechanics, had made it work beyond a couple of prototypes that transported steel balls only a few feet across a room. But even those crude early models could not have functioned at all without the basic components that preexisted the Totality Concept.

Mohandas Lakesh Singh, the project's overseer, experienced the epiphany and made that breakthrough. Armed with this knowledge, under Lakesh's guidance the quantum interphase mat-trans inducers opened a rift in the hyperdimensional quantum stream, between a relativistic here and there. The Cerberus technology did more than beam matter from one spot in linear space to another. It reduced organic and inorganic material to digital information and transmitted it along hyperdimensional pathways on a carrier wave.

In 1989, Lakesh himself had been the first successful long-distance matter transfer of a human subject, traveling a hundred yards from a prototype gateway chamber to a receiving booth. That initial success was replicated many times, and with the replication came the modifications and improvements of the quantum interphase mat-trans inducers, reaching the point where they were manufactured in modular form.

The latest modification was a miniaturized version of a mat-trans unit, employing much of the same hardware and operating principles. The gateways functioned by tapping into the quantum stream, the invisible pathways that crisscrossed outside perceived physical space and terminating in worm holes. The interphaser interacted with the energy within a naturally occurring vortex and caused a temporary overlapping of two dimensions. The vortex then became an intersection point, a discontinuous quantum jump, beyond relativistic space-time.

According to Lakesh, evidence indicated there were many vortex nodes, centers of intense energy, located in the same proximity on each of the planets of the solar system, and those points correlated to vortex centers on Earth. The power points of the planet, places that naturally generated specific types of energy, possessed both positive and projective frequencies, and others were negative and receptive. He referred to the positive energy as *prana,* which was an old Sanskrit term meaning "the world soul." Lakesh was sure some ancient peoples were aware of these symmetrical geo-energies and constructed monuments over the vortex points in order to manipulate them. He suspected the knowledge was suppressed over the centuries. Kane had no reason to doubt the suppression of such knowledge, even if he was skeptical of everything else.

Sardonicus squared his skinny shoulders and announced in his deep voice, "I really don't think I believe you."

"I really don't think I give much of a shit whether you do or not," Kane retorted indifferently. "We ar-

rived here while Mina was being attacked by
screamwings—the basilisks. She survived your little
test, so take her back to the institute and leave us
alone. We'll be out of sight and out of mind soon
enough.''

Murmuring passed among the people again.
''You're very wrong, Kane,'' Sardonicus declared.

Kane cocked his head quizzically. ''Which part?''

''You did the exact opposite of saving this girl's
life. In actual fact, you've caused it to be forfeit. By
interfering with the therapy, you've triggered in her a
dissocial reaction. It was her responsibility to survive
or not. Since you took that away from her, she now
lacks a sense of responsibility to the community and
can't be allowed to return.''

Grant's eyes narrowed, his index finger hovering
over the trigger stud of his pistol. ''I hope that doesn't
mean what I think it means.''

Sardonicus replied, ''You hope in vain. Groundskeeper Hogan—''

The big man who had lifted Mina out of the gully
instantly placed the sharpened end of his iron rod
against the girl's neck. The point depressed the flesh
at the hinge of her jaw, right above her carotid artery.

Mina's eyelids fluttered for an instant, like the
wings of a panicked butterfly, but she didn't otherwise move. She stood motionless, not even appearing
to breathe.

''However,'' Sardonicus continued, ''additional
therapy sessions might reverse her affliction...on the

condition you come with me to the sanatorium willingly.''

''Let me guess the rest,'' Brigid intoned with cold sarcasm. ''If we don't come with you willingly, you'll kill her right here and now.''

Sardonicus's grin seemed to widen, his teeth flashing like a pair of polished saw blades. ''Exactly.''

''If you do kill her right here and now,'' grated Kane, ''I'll damn sure do the same to you.''

Sardonicus sniffed disdainfully. ''Classic aggressive personality with underlying sociopathic behavior models. Surely you realize that she'll be just as dead as I will be. Do you think that will be an equitable exchange—my death for hers?''

''Why do you want us to go with you?'' Grant demanded hotly.

''Chain-of-command protocols,'' Sardonicus replied smoothly. ''It's the purview of Chief of Staff Eljay to decide what's to be done with interlopers—not that he's ever been faced with such a situation.''

The timbre of the man's voice changed subtly, but Kane caught the edge of resentment in his words nevertheless. He stored the observation away in case it could come in useful.

''And,'' Sardonicus went on, ''since you're not rag-assed wanderers, he may decide it's in the best interests of the valley if you join the community.''

A chuckle lurked at the back of his throat as he added, ''Providing you pass the entrance exams.''

Cold fingers of dread caressed the base of Kane's

spine and tickled the back of his neck. Sardonicus stopped trying to stifle his chuckle and threw back his head and laughed. His eyes shone brightly. Kane recognized the quality of the laugh and the light burning in Dr. Sardonicus's eyes. They were those of a madman. He knew with a grim certainty that the man's threat to kill Mina was not an empty bluff, regardless if it meant his death, as well.

Inhaling deeply through his nostrils, Kane turned slightly so he could read the expressions on his friends' faces. Unsurprisingly, they were inscrutable. Grant's face in particular was as immobile as if it were carved out of mahogany.

"Are you going to leave this up to me?" he asked irritably from one side of his mouth.

Neither Brigid nor Grant responded for a long tick of time. Then Brigid took a step forward. "All right, Doctor. Stop the posturing. We'll go with you."

Hogan still kept the point of his iron rod pressed against Mina's neck. Sardonicus quirked questioning eyebrows at Kane and Grant. Slowly, the two men lowered their weapons. Just as slowly and deliberately, Hogan removed the metal skewer from the girl's throat.

Sardonicus uttered a strange sobbing sound that Kane interpreted as a laugh of relieved triumph. He spoke to the other men in the group, and they bent over, extending the iron bars down into the gully, hooked ends foremost.

Kane and Grant pushed their Sin Eaters back in the

forearm holsters. Kane waved Brigid forward. "Ladies and decision makers first."

As Brigid reached for the hook, Sardonicus snapped, "Bring your mechanism."

Without even an instant of hesitation, Brigid shot back, "You don't want me to do that…not unless you want your precious valley contaminated."

Sardonicus narrowed his eyes to suspicious slits, but he didn't interrupt as Brigid went on, "The interphaser emits radioactive particles. They're deadly. Your water and crops will be poisoned and so will your people."

She ran a careless hand over the front of her shadow suit. "This material protects us from the radiation."

Sardonicus flicked his gaze from Brigid to the ticking pyramid as he pondered whether to believe her. Brigid tossed back her mane of hair in a careless gesture. "I'll bring it along if you insist, but it'll be a damn shame to toxify the Valley of the Divinely Inspired after it managed to survive the days of doom and the endless nights."

Sardonicus jerked slightly in reaction to her words. "Leave it, then. If Chief Eljay wants to see it, he can send somebody back for it."

Kane hid a smile of admiration as Brigid grasped the hook and was levered out of the gully. A couple of years before she wouldn't have been capable of lying so easily or convincingly. But, he reflected, she'd learned how to do it the hard way.

It required two men and two rods to lift Kane out of the X-shaped depression in the earth. When Grant's turn came, only Hogan reached down with his hooked bar. He smiled challengingly into Grant's upturned face. Grant tipped the scales at around 230 pounds and glared up into Hogan's eyes, silently daring him to try to lift him by himself.

Hogan took the dare. Muscles swelled and bulged along his arms as he began raising Grant to the over-hanging ridge. Although the man tried hard not to allow the exertion to show on his face, little veins stood out in relief on his shaved temples. Grant noted it with a certain amount of satisfaction, but he continued to maintain his neutral expression.

When they were all atop the ridge, Sardonicus held out his hands toward Kane and Grant. "Your weapons."

The two men didn't move for a moment. Hogan swiftly placed the sharpened tip of his bar against Brigid's throat, just above the high collar of her garment. Kane quashed the surge of anger. "This is getting old," he muttered, then unbuckled the straps and peeled back the Velcro tabs of his holster.

Brigid didn't look afraid, only exceptionally annoyed. Kane remembered how she had once wryly referred to herself as "Brigid Baptiste, girl hostage."

Grant removed his gun and they draped their holsters over the outstretched arms of Sardonicus. The grinning man nodded approvingly. "Very cooperative, very encouraging. I may have been too hasty in my initial diagnosis. There may be hope for you after all.''

He turned and marched down the slope, toward a distant collection of buildings. The three captives were bracketed by men holding the metal bars like spears. Kane doubted the filed-down points could penetrate their shadow suits, but the impacts of the stabbing thrusts would at the very least knock the wind out of them. And their heads were unprotected.

As they were herded along, Kane said softly to Brigid, ''Looks like you'll get in some anthropological fieldwork after all, Baptiste.''

She smiled ruefully. ''Isn't it funny how it always seems to work out that way.''

Chapter 5

Dr. Sardonicus whispered instructions to a young woman, and she glanced once at the three strangers before loping down the hillside. She ran quickly toward the distant collection of buildings.

Kane, Brigid and Grant were nudged down the ridge by their warders. Groundskeeper Hogan seemed to pay a lot of attention to Grant, poking him frequently in the small of the back with the point of his iron bar. Grant's jaw muscles bunched as he clenched his teeth, but he otherwise pretended that Hogan's prodding meant less than the buzz of an insect.

Once the group reached the base of the slope, the footing became more secure, the terrain less rugged and rocky. Sardonicus and Mina took the lead, striding along purposefully hand in hand. The girl did not so much as glance over her shoulder at the three people who had saved her from the screamwings. Kane wasn't angry about her sudden disinterest in them, but he was a little disgusted.

People in the isolated settlements lived in insular worlds, a universe completely separated from the rest of the continent, and the inhabitants of the valley were no different. Their world was the Valley of the Divinely Inspired, and changes, rebuilding processes, old and new barons were of absolutely no interest and in effect didn't exist for them. Theirs was a microcosmic kingdom, and anyone desiring to live among them had to think like them, believe like them and be like them.

The group of people walked across a meadow green with rich grass. Cattle grazed inside split-rail fences. Cultivated fields made a patchwork pattern over the terrain. Flagstone footpaths wound through a park of sorts with manicured lawns, neatly trimmed hedgerows and shade trees. Near the riverbank were benches, just as Mina had said, and even food stalls.

Brigid, Grant and Kane were struck by the overall cleanliness of the valley. They saw no litter anywhere, and all the shrubbery and undergrowth was trimmed neatly back. Almost all of the Outland settlements they had ever visited were little more than squalid collections of ramshackle dwellings and open, stinking cesspits. There was usually no discernible difference between a settlement's living areas and its garbage dump.

Grant muttered, "This isn't your typical Outland ville."

Kane grunted. "Yeah. It doesn't smell like shit, for one thing."

One of their guards overheard and favored Kane with a smoldering glare of anger. Kane met the glare with an expression of wide-eyed innocence. When the man turned around, Brigid whispered, "Let's try something different this time around—let's not make them mad enough kill us until we've gotten some information.''

Although Brigid's tone was icy, the corners of her mouth twitched as if she were trying to repress a smile, despite the tension of the situation. Kane only chuckled, not in the least offended by her rebuke.

For a long time at the beginning of their relationship, it was very difficult for Kane and Brigid not to give offense to each other. Both people were gifted in his or her own way. Most of what was important to people in the twenty-second century came easily to Kane—survival skills, prevailing in the face of adversity and cunning against enemies. But he could also be reckless, high-strung to the point of instability and given to fits of rage.

Brigid, on the other hand, was compulsively tidy and ordered, with a brilliant analytical mind. However, her clinical nature, the cool scientific detachment upon which she prided herself, sometimes blocked an understanding of the obvious human factor in any given situation. Regardless of their contrasting personalities, Kane and Brigid worked very well as a team, playing on each other's strengths rather than compounding their individual weaknesses.

As they approached the white walls of the sanatorium, people came out of an open courtyard to mill around and stare at them in wide-eyed wonder. They pointed and whispered at the procession. The citizenry, although simply dressed, had a well-scrubbed appearance. However, all the men, women and children seemed subdued.

The sanatorium was a sprawling complex, very clean and dignified. Dr. Sardonicus led them through a breezeway and into a circular open area. Stadium-style seats sloped symmetrically upward from all directions like an amphitheater. The floor was of sand, and it showed dark, wet stains in places. Two heavy-barred metal doors faced each other at opposite ends of the amphitheater. From behind one of them came a high-pitched chittering and the leathery rustle of wings.

A great bloated frog of a man was seated in the first row. A contingent of armed guards stood around him in a semicircle. Unlike all the other males they had seen so far, this man had hair, long, thin and silver streaked and parted in the middle. It framed a chubby-cheeked face with pendulous lips between the splayed nostrils of a spatulate nose. He breathed through his partially open nose, little bubbles of saliva forming and popping continuously on his fat lower lip. He was dressed in a shapeless white gown, and even his strangely small hands were encased in white gloves. When he caught sight of the group entering the amphitheater, he perched a pair of gold-framed pince-nez on the bridge of his nose.

Sardonicus gestured sharply behind him, and two of the overalled men crossed their metal bars in front of Brigid, Kane and Grant, forcing them to halt. He led Mina to the froglike man where they conferred in hushed, hurried whispers for several moments. The white-gowned man poked and picked at the blasters and power holsters with only a mild interest.

"This looks like an operating theater with the roof removed," Brigid said quietly.

"Would a sanatorium have something like that?" Grant asked.

She shrugged. "If the place was licensed to perform surgery, I suppose so."

She started to say more, but the white-gowned man lifted a wooden staff and pointed it toward them. The end bore a stylized design of two snakes intertwined, with their heads facing each other. Over his shoulder, Sardonicus declared, "Chief of Staff Eljay will see you now."

The three captives walked toward him, coming to a halt when he gestured with the caduceus again. The white-gowned man was seated in a such a way they had to look up to him. It was an old psychological ploy intended to intimidate, and none of them were fooled by it.

Without preamble, Eljay asked, "What are you doing in our valley?" His voice was resonant, but not particularly deep.

Brigid spoke before her companions could come up with responses. "We were simply trying to leave when the good doctor insisted we come with him."

"Standard procedure," Eljay responded flatly. He pursed his wet, fleshy lips as if he tasted something sour. "But that wasn't the question, and you didn't give me an answer. Should I repeat it, or rephrase it?''

Grant made a low rumbling noise deep in his chest. He could be theatrical when it suited his purposes. Now he stared unblinkingly into the face of Chief of Staff Eljay and announced, ''We come as friends or we come as enemies. The choice is yours.'' He used his Mag voice, an old trick he used to establish authority .

Eljay didn't appear to be impressed. ''You didn't come across the Waste.''

''That's true,'' Brigid replied matter-of-factly, then fell silent.

Eljay eyed them all critically, as though he found something in their appearance or manner substandard. His next question surprised and confused them all. ''Are you familiar with the practice of distributive analysis?''

Before any of them could so much as shake their heads, Eljay said crisply, ''It's a question-and-answer technique. The queries are directed by the psychotherapist along the lines suggested by the patient's symptoms, problems, attitudes and fantasies. You apparently are fantasizing that you're in charge here. That shows a cognitive disorder. The only way it can be effectively treated is if you cooperate with me.''

''Is that what's going on here?'' Kane ventured. ''A therapy session?''

Eljay regarded him bleakly. ''Everything in the Valley of the Divinely Inspired revolves around therapy, young man. That's how we have survived and thrived. That's why we have no dysfunctional citizens among us. In order for me to provide both a diagnosis and prognosis for you three, you must cooperate.''

Kane stopped short of rolling his eyes skyward, but Grant snorted derisively.

Brigid interposed, ''We're here under duress, through coercion. Therefore, due to those circumstances, any diagnosis you'd make would be highly questionable as to its accuracy.''

For the first time Eljay showed an emotion other than disapproval. His pendulous lips creased in a cold smile. ''A very good point. However, I can change the circumstances by permitting you to be admitted for elective observation and treatment.''

Brigid matched his frosty smile. ''Isn't forcing us to participate in an *elective* program something of a contradiction?'' Her emphasis on the word *elective* fairly dripped with sarcasm.

Eljay seated his pince-nez more firmly on his nose and blinked at her over the frames. ''It's a form of counterinvestment, I must admit. However, I'd had good luck with it in the past. For example—'' he pointed the caduceus toward Sardonicus ''—the doctor here once suffered from hebephrenia, a variety of schizophrenia marked by exceptionally foolish behavior and compulsive laughter. He laughed all the time and even thought it would be a joke to replace his bad teeth with steel ones. A very wasteful undertaking.''

"And it hurt like hell, too," Sardonicus said flatly.

Eljay didn't appear to have heard him. "Ordinary therapies only exacerbated the problem. He just laughed during the sessions, a very disquieting outcome. So I applied counterinvestment to his condition. If he was compelled to laugh at everything yet constantly trying not to, I determined the best course of treatment was to make it easier for him."

Lifting an index finger to the corners of his mouth, Eljay made two sharp, upcurving motions. "I gave him a perpetual grin. After the surgery, the acute symptomology all but disappeared...didn't it, Doctor?"

Sardonics dipped his shaved head in a short bow. "It did indeed. I find very little worth laughing about now."

Kane murmured, "I can't imagine why."

Eljay swept the snake-decorated staff to encompass the ampitheater. "So, if I force you three interlopers to undergo elective therapies, you'll be able to face your disorders and become valuable members of our community."

Affecting a bored, almost detached tone, Brigid Baptiste asked, "What do you propose as the first step in counterinvestment therapy?"

Eljay pursed his lips again as if pondering the matter. "I should say an object lesson would be the most beneficial. Psychodrama will allow you to gain insight and render you more tractable and cooperative."

"What the hell is pyschodrama?" Grant demanded.

Eljay's head swiveled toward him, eyes flicking up and down his body in swift appraisal. "Essentially, patients assume roles that provide them with the opportunity to act out their internal conflicts and reveal repressed material. I'd judge you have a severe problem dealing with authority figures. Therefore, one of my staff—oh, let us say Groundskeeper Hogan—will assume an authoritarian role. You will then act out your resentment. By working together, you will eventually come to terms with your problem."

He paused, smiled slyly, and added, "If you survive the first session, that is."

"You're talking trial by combat," Brigid snapped angrily. "A gladiatorial contest."

Eljay shrugged as if the matter were of little importance. "What were the gladiatorial games of ancient Rome but elaborately staged psychodramas?"

Kane cleared his throat. "If Grant survives, what's the payoff…besides his life?"

"All of you will be allowed to remain here as patients. Who knows, perhaps as your therapy progresses you might even become valued members of the sanatorium's staff…like good Dr. Sardonicus."

Grant glared at Eljay from beneath his furrowed brow. "Let me get this straight," he growled. "If I fight and win, that'll make us worthy to stay here and undergo even more therapies?"

Eljay nodded. "That is so."

In a remarkably gentle tone, Kane inquired, "Wouldn't it be easier and a lot more efficient to just—and it's a wild concept, I know—let us go back to where we came from?"

Eljay's response was short and brooked no debate. "No."

As if his one-word reply were a signal, two of the men suddenly placed the points of their metal bars against the backs of Kane's and Brigid's heads, right where their necks joined with their skulls. Kane winced at the painful pressure, knowing that the sharpened tip could easily pierce flesh and muscle and continue into the base of his brain. He and Brigid might not die due to the injuries, but they would probably wish they had.

Grant's lips drew back from his teeth in a silent snarl. He took a step toward the man behind Brigid, but Hogan blocked his way, laying the point of his iron rod lightly against his chest. Grant reached up to knock the shaft aside, but subsided when he saw Brigid stiffen at the increased pressure on the back of her neck. She didn't cry out but only because she clamped her lips tightly together. For a long, stretched-out moment the tableau held.

"Your choice," Eljay said diffidently as if he were fast losing interest in the situation.

In a studiedly nonchalant voice, Kane said, "Grant, do as he says. Just take care of that asshole fast so we can get back home in time for supper. I'm getting hungry."

Staring steadily into Hogan's eyes, Grant rumbled menacingly, "Sounds like a plan."

Grant stood aside as Kane and Brigid were marched out of the arena and into the seats. They sat on the benches with the two men still standing behind them, iron spears poised to thrust into their brains. Mina and Sardonicus joined Chief of Staff Eljay, sitting on either side of him. Eljay fondled Mina's leg absently as people filed into the stadium, taking seats all around. The crowd watched Grant in silence. They didn't seem anxious to watch the impending combat nor did they seem disturbed by the prospect. The attitude seemed to be one of performing a duty.

Hogan gestured to one of them guarding Chief of Staff Eljay. The man flung his sharpened iron bar, and Hogan caught it deftly. Putting his own weapon on the ground, he held the length of metal in front of him at arm's length, hands gripping either end. Gazing at Grant, he methodically began to exert pressure on the bar. His facial expression didn't change even as the muscles in his arms, chest and forearms bulged and bunched. With a faint creak, the bar slowly bent into a U shape. He flung it at Grant's feet.

"I can do the same to you," Hogan said grimly. He didn't even appear to be breathing hard.

Grant eyed the bar dispassionately. He picked up the rod, looked at it with only mild interest, secured a tight grasp on each end, then began to straighten it. It required every iota of strength in his upper body and all his concentration to keep the exertion from showing on his face. When he had bent the bar more or less straight again, he placed the sharpened end in the ground and leaned on the crooked end as if it were a cane. A few appreciative laughs came from the spectators.

"What are the rules?" Grant asked.

Hogan grunted as if Grant's question were extraordinarily naive. He stooped over as if to pick up his iron bar, then dug his fingers into the sand and flung a handful into Grant's face. "There are no rules."

Chapter 6

Grant spit and sputtered, his eyes stinging. Instinctively, he whipped up the iron rod and blocked a vicious swipe from the hooked end of Hogan's bar. Metal clanged loudly, and the impact sent painful shivers up and down Grant's arm.

He backpedaled rapidly, trying to clear his vision with frantic wipes of his fingers. He caught a blurred glimpse of Hogan thrusting swordlike with his weapon toward his face.

Grant parried as Hogan moved in with speed amazing for a man of his bulk. He swung, thrust and slashed, using both ends of his bar. The hook grazed the side of Grant's head and tore out a few gray-sprinkled kinks.

Grant cursed and tried to go on the offensive, but his eyes leaked tears. All he could do was parry Hogan's blows as he backed toward the curving walls. Sparks danced and flew, and the steady clanging of iron against iron filled the amphitheater.

Hogan broke off the attack and stepped away, spinning and whirling his metal rod as if it weighed no more than a hollow reed. Grant backed away, keeping his eyes on the man's feet. The whirling piece of metal hummed through the air in a blurry circle. He knew better than to stare at it, because the spinning motion induced a mild hypnotic effect.

The spectators didn't cheer the display of skill. Anger grew within Grant. No matter the euphemism Chief of Staff Eljay applied to the ordeal, it was still bread and circuses for the masses. He knew that in the wild old preunification days, a number of self-styled barons set up gladiatorial games, most of them using murky old traditions about the survival of the fittest for justification. Despite all their other flaws—and they were almost countless—the oligarchy of the nine barons had put a stop to that kind of organized barbarism.

In a low, grim voice, Grant intoned, "Hogan, as a general rule I win games like this. And as a general rule, the losers always die. You really don't want me to prove that to you."

Hogan uttered a barking laugh of contempt. He sidled forward, feinting with the spear point toward Grant's face in short little jabs. As he recoiled, the man spun the rod and hooked Grant's ankle. He jerked, and, arms windmilling, Grant slammed heavily onto his back. Only the loose sand kept the wind from being knocked out of him.

He rolled frantically to the right as Hogan stabbed down. The point bit deeply into the ground, the sharpened tip scraping along the side of Grant's face, nicking his earlobe. He kept rolling, but Hogan didn't pursue him.

Dizzy, spitting out grit, Grant got to his hands and knees. He saw Hogan strutting in a lordly fashion a few feet away. He whirled his bar over his head as he played the crowd, face split in a silent laugh. Grant mopped blood from the side of his neck and felt just a little sick. The man was toying with him, intending to humiliate him before killing him. The anger that had been growing within Grant suddenly burst in a wild flame of rage.

Muscles coiling, he sprang to his feet and bounded toward his adversary, his iron bar held before him like a sword. Hogan pivoted to meet him, and the two lengths of thick metal collided with an unmusical clang.

Hogan took the offensive again, crowding Grant with a flurry of thrusts, strokes and feints. He was tireless. On he came, on and on, forcing Grant away from the wall and into the center of the arena. Grant kept retreating. It was all he could do, all he could manage, the only way to stay alive. He began to feel a tinge of fear replacing the fury.

Reversing his bar, Grant lunged forward in a bull-like rush, trying to impale his opponent. It was his personal philosophy—strike fast, strike once, then get the hell clear. Hogan sidestepped swiftly and tried to trip him with the hook as he rushed past. Grant managed to leap over it, but the toe of his boot caught in the curve of metal and he staggered, off balance for a moment.

He heeled around, blocking a blow from Hogan

that would have split open his skull. His adversary
seemed to know that his body was protected, so he
concentrated his attack on his head.

Grant moved carefully backward, seeking to get his
back to the wall again, but before he could get in
position, Hogan bounded forward, hammering away
with his iron bar in a never-ending flurry of deadly
strokes.

Grant parried and blocked with his rod, not having
the chance to strike a blow himself. His lungs felt like
balloons filled with dry ice, and his muscles quivered
and spasmed. It occurred to him that the man was not
human, that he was made of the same stuff as his
weapon—iron.

Grant had fought hand to hand in a lot of places.
He'd learned from Mag trainers, Pit carjackers and
even a few cornered outlanders. Always he had come
out the victor in one-on-one combat. Now he wondered if had met his match at last.

Putting his back to the wall, Grant did the only
thing that occurred to him. Using the wall as a spring-
board, he tucked his head against his chest, dropped
his bar and dived forward. He heard a lethal blow
whisper over his head, brushing the back of his skull,
then he cannonballed his entire weight into Hogan's
midsection.

The man staggered, but he didn't fall even as Grant
sought to drag him down. His knee came up hard
against Grant's forehead and, at the same time, the

point of the rod in his right hand stabbed down at his upper back.

Grant gritted his teeth, feeling the sharp point slam between his shoulder blades. Only the tough fabric prevented it from impaling him. Getting his legs under him, he secured a grip on Hogan's thighs and wrenched upward, lifting him completely off his feet, then dumping him onto his back. Air left his lungs in an agonized grunt.

Grant grappled with the man, locking Hogan's right wrist under his left arm and heaving up on it with all his upper-body strength, trying to get him to drop his weapon even if it meant breaking his arm at the elbow. Hogan cried out in pain and jacked up a knee, seeking to pound Grant's testicles, but he shifted so it impacted painfully on his upper thigh.

Grant maintained the pressure on the captured arm, but the man's grip on the iron shaft didn't loosen. Hogan swung at his adversary's face with a knotted fist. Grant shifted position and took the blow on his shoulder. Hogan pounded his fists into Grant's midsection, sending waves of pain-induced nausea through him.

The man heaved his body back and forth, throwing himself from side to side as he fought to wriggle out of Grant's hold. His fingers finally opened and the metal rod slipped from his hand. Face contorted in a bare-toothed snarl, Hogan levered up from the waist and head-butted Grant on the underside of his chin.

Little multicolored pinwheels spiraled behind Grant's eyes.

Even as Grant fell over, he twisted and closed a leg-scissors lock around Hogan's neck. He heaved violently, seeking to drive the crown of the man's head into the ground. Hogan dug his toes into the sand. Grant stopped trying to throw him. He applied more pressure, devoting all of the strength in his powerful leg muscles into choking the life out of his opponent. Knots, lumps and ropes of sinew rippled along his massive legs.

A drawn-out, gagging gasp burst from Hogan as he clawed frantically at Grant's boots, then grasped his ankles and tried to wrench them apart. When that failed, he swatted out for his rod but it was far out of his reach.

Grant continued the compressing, strangling pressure. Hogan's eyes distended, his tongue slowly protruded and his face darkened. Grant groped for his own weapon, found it and jabbed at Hogan's face. The man squirmed violently backward, squeezing out between Grant's locked legs. The tip of the metal bar split the man's skin between his eyes, and he was immediately blinded by a flood of blood.

Hogan roared hoarsely in pain and outrage. With a surge of maddened strength, he fought his way out of the scissors lock and got to his feet.

The groundskeeper stumbled backward on rubbery legs, swiping at the flow of wet scarlet pouring over his eyes. He bellowed a few unintelligible words, but

Grant knew it wasn't a cry of surrender. He surprised and impressed Grant with his fortitude.

Hogan cleared his vision with furious swipes with the heels of both hands, then rushed forward. Grant twisted on his knees, planting the hooked end of his bar firmly in the sand, inclining the point toward the rushing groundskeeper. He heard Eljay yell Hogan's name, but before the man could respond, the sharpened end impaled the man just below the rib cage.

So furious was his rush that the pointed tip plunged through his torso and burst through his back in a spray of crimson droplets. Hogan kept lunging, bowling Grant over and staggering half a score of feet onward. Only slamming into the arena wall kept him from falling.

Grant leaped to his feet, half expecting Eljay to send a swarm of guards into the amphitheater to avenge their champion. But Hogan stayed on his feet. He turned to face Grant, actually flashing him a grin with red-filmed teeth. He fingered the bar transfixing him like a pin through a butterfly. He looked at it as if it were some new article of clothing he had been coaxed into wearing and only now realized it was uncomfortable.

He walked toward Grant, making odd noises in his throat. The crowd was completely silent as they watched Hogan stroll about impaled by the iron bar. No one made an effort to help him, to speak to him, to pull out the bar in his guts.

Trembling with fatigue, Grant watched him, knowing the man was hemorrhaging internally. He felt a quiver of pity for Hogan, but he had warned him up front. He brushed blood from the side of his face and kept his eyes on Hogan as his stride began to falter. He stumbled like a broken wind-up toy.

The man fell to his knees almost at Grant's feet. Reaching out, he grasped his metal bar and pulled it toward him. He offered it to Grant, hooked end first. After a few seconds of hesitation, Grant took it. Hogan laboriously lifted his head so he could gaze into Grant's face. He coughed, and a stream of liquid vermilion spilled over his lips. In a wheezing voice, he said, "You have won and I render unto you my tool of service."

Grant grunted, "Thanks."

Hogan's eyes acquired a glassy sheen. He pitched his voice to a low, strangulated whisper. "It isn't over for you or your friends. Chief Eljay will already be planning treachery."

Grant nodded. "I figured that out for myself."

Hogan's lips stretched in an ingenuous smile. "I hope you don't hold this against me." Then he fell forward dead. His weight pushed the reddened shaft the rest of the way through his body. It protruded from his back like a giant scarlet thorn.

Grant gripped the bar in his hands so tightly the metal creaked, but he kept his face impassive as he surveyed the spectators. They met his gaze bleakly, then almost as one they cast their eyes toward Chief of Staff Eljay. Silently, they waited for his reaction.

Grant understood they would tailor their responses to whatever Eljay said and did. They were his flesh-and-blood mirrors. He glanced toward Kane and Brigid and noted that even the sec men standing behind them had their attention focused on Eljay.

Ponderously, Eljay pushed himself to his feet by the arms of his chair. He scowled toward Grant, then motioned him forward with an imperious jerk of his caduceus staff.

Grant advanced at a slow, almost reluctant walk. Then he increased the length of his stride and the speed of his gait. Within seconds he was running flat out toward Eljay's box, whipping his right arm up and back, holding the iron rod like a javelin.

He glimpsed Eljay's eyes widen in sudden alarm above the rims of his pince-nez an instant before he hurled the length of metal in a looping overhand, using all of his momentum and upper-body strength to propel it from his hand.

The iron bar was heavy, poorly balanced, not suited for much beyond a tool of mutilation and maiming. But Grant threw it straight and true. The sharpened, filed-down point made a crunching sound as it embedded itself in Eljay's breastbone.

Chief of Staff Eljay fell back into his chair, uttering a bleat of confused pain. Synchronized with his outcry, Kane and Brigid moved. Kicking himself up and backward, Kane drove an elbow into the sec man's sternum. He ignored the spear point dragging along his back. He pivoted at the waist to wrest the shaft from the man's hands. He swung the hooked end at the side of the man's head, the outer curve shattering his skull, splattering the benches with a bloody spray. His body landed heavily in the narrow aisle between two rows of seats.

Brigid surged up and out, slapping her hands over the top of the wall and using it as a brace to somersault over it. Her back-lashing feet caught the sec man in the face, knocking him over a chair. She landed in a crouch on the loosely packed sand of the amphitheater.

Kane turned toward the other guard, even though his movements were hampered by the benches. His blow with the metal bar sent the sec man sprawling over two rows of seats and into the arena. He howled as he fell, clutching at a broken arm.

The people in the amphitheater cried out in panic and terror. They began a jostling, milling stampede for the nearest exists. At least a dozen overall-wearing men wielding the hooked rods leaped into the arena and approached Grant and Brigid.

Grant sidestepped to the broken-armed man writhing in the sand, stamped on the hooked end of his weapon and flipped it up off the ground. He caught it easily and put himself in front of Brigid.

The sec men paused, staring disconcertedly at Grant. He was pretty certain they had never had to fight, and the last thing they ever expected to face was a black giant who had killed the strongest member of their community. After a moment of hesitation, they came on bravely enough, spreading out across the open ground, intending to encircle the two outsiders and trap them against the wall.

Kane vaulted into the arena and he and Grant waded in, swinging wildly. Their first two blows dropped a pair of men with broken heads. A sharpened point was thrust at Kane's face, but he knocked the rod out of the man's hand with one swing and caved in his ribs with the backswing. The sec men swarmed around Grant and Kane. The two men used their feet and knees and elbows, the crowns of their heads and their hands, flat and knotted into fists.

As outnumbered as they were, Kane and Grant should have been beaten to death within the first half minute. The fight lasted far longer than that because they knew more dirty tricks and had no compunction about bringing them into play.

Mina's voice suddenly cut loudly through the mad babble of yelps of fear and pain. *"Brigid!"*

Brigid turned just as the girl threw her a holstered Sin Eater. As she reached up to catch it, she noticed that Dr. Sardonicus had not stirred from his chair. He sat motionless, making no attempt to restrain the girl.

Brigid snatched the weapon out of the air and fumbled with the inner lock catch to override the tendon actuators. She glimpsed one of the sec men running in a crouch toward Kane's unprotected back, iron bar held for a skull-fracturing blow.

The Sin Eater popped from its molded plastic case, the trigger stud coming into contact with her index finger. The single shot was deafeningly loud, a painful wave of ear-knocking sound. The 248-grain wad of lead caught the sec man dead center, impacting at 335 pounds of pressure per square inch. The bullet smashed his ribs and clavicle, ripped both lungs apart, and the hydrostatic shock stopped his heart. He didn't cry out. He just left his feet, flying backward into the men behind him.

The guards all rocked to an unsteady halt, feet skidding in the sand. One man tripped over Hogan's legs. Almost immediately a great hush fell over the amphitheater as if a vast bell jar had suddenly been lowered, muting all sound. Everyone, from the fleeing spectators to the sec men, stood motionless, their faces registering profound shock at the brutal thunderclap that had struck down one of their own.

Kane took advantage of the paralysis to pull himself into Eljay's box. Mina meekly handed him the other side arm. Dr. Sardonicus looked up at him with his frozen grin and said mildly, "Well...this has never happened before."

Kane started to strap the holster to his forearm, realized it was Grant's and didn't bother. Darkly, he replied, "It's way past time."

Grant and Brigid backed up to the wall. She handed Grant the Sin Eater, and he hefted it briefly, then held it up toward Kane. "Trade you."

The two men swiftly exchanged weapons, attaching them to their arms. Kane nodded in Mina's direction.

"Thanks. Your status has risen with us at least, if that means anything."

He turned toward Eljay, a bit surprised to see the man was still alive. Over the rims of his spectacles, he stared down at the length of metal impaling his chest. His shaking hands rose to grasp the rod, but he didn't try to pull it out. He simply held it, fingers caressing and fondling the shaft. He lifted his face and looked at Kane, the saliva bubbles on his lips now crimson hued.

Hoarsely, he said, "Dissociative reaction…with an underlying but extreme explosive diathesis."

"If you mean Grant was pissed off," Kane replied, "yeah, I can't argue with that diagnosis."

Grant heaved himself up over the wall, followed by Brigid. He glared wrathfully at Eljay, then Sardonicus. "Did you fused-out stupes really think I would fight so I could join your fucked-up little society? What the hell makes you think anybody in their right minds would do that? What kind of books have you been reading?"

He shook his head in contempt. "Talk about delusions."

Eljay didn't hear him. His head fell forward and he sagged in his chair. Sardonicus stood and peeled back one of the man's eyelids, made a "tsk" sound of fake sympathy, then picked up the caduceus.

"Looks like you're the chief of staff now," Brigid informed Sardonicus.

She glanced toward Mina. "Unless you want to recommend somebody else for the job."

Before the girl could reply, Sardonicus draped an arm around her slim shoulders and pulled her to him. "She knows I'm the most qualified."

"Yeah," said Kane sourly. "But do we?"

"She will not be harmed," Sardonicus assured them. "The entire Valley of the Divinely Inspired owes this child a great debt. Without her, the chains of Eljay's tyranny could not have been broken."

"Very inspiring," Brigid observed dryly. "How do we know you won't just forge new ones as soon as we're gone?"

Sardonicus laid the double-facing snakes over his heart. "I pledge to you on my Hypocritic oath that a new, kinder and gentler community will arise from the ashes of this one."

"It's Hippocratic oath," Brigid corrected him. She looked into his grinning face and added coldly, "But more than likely you were right the first time."

Grant said to Mina, "You wanted to know what lay beyond the Forbidden Waste. You're welcome to come with us and find out for yourself."

The girl nibbled at her underlip uncertainly, looking first at the body of Eljay then toward Dr. Sardonicus. She sighed in resignation. "I'll stay here. If things will be different from now on, there's no reason to leave."

"That's right," Sardonicus declared decisively. "It'll all be different from now on."

"You're very quick to make promises," Kane snapped. He stepped toward Sardonicus and jabbed him so hard in the chest with the barrel of his Sin Eater that the man stumbled, falling back into his chair. Towering over him, Kane intoned with deadly sincerity, "You'd better keep them. We can come back at any time, and you'll never know we're here until you see us."

Sardonicus swallowed hard, then bobbed his head repeatedly. "When you do return, you'll be welcomed as friends and liberators."

After exchanging goodbyes with Mina, the three exiles left the institution the same way they had entered it, crossing the arena to the breezeway. Kane peeled back a strip of fabric on his left wrist and consulted his digital chron. "We've been here two hours and eleven minutes. That's how long it took us to wreck this society."

"Something of a new record, even for us," Brigid commented breezily.

"Yeah," rumbled Grant. "It'll be hard to beat."

Kane cast a quick glance over his shoulder down the breezeway and into the amphitheater. People were dragging the dead and injured sec men away under Sardonicus's direction. He still stood beside Eljay's body, and the noonday sun glinted briefly from his burnished teeth. Kane shivered involuntarily from a sudden chill.

"What's the matter?" asked Brigid.

Kane shook his head, returning his gaze to the

ridgeline rising in the distance. "My instincts tell me we haven't seen the last of that fang-faced psycho."

Grant smiled without mirth. "What a coincidence. Mine are telling me the exact same thing."

Brigid tossed her hair back from her face. "More than likely all we actually accomplished here is to make another enemy. We should all be used to that by now."

Chapter 7

"Lakesh, I believe you're getting gray." Domi brushed the tips of her fingers through the thick hair at his temples. "Mebbe you'll have hair the same color as mine soon."

Lakesh propped himself up on an elbow, gazing down at the beautiful white face beneath him. A dew of sweat glistened below her up-slanting red eyes and above her sensually shaped mouth. Her eyes usually shone like rubies or drops of freshly spilled blood, but now they were dreamy and faraway. Her face, which normally appeared to have been sculpted from porcelain, held a soft look, all the harsh, chiseled angles sponged away by their lovemaking.

Her eyes closed on either side of her thin-bridged nose, the long sweeping lashes resembling pine-needle branches dusted with snow. Lakesh continued to gaze into her face, more than a little troubled by her observation. His hand went reflexively to touch his black hair. He certainly couldn't feel any difference.

Grinning, Domi pulled his head down, kissing him playfully on the end of his long, aquiline nose. "Don't worry. I loved you when you hardly had any hair at all. I can deal with a little gray. 'Sides, you're a scientist, a whitecoat. You're supposed to look distinguished.''

Lakesh wasn't mollified. Pushing himself off the bed, he crossed the room to the small mirror hanging above the built-in bureau. By the dim light he examined his reflection. For more than two-score years, since his resurrection from cryo-sleep, he always experienced a moment of disoriented shock when he saw a wizened, cadaverous face gazing back at him. For the first three years after his awakening, he was always discomfited by the sight of blue eyes staring out at him from his own face.

The year before the nukecaust, he had been diagnosed with incipient glaucoma, and although the advance of the disease had been halted during his century and a half in cryostasis, it had returned with a double vengeance upon his revival. The eye transplant was only the first of many reconstructive surgeries he underwent, first in the Anthill, then in the Dulce installation.

After his brown eyes were replaced with blue ones, his leaky old heart exchanged for a sound new one and his lungs changed out, arthritic knee joints had been removed and traded with polyethylene. By the time all the surgeries were complete, the mental image he'd carried of his physical appearance no longer coincided with the reality. From a robust, youthful-looking man, he had become a liver-spotted scarecrow. His glossy jet-black hair became a thin gray patina of ash that barely covered his head. The prolonged stasis process had killed the follicles of his facial hair, and he could never regrow the mustache he had once taken so much pride in.

His once clear olive complexion had become leathery, crisscrossed with a network of deep seams and creases that bespoke the anguish of keeping two centuries' worth of secrets. For a long time, Lakesh could take consolation only in the fact that though he looked very old indeed, he was far older than he looked.

But now he looked far, far younger than his chronological age, but he still felt a shock when he looked into the mirror. The shock was different, however, stemming as it did from fear. At the temples of his thick, jet-black hair he still saw a few gray threads, but his olive complexion was still unlined, holding few creases from either age or stress, although he certainly had a stockpile of both. The vision in his blue eyes was still sharp. He glanced with distaste at the pair of eyeglasses resting on top of the bureau. They were dark-rimmed with thick lenses and a hearing aid attached to the right earpiece. For the past decade he had worn them, knowing he resembled a myopic zombie. For the previous three months, though, they hadn't been necessary, and he realized the prospect that they might be again shook him far more profoundly than he expected. He murmured to his face, "Are you really that vain, Mohandas Lakesh Singh?"

Domi padded up silently from behind him, putting her arms around his waist. He felt the nipples of her small but perfectly shaped breasts pressing into his back. She placed a hand over his heart and felt its rapid, agitated rhythm. ''Don't be afraid,'' she said softly.

Inhaling a deep breath, trying to calm himself, Lakesh inspected his reflection with a more objective eye. His restored youth—or more accurately, his restored early middle age—was the only beneficial result of his encounter with Sam, the self-proclaimed imperator of the baronies. He still remembered with vivid clarity how Sam, who resembled a ten-year-old boy, had accomplished the miracle by the simple laying on of hands.

Lakesh knew the process was far more complex than that, but he could engage only in fairly futile speculation how it had been accomplished. He assumed Sam possessed the ability to transfer his biological energy to other organic matter, which in turn stimulated the entire human cellular structure. Beyond that, Lakesh could only guess. He theorized the energy transfer might have rejuvenated the MHC in the six chromosomal structures, resulting in turning back the hands of the metabolic clock by persuading the cells to reproduce and repair themselves.

Regardless of how Sam had done it, Lakesh knew his youth and vitality weren't bestowed without a price. At this juncture he didn't know what he would eventually have to pay out. The fact his hair showed touches of gray after such a short time indicated he either needed regular treatments or the process had a definite effective time limit.

His thoughts returned to the present when he felt Domi's hand fondling his belly, then groping lower. He turned and she smiled impishly up at him, her touch becoming more wanton. He felt himself responding, but he couldn't feel shame about it.

Petite in build, barely five feet tall, Domi was certainly beautiful despite the scars marring the pearly perfection of her skin, particularly the one shaped like a starburst on her right shoulder. She was waiflike, almost childish with her firm, pert breasts and gamine slim legs. An outlander by birth, she was always at ease being nude in the company of others, and if those others didn't share that comfort zone, she couldn't care less.

One of the genetic quirks of the nukecaust aftermath was a rise in the albino population, particularly down south in bayou country. Albinos weren't exactly rare anywhere else, but they were hardly commonplace.

The former Pit Boss of Cobaltville, Guana Teague, had found Domi particularly unique and smuggled her into the Pits with a forged ID chip. In exchange, she gave him six months of sexual service. When seven months had passed without his releasing her from their agreement, she terminated the contract by cutting his throat.

Lakesh crushed her fiercely to him to stop her attempts to arouse him and because he knew both of them couldn't continue to be unaccounted for without arousing the suspicions of the other Cerberus personnel.

"Cease and desist, darlingest one," he whispered, kissing the top of her white head. "Duty calls."

"What duty?" she demanded. "Stand around and listen to machines go click-click-click?"

He chuckled self-consciously and pushed her away, holding her at arm's length. "That click-click-click holds several worlds of meaning, at least to me."

The little albino girl pretended to pout, watching as Lakesh pulled on the standard duty uniform of the Cerberus personnel, a one-piece white bodysuit. Sullenly, Domi asked, "Why do we hide what we do?" Under stress, her abbreviated mode of Outland speech became more pronounced.

"Perhaps there is no good reason at present," Lakesh answered, zipping up the front of the suit. "But the future is always murky. I'd rather not risk complications, not when matters are running smoothly here for the very first time in my memory."

"What complications?" Domi demanded impatiently. "Everything is different now. Grant doesn't want me and I'm okay with that now. It took me a while, but I accepted it. The barons are too busy rebuilding after the war to look for us. 'Sides, the imperator knows where we are and he hasn't come calling."

"That may have more to do with the way I rephased our gateway's matter-stream harmonics." Despite the easy answer, Lakesh suspected Sam could overcome such a security measure with little effort. He had already proved that he had access to a method of instantaneous hyperdimensional travel that apparently had little connection with the workings of the Cerberus mat-trans network.

Domi shook her head in annoyance at the technobabble. "Whatever the reason, things have been quiet for a while."

"All the more reason not to poke at a hornet's nest." Lakesh turned toward the door. "You can stay here if you like."

"And just wait for you to come back?" Domi planted her fists on her flaring hips and cocked her head at a defiant angle. "What you think I am? A gaudy slut?"

She employed the old euphemism for prostitute, but Lakesh knew she wasn't really offended. He had been fond of her since the day they first met, and over the past couple of years that affection had grown to love. He hadn't been able to demonstrate his feelings for her until recently. It was still a source of joy to him that Domi reciprocated his feelings and had no inhibitions about acting on them, regardless of the bitterness she still harbored over her unrequited love for Grant. In any event, he had broken a fifty-year streak of celibacy, and they repeated the actions of that first delirious night whenever the opportunity arose—usually when Kane, Brigid and particularly Grant were out in the field on the bench-marking expeditions.

Lakesh admired Domi's compact little body and felt himself responding to her nudity. He found himself very reluctant to exchange the muted light of the bedroom and the musky scent of a female for bright fluorescent lights and the antiseptic smell of the central control complex.

He sighed and shook his head ruefully. "Domi, you're not a gaudy slut. You only play at one, for which I am eternally grateful. But that act can be damnably distracting to a man with things to do."

Domi grinned and flounced back to the bed. "Then my job is done."

Lakesh returned the grin. "Only temporarily, darlingest one. Only temporarily."

Lakesh was still grinning when he stepped out into the corridor. He quickly wiped it off his face when he saw Reba DeFore approaching from the direction of the main operations complex. He quickly moved away from the door of his quarters just in case Domi made a noise or decided to pop out.

A sudden stabbing pain flared in his right knee. The pain was brief but it was familiar, and he fought to prevent a grimace from showing on his face. Arthritis pains had become more and more frequent as of late, particularly when he made swift moves. He could only hope DeFore hadn't noticed him wincing.

"Good afternoon, Doctor," Lakesh said. "Is the redoubt in order, health-wise?"

DeFore eyed him keenly. She wore her ash-blond hair pulled back from her face, contrasting starkly with the deep bronze of her skin. The installation's resident medic was stocky and buxom, but she looked good in the one-piece white Cerberus jumpsuit. "The people here, yes," she replied. "But the transponder telemetry from the field team caused a few jitters a little while ago."

He stiffened, looking past her to the T junction in the corridor. "Why wasn't I told?"

"Nobody knew where you were," she answered. "I didn't figure you'd be in your quarters in the middle of the day."

Lakesh decided not to address the comment. "What are the telemetric readings now?"

"Pretty much back to normal. Whatever stimulus caused them to spike is over." Narrowing her deep brown eyes, she reached up to touch his temple. "A little gray is showing. How are you feeling?"

With a sinking sensation in his stomach, he realized DeFore had indeed noticed his brief grimace. Gruffly, he replied, "Just fine. A little snow on the roof is perfectly understandable on a man on the high side of 250."

"It's not your roof I'm worried about."

Lakesh didn't respond to her sarcasm. Even after five years, he and DeFore still disagreed on a wide variety of matters. She had accused him of being overdemanding and high-handed, and sometimes he was sure she outright distrusted him, particularly after supplying Balam with the destination lock codes of the redoubt's gateway. Quite possibly she thought he was lying about the means of restored youth.

He couldn't blame her about that, not really. She didn't even pretend to understand how it had happened. The process Lakesh described flew so thoroughly in the face of all her medical training—as limited as it was—he might as well have relegated the cause to a angelic intervention.

All DeFore really knew was that a few months ago she watched Mohandas Lakesh Singh step into the gateway chamber as a hunched-over, spindly old man who appeared to be fighting the grave for every hour he remained on the planet.

A day later the gateway chamber activated and when the door opened Kane, Brigid Baptiste, Grant and Domi emerged. A well-built stranger wearing the white bodysuit of Cerberus duty personnel followed them. Lakesh still remembered how DeFore gaped in stunned amazement at the man's thick, glossy black hair, his unlined olive complexion and toothy, excited grin. She recognized only the blue eyes and the long, aquiline nose as belonging to the Lakesh she had known these past five years.

She was very dubious about the story of Sam. Lakesh claimed he had no idea how long his vitality would last. Whether it would vanish overnight and leave him a doddering old scarecrow again or whether he would simply begin to age normally from that point onward, he couldn't be certain. However, he told her he wasn't about to waste the gift of youth, as transitory as it might be, and she did notice Lakesh surreptitiously eyeing her bosom in a way he had never done before.

"You're not feeling any pains in your joints, are you?" she asked. "Your eyesight is still clear? Your hearing unimpaired?"

"No, yes and yes," he retorted impatiently. "Everything is working just fine."

DeFore nodded, but the angle of her eyebrows called his answers into doubt.

"Are you implying something specific or just trying to ruin my day as has been your habit lately?" he demanded.

Anger flashed briefly in the woman's eyes, and Lakesh instantly regretted his tone. She was one of the first group of Cerberus exiles and had always performed her duties splendidly. "I'm sorry," he said quietly. "You don't deserve that."

"That's for sure," she snapped. "But as for me implying something specific, I suppose I am. I'm worried about you. This restoration of yours can't be as simple as you made it out to be."

"I told you what happened," he said. "That's all I can do. Everything else is hypothesis."

"A laying on of hands," DeFore drawled with a deliberate, mocking slowness. "Very scientific."

"Actually, it was only one hand. His right, as I recall."

Despite his light tone, Lakesh repressed a shiver. He still retained exceptionally vivid memories of the incident when Sam told him he would be "moving energy in precise harmony and perfect balance."

He remembered how Sam laid his little hand against Lakesh's midriff and how a tingling warmth seemed to seep from it. The warmth swiftly became searing heat, like liquid fire, rippling through his veins and arteries. His heartbeat picked up in tempo, seeming to spread the heat through the rest of his body, a pulsing web of energy suffusing every separate cell and organ. He was aflame with a searing pain, the same kind of agony as when circulation was suddenly restored to a numb limb. His entire metabolism seemed to awaken to furious life from a long slumber, as if it had been jump-started by a powerful battery.

He still remembered with awe that after the sensation of heat faded he realized two things more or less simultaneously—he wasn't wearing his glasses but he could see his hand perfectly. And by that perfect vision, he saw the flesh of his hand was smooth, the prominent veins having sunk back into firm flesh. The liver spots faded even as he watched.

Later, Sam claimed he had increased Lakesh's production of two antioxidant enzymes, catalase and superoxide dismutase, and boosted his alkyglycerol level to the point where the aging process was for all intents and purposes reversed. For the first few weeks following Sam's treatment, his hair continued to darken and more and more of his wrinkles disappeared. But then the entire process came to a halt.

DeFore's voice broke into his reverie. "Since you

refuse to let me examine you on a regular basis, I can only take your word for the state of your health. But I know one thing—if aging is controlled by a kind of biological alarm clock, a sort of genetic switching system, and the hands of yours were turned back, it stands to reason they'll start moving in the normal fashion again.''

"And?'' Lakesh asked sourly.

"And,'' she retorted, "just as different kinds of clocks and watches are designed to run for different lengths of time after being wound, so different kinds of bodies are genetically designed to run for different periods. The mainspring of your body's clock could break at any time or it could go haywire. You could age ten years in ten seconds.''

He nodded. "I've considered that possibility.''

"But you're not going to do anything about it.''

He shook his head impatiently. "What can I do? Move into the infirmary while old Doc DeFore pokes and prods me and goes 'tsk-tsk' every few minutes?''

For the first time, DeFore smiled and some of the confrontational tension ebbed from her posture. "I'm not really offering a prognosis, Lakesh. I'm only expressing a physician's concern for a patient.''

Lakesh returned the smile. "Acknowledged and appreciated, doctor. I assure you when I start feeling my age, you'll be one of the first to know.''

She lifted an eyebrow. "*One* of the first?''

He hastily amended his statement. "*The* first. Are you satisfied?''

"No, but that's not unusual." She continued down the corridor. Lakesh watched her anxiously until she passed his quarters, and he expelled a relieved sigh.

He still didn't know why he felt compelled to keep his relationship with Domi a secret. With Grant's heart more or less pledged to Shizuka, even though she was more than a thousand miles away on the island of New Edo, the big man was probably too preoccupied with thoughts of her to give the more covert—and personal—activities of the redoubt more than his cursory attention.

Lakesh guessed his reluctance to let anyone know about his affair with Domi derived mainly from the habit of keeping so many secrets. As it was, he lived daily with the fear that he would anger Grant or Kane and they would expose his biggest secret—how there came to be exiles at Cerberus.

In the twentieth century Lakesh had been a major player in the conspiracy that led to the nuclear holocaust. After that, he became instrumental in establishing the baronial society and served as a trusted member of Baron Cobalt's inner circle. However, all that he'd seen and lived through, and everything he remembered from the past, altered Lakesh's alliances.

Instead of remaining a key facilitator of the unification program's aims and goals, he'd become its most dangerous adversary. Over the past forty years he'd put his plans into action. He acted on the fact that only he knew Redoubt Bravo, the seat of Project Cerberus, was still active when the nine barons believed it was unsalvageable. He manipulated the political system of the baronies to secretly restore the redoubt to full operational capacity. But having a headquarters for a resistance movement meant nothing if there were no resistance fighters.

The only way to find them was through yet more manipulation. Using the genetic records on file in villes, Lakesh selected candidates for his rebellion, but finding them and recruiting them were not the same thing. With his authority and influence, he set them up, framing them for crimes against their respective villes.

It was a cruel, heartless plan with a barely acceptable risk factor, but Lakesh believed it was the only way to spirit them out of their villes, turn them against the barons and make them feel indebted to him.

Only recently had Lakesh's practice been exposed. Grant, Kane and Brigid had staged something of a minimutiny over the issue, but nothing had been decisively settled. However, Lakesh was on notice his titular position as the redoubt's administrator was extremely weak.

Lakesh walked along the twenty-foot-wide corridor made of softly gleaming vanadium alloy. Great curving ribs of metal and massive arches supported the high rock roof. He entered the command center of the redoubt. The long, high-ceilinged room was divided by two aisles of computer stations. The central complex had five dedicated and eight-shared subprocessors, all linked to the mainframe behind the far wall.

Two hundred years ago, it had been an advanced model, carrying experimental, error-correcting microchips of such a tiny size that they even reacted to quantum fluctuations. Biochip technology had been employed when it was built, protein molecules sandwiched between microscopic glass-and-metal circuits.

On the opposite side of the center, an anteroom held the mat-trans chamber, its brown-hued armaglass walls as translucent as ever. He didn't even glance at the indicator lights of the huge Mercator relief map of the world that spanned one entire wall. Pinpoints of light shone steadily in almost every country, connected by a thin glowing pattern of lines. They represented the Cerberus network, the locations of all functioning gateway units across the planet.

Bry manned the main ops console, and he greeted Lakesh with an uncharacteristic display of hostility. "It's about time you got here."

Chapter 8

Lakesh sniffed diffidently. "I have other matters to occupy me aside from waiting around in here to hold your hand just in case a buzzer goes off or a light blinks. Besides, if a truly critical matter had arisen, you could have sounded a general alarm."

Bry maintained his accusatory glower for another moment, glaring up at Lakesh from beneath a mass of coppery curls badly in need of a trim. Then the slightly built man turned in his chair, back toward the four-foot VGA monitor screen. Knuckling his eyes, he intoned, "Sorry. I'm tired…every time we open a parallax point I get nervous."

Lakesh nodded as if in understanding, but he thought that since he now looked only a few years older than Bry did, the need to show deference to a learned elder and mentor wasn't quite as important as it had been.

He didn't put that sentiment into words. For the past couple of months, his former apprentice had become more testy, more challenging and even a bit disrespectful toward him. Lakesh figured Bry had always assumed he would be the resident technical genius of the redoubt in a short time. But now assuming that position, as nebulous as it was, seemed so far in the future it wasn't worth planning for. The man was certainly brilliant, which was why Lakesh had arranged for his exile, but Lakesh had no intention of butting heads with him over grazing rights to control of the redoubt. As far as Lakesh was concerned, who issued the marching orders to the personnel of the Cerberus redoubt wasn't particularly important any longer.

Lakesh turned toward Banks, who manned the satellite telemetric console. "Status."

The young black man with the neatly trimmed beard waved a hand toward three monitor screens upon which three white icons pulsed. "Normal readings."

The telemetry transmitted from Kane's, Brigid's and Grant's transponders scrolled upward. The digital data stream was then routed to the console on Banks's right, through the locational program, to precisely isolate the team's present position in time and space. The program considered and discarded thousands of possibilities within milliseconds. Banks punched in a sequence of numbers on the keyboard, and a topographical map flashed onto the monitor screen, superimposing itself over the three icons. The little symbols inched across the computer-generated terrain.

"We had some high-stress indicators a little while ago," Banks went on, "but they returned to normal after a few minutes. Whatever happened to cause the spikes is over now.''

"Good," replied Lakesh. "So far their bench-marking expeditions have been fairly free of incident. I'd prefer to keep in that way.''

Banks grinned. "I'm sure they do, too.''

Unlike Bry and the other gifted polymaths in the redoubt, Banks was not a tech-head. He was currently in training to serve as one, but computers and electronics weren't his field of expertise. Lakesh had arranged for his exile from Samariumville for two reasons—one was his training in biochemistry. The second, and by far the most important, was the strong latent psionic talents that had shown up on his career placement tests. Both attributes had proved invaluable during the three-plus years he had served as the warder for Balam. His telepathic ability was strong enough to screen out Balam's attempts at psychic influence, except for the one instance when he was able to insinuate himself into Banks's sleeping mind.

But now that Balam was gone, Banks needed to be trained in another area, several if possible. He was also under the tutelage of DeFore, learning the basics of medicine.

"I'd still feel a lot better if they were travelling by gateway,'' Bry muttered.

Lakesh didn't bother to reply. He felt a little sorry for the man. Bry was learning the hard way the meaning of Einstein's statement that physics had lost its walls. Einstein was obliquely calling to the attention of all physicists what philosophers had always known to be true, that the boundaries between space and time carried a large subjective element. Men either created these differences unconsciously for themselves and by their own power, or those invisible creatures called gods created the differences so that men might live by them.

More to appear busy than anything else, Lakesh stepped over to a vacant computer station and tapped the keyboard, patching into the security vid signals. He transferred the vid network to the exterior cameras. The monochromatic image of the plateau and the surrounding area showed very little but early-spring foliage and shadows cast by the cliff face overhanging the road. The shadows were deep and dark, which Lakesh always found appropriate, since the Cerberus redoubt was built into a peak of the Montana mountain range known colloquially as the Darks. In the centuries preceding the apocalypse, the mountains had been known as the Bitterroot Range. In the generations since the nukecaust, a sinister mythology had been ascribed to the mountains, with their mysteriously shadowed forests and deep, dangerous ravines. The wilderness area was virtually unpopulated. The nearest settlement was nearly a hundred miles away, and it consisted of a small band of Indians, Sioux and Cheyenne.

When Cerberus was built in the mid-1990s, no expense had been spared to make the installation a masterpiece of impenetrability. The trilevel, thirty-acre facility had come through the nukecaust in good condition. Its radiation shielding was still intact, and an elaborate system of heat-sensing warning devices, night-vision vid cameras and motion-trigger alarms surrounded the plateau that concealed it.

When Lakesh had reactivated the installation some thirty years before, the repairs he made had been minor, primarily cosmetic in nature. Over a period of time, he had added the security system to the plateau surrounding the redoubt. He had been forced to work in secret and completely alone, so the upgrades had taken several years to complete. Planted within rocky clefts of the mountain peak and concealed by camouflage netting were the uplinks with an orbiting Vela-class reconnaissance satellite and a Comsat. It could be safely assumed that no one or nothing could approach Cerberus undetected by land or by air—not that he expected anyone to make the attempt, particularly overland.

The road leading down from Cerberus to the foothills was little more than a cracked and twisted asphalt ribbon, skirting yawning chasms and cliffs. Acres of the mountainsides had collapsed during the nuke-triggered earthquakes nearly two centuries earlier. It was almost impossible for anyone to reach the plateau by foot or by vehicle, therefore Lakesh had seen to it that the facility was listed as irretrievably unsalvageable on all ville records. The installation had been built as the seat of Project Cerberus, a subdivision of Overproject Whisper, which in turn had been a primary component of the Totality Concept. At its height, the redoubt had housed well over a hundred people, from civilian scientists to military personnel. Now it was full of shadowed corridors and empty rooms, where most of the time silence reigned. It was possible that the handful of people who lived in the installation would be the last of their kind.

Lakesh had tried many times since his resurrection to arrest the tide of extinction inexorably engulfing the human race. First had been his attempts to manipulate the human genetic samples in storage, preserved in vitro since before the nukecaust to provide the hybridization program with a supply of the best DNA. He had hoped to create an underground resistance movement of superior human beings to oppose the barons and their hidden masters, the Archon Directorate. His only success had been Kane, and even that was arguable.

Still later, upon discovering the journal of Mildred Wyeth on a computer disk, Lakesh had seen to its dissemination throughout the Historical Divisions of the villes. At the same time, he wove the myth of the Preservationist menace, presenting a false trail made by a nonexistent enemy for the barons to pursue and fear. He created the Preservationists to be straw adversaries, allegedly an underground resistance movement pledged to deliver the hidden history of the world to a humanity in bondage.

Lakesh checked the area around the closed sec doors where the plateau debouched into the higher slopes, but saw only the grave sites of Cotta and Beth-Li Rouch.

He transferred the view to an interior camera, just inside the main entrance. The massive sec door was closed, locked tight. Vanadium alloy gleamed dully beneath peeling paint. The multiton door opened like an accordion, folding to one side, operated by a punched-in code and a lever control. Nothing short of an antitank shell could even dent it.

A large illustration of a froth-mouthed black hound was rendered on the wall near the control lever. Because the sec cameras transmitted in black and white and shades of gray, he couldn't see the lurid colors of the large illustration on the wall. But he'd so memorized the crimson eyes and yellow fangs his mind supplied the garish pigment the artist had used. Underneath the image, in an ornately overdone Gothic script, was written the single word: Cerberus.

The artist had been one of the enlisted men assigned to the redoubt toward the end of the twentieth century. Lakesh hadn't bothered to remove the illustration, partly because the paint was indelible and partly because the ferocious guardian of the gateway to Hades seemed an appropriate totem and code name for the project devoted to ripping open gates in the quantum field.

Lakesh never did have a clear idea of how many people not directly involved in Project Cerberus knew of the existence of the gateways. He presumed the President of the United States knew, as did the Joint

Chiefs of Staff. He knew secrecy was important. A device that could transport matter—like nuclear devices—was a more important weapon than the atomic weapons themselves. If a state of war existed, it was theoretically possible to invade the enemy nation and pour in troops, tanks, personnel carriers and whatever weapons tactics indicated.

Lakesh focused on the less destructive applications of the gateways. Given wide use, the mat-trans units could eliminate long-haul transportation of goods and even turn international travel into no more daunting a journey than opening and closing a door. He realized, of course, that many decades, perhaps even a century, would pass before the gateway units would be accepted by the public for tourist traffic. The transit phase was so unnerving that wide public acceptance was probably an impossibility.

Eventually, Lakesh hoped, the gateways would primarily be used for space exploration, replacing cumbersome, slow-moving shuttles that were restricted to the closer planets of the solar system.

But with the interphaser, the applications widened even beyond that. Jumping from any point on Earth, it was possible to establish a base anywhere on Earth and conceivably on the other planets, if corresponding vortex nodes could be matched up within the gateway and interphaser's targeting computers.

Even then, the mystery of the origin of the gateway technology haunted Lakesh. It would be many years before he came across the shocking fact that although the integral components were of terrestrial origin, they were constructed under the auspices of a non-human intelligence—or at least, nonhuman as defined by late-twentieth-century standards. Nearly two centuries would pass before Lakesh learned the entire story, or a version of it. Within a year, the proper terminology for the process was replaced in favor of the Cerberus network, or the Cerberus gateways.

He swiftly switched the view to the dining hall, seeing Farrell sitting by himself at a table, reading a book. The middle-aged man with the shaved head, scraggly goatee and gold earring studiously ignored Auerbach, who was picking through the frozen-food selections in the big freezer. Auerbach was a burly, freckled man with a red buzz cut who currently occupied the unenviable position of pariah among the redoubt's personnel. It was position he richly deserved, since a foolish infatuation with Beth-Li Rouch had very nearly resulted in the deaths of Kane, Grant and Brigid.

Depressing another key, Lakesh peeked in at the subterranean maintenance section. Wegmann dozed on a stool, his balding head resting against the huge wire cage enclosing the three ovoid nuclear generators. The big vanadium-shelled machines had provided the redoubt's power for the past two centuries and probably would continue to do so for the next five.

Though there was absolutely no reason to do so,

Lakesh opened the circuit to the room that had served as Balam's holding facility for more than three years.

The image of a wide, low-ceilinged room appeared on the screen. Most of the furnishings consisted of desks and computer terminals. A control console ran the length of the right-hand wall, glass-encased readouts and liquid crystal displays dead and unlit. A complicated network of glass tubes, beakers, retorts, bunsen burners and microscopes covered three black-topped lab tables.

Upright panes of glass formed the left wall. A deeply recessed room stretched on the other side of them. The cell was still illuminated by an overhead neon strip, glowing a dull red. He had considered disconnecting the lights to the cell on more than one occasion, but the power consumption was negligible. He wondered if there were a deeper meaning at hand, that by keeping the lights on, Balam would one day return—not that he was at all certain if he wanted him back.

Lakesh had never thought that during Balam's three and a half years of imprisonment in the glass-walled cell he would miss him when he was gone. Of course, it never occurred to him he would ever be gone. Lakesh hadn't thought that far ahead.

After a couple of years, he had ceased to view the entity as a prisoner or as a source of information about the Archon Directorate. Instead Balam became a trophy, a sentient conversation piece, like a one-item freak show.

In hindsight it was fairly apparent that Balam had chosen to remain in the Cerberus redoubt for reasons of his own. He had used his psionic abilities to manipulate Banks, his former warder, into initiating a dialogue when he probably could just as easily have manipulated the man into releasing him.

It certainly wouldn't have been the first time Balam and those of his kind tricked and lied to their human allies—or pawns.

Repressing a shudder, Lakesh transferred the vid network to the exterior cameras again. When it came to Balam, the only thing he could be certain of was that he could be certain of nothing.

He turned toward Bry. "What's the status of the interpolation on the last group of parallax point coordinates?"

Bry gestured to the stream of numbers and geometric shapes scrolling and flashing at dizzying speed across the monitor screen. "Encoding them into the main database now. Once we have them all collated and decyrpted, they can be fed into the Cerberus mat-trans directory and copied onto the interphaser's hard drive."

He frowned slightly and added, "Providing our bench-marking team brings the damn thing back and doesn't abandon it like they did the prototype."

"They didn't have much choice, as you recall," Lakesh argued.

Nearly two years before, Lakesh had embarked on the most audacious and desperate plan in a double lifetime filled with scheming. He had constructed a small device on the same scientific principle as the mat-trans inducers, an interphaser designed to interact with naturally occurring quantum vortices. Theoretically, the interphaser opened dimensional rifts much like the gateways, but instead of the rifts being pathways through linear space, Lakesh had envisioned them as a method to travel through the gaps in normal space-time.

He had hoped to open a rift that intersected with the home dimension of the Archon Directorate, if indeed the entities were pan-dimensional rather than extraterrestrial. The interphaser had not functioned according to its design, and due to interference caused by Lord Strongbow's similar device, the so-called Singularity, its dilated temporal energy had sent Kane, Brigid, Domi and Grant on a short, disembodied trip into the past.

Although the interphaser had been lost, its memory disk had been retrieved, and using the data recorded on it, Lakesh had tried to duplicate the dilation effect by turning the Cerberus mat-trans unit into a time machine.

Such efforts were not new. A major subdivision of the Totality Concept had been devoted to manipulating the nature of time. Operation Chronos was built on the breakthroughs of Project Cerberus, but it had not been as successful. During development of the mat-trans gateways, the Cerberus researchers observed a number of side effects. On occasion, traversing the quantum pathways resulted in minor temporal anomalies, such as arriving at a destination three seconds before the jump initiator was actually engaged.

Lakesh found that time could be measured or accurately perceived in the quantum stream. Hypothetically, constant jumpers might find themselves physically rejuvenated, with the toll of time erased if enough ''backward time'' was accumulated in their metabolisms. Conversely, jumpers might find themselves prematurely aged if the quantum stream pushed them farther into the future with each journey. From these temporal anomalies Operation Chronos had the starting point, using the gateway technology, to develop time travel.

The Operation Chronos scientists employed a practice they termed ''trawling,'' focusing on subjects in the past and pulling them forward to the twentieth century. Although not directly connected with the time-travel experiments, Lakesh had heard rumors of their many attempts and failures.

Without access to the specs and data of Operation Chronos, Lakesh could not duplicate what they had done, so he determined to circumvent it. He saw to the creation of the Omega Path program and linked it with the mat-trans gateway.

The concept was sound—to dispatch Kane and Brigid back through time to a point only a month before the nukecaust so they could hopefully trigger an alternate event horizon and thus avert the apocalypse.

The Omega Path had worked, at least insofar as translating them into a past temporal plane, but they came to learn it was not their world's past, but another's, almost identical to it. Any actions they undertook had no bearing on their world's present and future.

Lakesh could only speculate on what had happened, and on the system of physics at work. Operation Chronos had functioned on the chronon theory, that time was not continuous but made up of subatomic particles jammed together like beads on a string. According to the theory, between each bead, each individual unit of time might exist in an infinite series of parallel universes, fitted into the probability gaps between the chronons.

Bry lifted one of his knobby shoulders in a half shrug as if he found Lakesh's rebuke not only irrelevant but boring. "The thing is, these parallax points of yours are just as limited in their own way as the mat-trans units. Sure, the gateways only offer transport from a transmitting unit to a receiving unit. But the parallax points only activate naturally occurring vortices, electromagnetic anomalies. The nodes we've mapped so far have no real strategic value. Like Grant said, most of them are in the ass end of nowhere in unhabited and uninhabitable places."

He shrugged again. "At least the mat-trans system, even the unindexed gateways not part of the official Cerberus network, takes you to redoubts, not deserts or earthquake fault lines."

Most of the gateways were located in Totality Concept redoubts, subterranean military complexes scattered over the face of America. Even during the height of the Totality Concept researches, only a handful of people knew the redoubts even existed, and even fewer knew all their locations. The knowledge had been lost after the nukecaust, rediscovered a century later, then jealously, ruthlessly guarded. There were, however, gateway units in other countries—Russia, Mongolia, Tibet, England, South America.

Lakesh smiled a little challengingly at his former apprentice. "We've had this discussion before, Mr. Bry. Or at least talked around it. What's really bothering you is the origin of the parallax points data."

Bry scowled up at him. "That's my point—excuse the pun. We don't really *know* its origin, do we? I don't see any reason to bring that up again, but if you want to rehash it—"

Lakesh held up a pair of conciliatory hands. "No need. I may not have Brigid Baptiste's total recall, but I can easily recollect your major objections without putting a strain on my memory."

He began ticking them off on his fingers, one at a time. "One, we found the data in Redoubt Yankee, the primary Operation Chronos facility on one of the Santa Barbara Islands. It had been commandeered by Sindri, and in fact, without his reference to the program, we wouldn't know anything about the parallax points.

"Two," Lakesh continued, "Sindri denied having anything to do with the program, so our prime suspect is eliminated. We don't know who was responsible for writing it, and since it derives from an unknown source, we're taking a big risk putting our faith in it.

"Three, some of these parallax points have exceptionally questionable longitudes and latitudes. Anyone who travels them may very well find themselves opening a vortex on the bottom of the ocean or atop Mount Everest."

He raised questioning eyebrows at the tech. "Have I missed anything?"

Bry held up four fingers. "Four, the interphaser is a delicate and cantankerous piece of machinery. It could malfunction and leave our bench-marking parties stranded in the middle of the Sahara, or it could do to them what the first one did—trigger a spatial and temporal anomaly and boot them all on an unscheduled trip through time."

"It won't," Lakesh broke in, his voice rising. "This version of the interphaser is completely retooled from the prototype. Besides, I seriously doubt they'll interface with the radiations of another tinkered-together Singularity."

"I don't know about that," Bry said doubtfully. "According to you, the imperator can open up localized worm holes. That's how Brigid, Grant and Kane were transported from the Pacific to China."

"I was there," Lakesh said a touch acidly. "I saw

it myself. I don't need the reminder. That's why the parallax points program is so important.''

Bry still looked skeptical. Even though Lakesh had explained the event to him, the man wasn't certain of what happened on that day. According to Lakesh, Sam, the self-proclaimed imperator, could manipulate the energies of what he called the ''Heart of the World,'' an encapsulated packet of the quantum field.

Buried beneath the Xian pyramid in China, the Heart was described as containing the energies released in the first picoseconds following the Big Bang, channeling the matrix of protoparticles that swirled through the universe before physical, relativistic laws fully stabilized. It existed slightly out of phase with the third dimension, with the human concept of space-time. From this central core extended a web of electromagnetic and geophysical energy that covered the entire planet. Sam himself claimed he had transported Kane, Brigid and Grant from Thunder Isle to Xian by opening a localized worm hole in the energy web.

However, he had transported them from the primary Operation Chronos installations while the temporal dilator was still powered up. Lakesh did not think the two events were unconnected.

''Is there anything else?'' Lakesh asked.

Bry smiled mirthlessly and extended his thumb. ''Five, so far, we've been able to align the phase harmonics of the vortices with the normal materialization process of the gateways. But I don't we think we can count on—''

The rest of his words were drowned out by a deep humming tone vibrating from the gateway chamber in the anteroom. Console lights flashed, and power-gauge needles wavered. Looking at the deep brown-hued armaglass door of the jump chamber, they saw swirls of light fluttering on the other side. The droning hum climbed, faltered, then tried to climb again.

Bry half rose from his chair, squinting toward the free-standing enclosed arrangement made of eight-foot-tall slabs of armaglass. ''I don't like the sound of that,'' he murmured. He glanced tensely over at Lakesh. ''This is what I was trying to tell you—the interphaser's carrier signature isn't being completely recognized by the gateway's transition in-feed lock!''

Chapter 9

Green sine and cosine waves stretched and rotated across the readouts of the instrument panel. The design didn't conform to the symmetry of the rest of the control consoles in the complex. Dark, long and bulky, like an old-fashioned dining table canted at a thirty-degree angle, it bristled with thousands of tiny electrodes and a complex pattern of naked circuitry. A switchboard contained relays and the readout screens.

The instrument panel over which Lakesh leaned had been built and installed well over a year before to oversee the temporal dilation of the Omega Path program. Since the energy outputs of the parallax points and the temporal dilator were of similar frequencies, it hadn't been much of a task to put the system back into use.

Lakesh glanced up, peering through the open door of the anteroom to the mat-trans chamber beyond. The phase transition coils enclosed within the elevated platform produced the steady, high-pitched drone, an electronic synthesis between the device's hurricane howl and down-cycling hum.

Because of the translucent quality of the brown-tinted armaglass shielding, he could see nothing within it except vague, shifting shapes without form or apparent solidity.

He knew the chamber was full of the plasma bleed-off, the ionized wave-forms that resembled mist. So far, all was as it had been in the tests and preliminary experiments. As had been done with the Omega Path, the mainframe computers were reprogrammed with the logarithmic data of the parallax points. The program prolonged the quincunx effect produced by re-materialization, stretching it out in perfect balance between the phase and interphase inducers.

Lakesh wasn't too concerned about the imperfect synchronization between the frequencies of the inter-phaser and the mat-trans unit. He had the utmost faith in Bry, who worked the controls, increasing the matter-stream conformals. Within seconds, the discordant whine melded into a smooth drone, then the flares of light faded.

Lakesh waited, listening to the muffled whining of the interphase transition coils cycling down beneath the platform. He heard the clicking of solenoids, and the heavy armaglass door swung open on its counter-balanced hinges. Mist swirled and thread-thin static-electricity discharges arced within the billowing mass. Looking like shadows in a fog bank, Brigid, Grant and Kane stepped one by one off the platform and into the ready room.

Lakesh left the instrument panel and went to stand by the door as they entered the control complex. He greeted and examined them quickly as they passed by, relieved they all appeared to be uninjured. He saw the dried blood caked on the side of Grant's neck and caught his breath.

He moved in front of the big man, reaching out to touch the fresh cut on his earlobe. "What happened?" Lakesh asked.

Grant regarded him with a combination of amusement and surprise, but he allowed Lakesh to tentatively touch the wound. "Nothing much. We had a little disagreement with some folks we met. It all worked out."

Lakesh inhaled a calming breath. "What kind of folks? The usual bunch of robbers and Roamers?"

Kane grinned lopsidedly. "Not exactly." He quickly explained about the isolated Valley of the Divinely Inspired, not embellishing or omitting any details. Lakesh nodded throughout his recitation as if the tale were a familiar one. In many ways, it was.

"But you're all unhurt?" he asked.

Grant heaved the broad yoke of his shoulders in a shrug. "Pretty much, yeah."

Lakesh eyed Grant's cut critically, agreeing silently the injury was superficial. But he said, "Perhaps so, but I suggest you let DeFore make the final determination." With a sigh, he added, "I suppose it was too much to hope that all of your forays would be free of violence."

"It was a matter of playing the odds," Brigid said.

"Speaking of which, the interphaser's uplink failed on us. I had to reboot the whole system."

Face creased in a frown, Bry threw Lakesh an I-told-you-so look and rose from his station. He strode swiftly into the ready room. "I was afraid something like that would happen. All those damn retooled microchips."

Lakesh stiffened at the mumbled criticism but he didn't respond as the man entered the jump chamber. The little pyramid sat on the hexagonal floor, wisps of vapor curling around its metal skin. Bry reached down for it. A tiny spark popped. He recoiling, cursing, shaking his stinging hand. He looked at Lakesh accusingly.

Lakesh grinned. "You never take static buildups into consideration, Mr. Bry."

Bry rubbed his fingertips together as if he were trying to rid them of lint. "You could have reminded me," he said reproachfully.

"And distract you from the problems of retooled microchips?"

Lakesh turned back to Brigid, Grant and Kane. Brigid stood at Bry's station, gazing at the numbers and shapes flickering over the big monitor screen. "Still interpolating?"

"Yes," Lakesh answered a little defensively. "It's a very complicated and time-consuming process."

"Not to mention," Grant put in, "a little time-wasting."

A laugh, quickly stifled, came from Bry in the jump

chamber. Lakesh ignored him. "Friend Grant," he said severely, "unraveling all of the parallax points is our only possible defense against an incursion of the imperator's forces."

"An incursion," Kane interjected, "which hasn't come yet, even after all this time. I don't think it will. I don't think either Sam or Balam considers us much of a threat anymore."

"That's because we haven't been one since Sam took power," Brigid stated. "We haven't interfered as he consolidated his power over the barons or made a move against Dreamland."

"We don't know how many barons have thrown in with him," argued Kane. "Sharpe and Snakefish for sure...Baron Samarium is still a maybe, and the loyalties of the others are complete unknowns. Cobalt is out of the picture entirely—"

"We think," Grant broke in. "Since his ville was overthrown, we don't know if he's alive or dead or hiding out. The only thing we do know for sure is he's the most dangerous of the bunch—and the only one who holds a personal grudge against us here at Cerberus."

Lakesh smiled sourly. "At this juncture, if Baron Cobalt still lives, he would most likely be preoccupied with a vendetta against Sam. The imperator managed to do what we only dreamed of—unseating him."

None of the three could disagree about that, but by the same token, none of them felt particularly good about an imperator controlling the villes instead of a group of hybrid barons, either. The ancient Roman Empire was governed by a senate, but ruled by an emperor, sometimes known as an imperator. This person served as the final arbiter in matters pertaining to government.

A few months before, they learned about a mysterious figure called the imperator who intended to set himself up as overlord of the villes, with the barons subservient to him. That bit of news was surprising enough, but it quickly turned shocking when they found out that Balam, who they had thought was gone forever, was the power behind the imperator.

Several months earlier, during a council of the barons in Front Royal, Baron Cobalt put forth the proposal to establish a central ruling consortium. In effect, the barons would become viceroys, plenipotentiaries in their own territories. Since the barons were accustomed to acting as the viceroys of the Archon Directorate, the actual proposal didn't offend them.

All of them, barons and the Cerberus exiles alike, had believed the barons were under the sway of the Archons, a nonhuman race that had influenced human affairs for thousands of years. Allegedly, the sinister thread linking all of humankind's darkest hours led back to a nonhuman presence that controlled humanity through political chaos, staged wars, famines, plagues and natural disasters. The nuclear apocalypse of 2001 was all part of the Archon Directorate's strategy. With the destruction of social structures and severe depopulation, the Archons established the nine barons and distributed predark technology among them to consolidate their power over Earth and its disenfranchised, spiritually beaten human inhabitants.

But over the past year or so, all of them had learned that the elaborate back story was all a ruse, bits of truth mixed in with outrageous fiction. The Archon Directorate didn't exist except as a vast cover story, created in the twentieth century and grown larger with each succeeding generation. The only so-called Archon on Earth was Balam, the last of an extinct race that had once shared the planet with humankind.

After three years of imprisonment in the Cerberus redoubt, Balam finally revealed the truth behind the Directorate and the hybridization program initiated centuries before. Balam claimed that the Archon Directorate existed only as an appellation and a myth created by the predark government agencies as a control mechanism. Lakesh referred to it as the Oz Effect, wherein a single vulnerable entity created the illusion of being the representative of an all-powerful body.

Balam himself may have even coined the term Archon to describe his people. In ancient Gnostic texts, *archon* was applied to a parahuman world-governing force that imprisoned the divine spark in human souls. Kane had often wondered over the past few months if Balam had indeed created that appellation as a cryptic code to warn future generations.

Even more shocking was Balam's assertion that he

and his ancient folk were of human stock, not alien but alienated. They still didn't know how much to believe. But if nothing else, none of the Cerberus personnel any longer subscribed to the fatalistic belief that the human race had had its day and only extinction lay ahead. Balam had indicated that wasn't true, but was only another control mechanism.

Though the myth had been exposed, the barons, the half-human hybrids spawned from Balam's DNA, still ruled. Although each of the fortress-cities with its individual, allegedly immortal god-king was supposed to be interdependent, the baronies still operated on insular principles. Cooperation among them was grudging despite their shared goal of a unified world. They perceived humanity in general as either servants or as living storage vessels for transplanted organs and fresh genetic material.

The barons were not in favor of Baron Cobalt's proposal to be recognized as the imperator. However, they really didn't have much of a choice—Cobalt had arranged matters that way. After the destruction of the Archuleta Mesa medical facilities, the barons were left without access to the ectogenesis techniques of fetal development outside the womb. Not only was the baronial oligarchy in danger of extinction, but so was the entire hybrid race.

Baron Cobalt occupied Area 51 with the spoken assumption of taking responsibility to sustain his race—but only if he was elevated to a position of high authority, even above his brother barons. It wasn't a matter of making an incursion into another baron's territory, as most of Nevada was not part of an official baronial territory.

Since Area 51's history was intertwined with rumors of alien involvement, Baron Cobalt had used its medical facilities as a substitute for those destroyed in New Mexico. Of course, he couldn't be sure if the aliens referred to by the predark conspiracy theorists were the Archons, but more than likely they were, inasmuch as the equipment that still existed was already designed to be compatible with the hybrid metabolisms.

In any event, Baron Cobalt reactivated the installation, turning it into a processing and treatment center without having to rebuild from scratch, and transferred the human and hybrid personnel from the Dulce facility—those who had survived the destruction there, at any rate.

However, the medical treatments that addressed the congenital autoimmune system deficiencies of the hybrids weren't enough to insure the continued survival of the race. The necessary equipment and raw material to implement procreation had yet to be installed. Baron Cobalt had unilaterally decided that the conventional means of conception was the only option to keep the hybrid race alive.

Because of those metabolic deficiencies, the barons lived insulated, isolated lives. The theatrical trappings many of them adopted not only added to their semidivine mystique, but also protected them from contamination both psychological and physical.

Although all the hybrids were extremely long-lived, cellular and metabolic deterioration was part and parcel of what they were—hybrids of human and Archon DNA. Just like the caste system in place in the villes, the hybrids observed similar distinctions of rank.

The hybrids, at least by their way of thinking, represented the final phase of human evolution. They created wholesale, planned alterations in living organisms and were empowered to control both their environment and the evolution of other species. And the barons were the pinnacle of that evolutionary achievement, as high above ordinary hybrids as those hybrids were above mere humans.

When Baron Cobalt dangled the medical treatments before his fellow barons like a carrot on a stick, war was the inevitable result—particularly after Sam, supported by none other than Balam, hijacked not only Cobalt's plan but also the title of imperator.

Bry returned to the operations center, holding the interphaser between two hands. He walked carefully, as if the machine were made of spun sugar and cobwebs. Lakesh was irritated by the exaggerated caution the man displayed. Acidly, he said, "It's not a Fabergé egg, Mr. Bry. No need to handle it like one."

Kane and Grant swapped grins. Lakesh caught the exchange and demanded, "Is there a joke I'm missing?"

Kane stared into Lakesh's bright blue gaze, but the man never flinched. He still hadn't grown accustomed to dealing with a robust—relatively speaking—Lakesh whose eyes weren't covered by thick lenses and whose voice no longer rose to a reedy rasp. He also had to consciously catch himself from addressing Lakesh as "old man." It had become a habit over the past couple of years, and he found it was hard to break.

"Actually," Kane said, "you're the joke."

Lakesh's eyebrows rose toward his hairline. "Am I, indeed?"

"You have a sense of humor about everything—except one of your own creations. You could spend years making a high-tech, computerized jack-in-the-box and then wonder why everybody laughed."

A wry smile creased Lakesh's lips. "I suppose I do tend to wear blinders when it comes to my work."

The computer station emitted a beep, signaling its function was complete. Lakesh joined Brigid at the terminal.

"Good, another set of coordinates to add to the main database," he said.

Brigid didn't reply. She stared intently at the columns of numbers and the bisected sphere glowing on the screen. Faint lines of consternation appeared on her forehead. She pursed her lips, murmuring, "Something's not right."

Lakesh glanced at her in annoyance. "Is everybody going to criticize my work today?" He started to say more, then he looked toward the numerical sequence and geometric forms displayed on the monitor. "What do you mean?" he demanded.

His fingertip traced the first line of digits. "We've got a set of rectangular and polar coordinates, equatorial meridians, latitudes and longitudes..." His words trailed off, his eyes narrowing. Almost unconsciously, he muttered, "Something's not right."

Brigid said, "We may have all of those, but we don't have the terrestrial correlations. Not unless the Mare Vaporum is outside of Salt Lake City." She looked at him, saying blandly, "And I don't think it is."

Kane and Grant stepped closer. "What's the problem?" Kane asked. "You can't find a parallax point in all that digital gobbledygook?"

Lakesh straightened and with his eyes still fixed on the screen intoned, "No, we can find it. The only problem is, it's not on Earth."

The corner of his mouth lifted in a slightly abashed smile. "It's on the Moon."

Chapter 10

"No," Kane said flatly. "No."

"No, *no*," Grant growled. "As in *no* fucking way."

Lakesh pretended not to have heard the two men. His eyes alight, he tapped a few buttons on the keyboard in front of him. A sectionized sphere appeared on the screen, and curving, irregular lines crawled across its diameter. Blocks of copy appeared at random intervals. Kane read only a few of them, unfamiliar phrases like *Mare Frigoris, Montes Carpatus* and *Oceanus Proscellarum,* before he said again, this time with a good deal more vehemence, *"No."*

Lakesh laughed, as if Kane and Grant were putting on a vastly entertaining comedy act. "This bears my theory out," he announced.

"And which theory was that again?" Grant demanded haughtily. "I mean which one was it this week?"

"Hyperdimensional mathematics," Lakesh answered calmly, "provides a fundamental connection between the four forces of nature. In our universe, energy flows downhill, from hot to cold, from higher to lower energy. A spinning celestial body, such as a planet, would have a connection to uphill and down-hill energy flows, from an invisible higher dimension to a lower one, in which we live.

"As you know, I always believed there are many vortex points located in generally the same proximity on each of the planets of our solar system, and these nodes correlate to vortex centers on Earth."

He touched the screen where a single red dot, like a pinhead of blood, pulsed in the center of an area labeled Manitius. "And there is the correlating point on the Moon."

Brigid, smiling at Lakesh's delight, leaned her hip against a desk. "I understand your excitement, Lakesh, but just because there's a parallax point on the Moon doesn't mean it's of strategic value. Other than a 'because it's there' approach, I don't see much reason to activate it."

"Me, either," rumbled Grant. "We've already been to Mars, and that place was about as hospitable as Washington Hole. The Moon is probably worse."

"At least it would be closer," Lakesh commented distractedly. "Regardless, whoever wrote this program included it and presumably activated it themselves."

"Presumably," Kane echoed sarcastically. "How do you know they didn't step into a hard vacuum and suffocate or explode?"

Lakesh removed his enthralled gaze from the screen. "I don't think they did, either, so more than likely nor would you."

Grant angled a challenging eyebrow. "And why not?"

"Because there's a base there, in Manitius Crater, remember?"

"How the hell could I?" Grant shot back. "The closest we've ever been to the Moon is *Parallax Red*—" He suddenly stopped talking and his eyes grew thoughtful.

Lakesh nodded genially. "That's right. Remember the briefing once we found the mat-trans destination code for *Parallax Red?*"

Kane sifted through his memory and looked hopefully toward Brigid. Her eyes narrowed as she intoned, "If I recall correctly—"

"And there's no reason you wouldn't," Lakesh interposed.

"You told us the official U.S. space program had been used to conceal the objective of the real space program from the public. Joint ventures between the American and Russian military that attempted to colonize both the Moon and Mars."

Grant nodded. "Right. You mentioned something called Alternative Three, which claimed alien abductees were lifted off Earth to build secret bases. The abductees served as mind-controlled slave-labor construction workers, not for aliens but for a covert, ultrasecret arm of the government. According to this theory, NASA was simply a smoke screen, diverting attention from a U.S. and USSR joint space program.

Part of that program was the construction of the *Parallax Red* space station.''

Brigid picked up the thread. ''The early shuttle-craft program ferried construction materials to a point in the Moon's orbit, where they were retrieved using short-range unmanned vessels by engineers living in the secret lunar base in the Manitius Crater region. From there, they were conveyed to Lagrange Region 2, where the space habitat was being built.''

She shrugged. ''I admit, it's an intriguing prospect to visit the Moon, Lakesh, but I agree with Kane and Grant on this one. We're still marking the vortex centers on Earth. Let's save the extraterrestrial ones for later.''

Lakesh tugged at his long nose and said contemplatively, ''Two centuries ago, an astrophysicist named Ziolkovsky described the Earth as the cradle of mankind but remarked that one cannot live forever in the cradle. There's no reason why we can't send a remote probe out of the cradle…preselect the timing program on the interphaser to reopen the vortex a few minutes after it closes.''

Bry turned, mouth and eyes wide. ''You'll open a worm hole from here to the Moon? Why can't we see if there's a functioning lunar gateway in the Cerberus index?''

''There isn't. I checked a long time ago.''

Bry struggled to control his rising consternation. ''What are you trying to do, Lakesh? If you open a worm hole here, everything that's not nailed down will be sucked through and into the vacuum! Us included!''

Lakesh snorted disdainfully. ''The interphaser will be shielded inside the gateway chamber as always. It's hermetically sealed, so there's no danger of anything you hold dear being sucked.''

Kane laughed and walked toward the exit. ''I'll let you two work it out. I'm getting out of this second skin and taking a shower.''

Grant fell into step behind him. ''Me, too.'' He paused and asked over his shoulder, ''Anybody see Domi around today?''

Lakesh hesitated before saying, ''I saw her earlier.''

Grant narrowed his eyes at the vagueness of Lakesh's response, waited for him to say something else, and, when it wasn't forthcoming, he left the operations complex. Once out in the corridor, he and Kane made for the armory. Grant was silent as they walked, seemingly preoccupied with working at the buckles and tabs of his Sin Eater's power holster. Kane knew Grant was bothered, either disquieted or irritated. The two men had partnered together for nearly fifteen years, and they had learned to be sensitive to each other's moods.

''Do you want Domi for any reason in particular?'' Kane asked casually.

Grant grunted flatly, ''No.'' A few seconds later he said, ''I just haven't seen her around in the past couple of days.''

"It's a big place. Maybe you haven't looked everywhere."

Grant's eyes suddenly glittered with annoyed suspicion. "What's that supposed to mean?"

Kane sighed wearily, in exasperation. "Not a thing. I'm just saying if you really wanted to find her, you could."

After an awkward moment of silence, Grant matched Kane's sigh with one of his own. "I know."

They walked on down the corridor past the vehicle depot and workroom and entered an open doorway. Kane depressed the flat toggle switch on the door frame with his thumb, and the overhead fluorescent fixtures blazed on, flooding the armory with a white, sterile light.

The big square room was stacked nearly to the ceiling with wooden crates and boxes. Many of the crates were stenciled with the legend Property U.S. Army.

Glass-fronted gun cases lined the four walls, containing automatic assault rifles, many makes and models of subguns and dozens of semiautomatic blasters. Heavy assault weaponry occupied the north wall, bazookas, tripod-mounted M-249 machine guns, mortars and rocket launchers.

On the day of their arrival at the redoubt, Lakesh told them that all of the ordnance was of predark manufacture. Caches of matériel had been laid down in hermetically sealed Continuity of Government installations before the nukecaust. Protected from the ravages of the outraged environment, nearly every piece of munitions and hardware was as pristine as the day it rolled off the assembly line.

Lakesh himself put the arsenal together over several decades, envisioning it as the major supply depot for a rebel army. The army never materialized—at least not in the fashion Lakesh hoped it would. Therefore, Cerberus was blessed with a surplus of death-dealing equipment that would turn the most militaristic baron green with envy, or give the most pacifistic of them heart failure—if they indeed possessed hearts.

Kane and Grant hung their power holsters on hooks inside a gun case that stood between the two suits of Magistrate body armor mounted on metal frameworks. They stood there like silent, grim sentinels. Though relatively light, the black polycarbonate was sufficiently dense to deflect every caliber of projectile, up to and including a .45-caliber bullet. It absorbed and redistributed a bullet's kinetic impact, minimizing the chance of incurring hydrostatic shock.

The armor was close-fitting, molded to conform to the biceps, triceps, pectorals and abdomen. The only spot of color anywhere on it was the small, disk-shaped badge of office emblazoned on the left pectoral. It depicted, in crimson, a stylized, balanced scales of justice, superimposed over a nine-spoked wheel. It symbolized the Magistrate's oath, of keeping the wheels of justice in the nine villes turning.

Like the armor, the helmets were made of black polycarbonate, and fitted over the upper half and back of the head, leaving only portions of the mouth and chin exposed.

The slightly convex, red-tinted visor served several functions—it protected the eyes from foreign particles and the electro-chemical polymer was connected to a passive night sight that intensified ambient light to permit one-color night vision.

The armor served as a symbol of their past, when they were enforcers of the ville laws and Baron Cobalt's edicts, legally and spiritually sanctioned to act as judges, juries and executioners.

All Magistrates followed a patrilineal tradition, assuming the duties and positions of their fathers before them. They didn't have given names, each taking the surname of the father, as though the first Magistrate to bear the name were the same man as the last.

As Magistrates, the courses their lives followed had been charted before their births. They were destined to live, fight and die, usually violently, as they fulfilled their oaths to impose order upon chaos. By a strict definition, Grant and Kane had betrayed their oaths, but as Lakesh was wont to say, "There's no sin in betraying a betrayer."

The bromide was easy enough to utter, but to live with the knowledge was another struggle entirely. Nearly two years previously, when they broke their lifetimes of conditioning, the inner agony was almost impossible to endure. The peeling away of their Mag identities, their Mag purpose, had been a gradual process, but now, when Kane thought of his years as a

Magistrate, it brought only an ache, a sense of remorse over wasted years.

Superficially, Grant had handled his status as renegade better than Kane, but the man was always stoic in the face of physical and emotional pain. Grant had followed Brigid's lead, who was the most adaptable of the three of them, and he seemed devoted to the new work Cerberus offered.

But old Mag habits died very hard. Kane managed to push most of them to the back of his mind, storing them with his memories of all the other things that were past and he wasn't particularly anxious to think about.

Kane closed the gun-case door and asked, "You finally got around to telling Domi about Shizuka, right?"

"You know I did."

Kane turned to face him, grinning crookedly. "Since she didn't do a Guana on you, I guess she accepted it."

Kane employed a bit of personal vernacular, referring to Guana Teague, the former Pit Boss of Cobaltville. Teague was crushing the life out of Grant beneath his three-hundred-plus pounds of flab, when Domi had expertly slit his throat.

After that, Domi attached herself to Grant, viewing him as a gallant black knight who rescued her from the shackles of Guana Teague's slavery, even though, in reality, quite the reverse was true. As something of a memento, she always carried the hunting knife with the nine-inch serrated blade that had done the deed.

For more than a year, she made it fiercely clear that Grant was hers and hers alone, even though Grant fought hard to make sure there was nothing but friendship between him and the albino girl. He tried to make the gap in their ages the reason he didn't want to get involved with her, sexually or otherwise. Domi had been patient and understanding for a year until she grew tired of waiting.

He knew he had hurt Domi dreadfully when she spied him and Shizuka locked in a passionate embrace. He didn't speak to her about it. Part of his reluctance was due to shame, another part due to pride, but more than anything else, fear made him hold his tongue.

It was Grant's habit to keep some emotional distance between himself and everyone he knew, even Kane. The reason was simple—if one were lost, the other could go on.

"I really don't know if Domi accepted it or not," Grant intoned. "She hardly said anything at all. She just looked at me. She won't talk to me about anything unless it's absolutely necessary. She's never in the galley when I'm there, or down in the pool."

Despite his uninflected tone, Kane knew Grant was feeling guilt and remorse, despite pledging his devotion to Shizuka, whose heart and soul were inextricably bound to New Edo. Those ties were even stronger now after she had averted a rebellion and defeated an invasion of Magistrates dispatched by Baron Snakefish. She would never leave as long as she perceived New Edo needed her. Kane knew the notion of remaining on the little island monarchy definitely appealed to Grant, but he had never even mentioned whether it was an option.

"She'll get over it," Kane said, hoping he sounded reassuring. "She'll start talking to you again."

Grant shrugged. "She never even told me about what she went through in Dreamland." His dark eyes suddenly bored into Kane's pale ones. "Neither did you, come to think of it."

Trying to prevent his sudden tension from creeping into his voice or posture, Kane said offhandedly, "I told you all there was to tell. Cooling my heels in a cell for two weeks doesn't make for an exciting memoir."

"Right." Grant drawled out the word, then turned and left the armory.

Kane lingered for a minute, allowing Grant time to reach his quarters. He turned out the lights and made it to his own suite of rooms without seeing anyone. In his quarters, Kane stripped out of the shadow suit by opening a magnetic seal on the right side. The garment had no zippers or buttons, and he peeled off the one continuous piece from the hard-soled boots to the gloves.

He stepped into the shower, deliberately turning his mind from Grant's heavy-handed implication that both he and Domi were withholding information about their captivity in Area 51. He tried to wash away the memories, but he knew they still clung to him like an odor. Although it was early in the day, he decided to nap. He was accustomed to going without sleep for long periods; he was also accustomed to catching sleep whenever he could to build up a backlog. He was awakened almost immediately, it seemed, by a scream.

Jackknifing up from the bed, Kane wondered for an instant if the scream had been real or one from a dream—God knew, there were plenty tucked away in the recesses of his memory. The scream was repeated, and he quickly identified the noise as an alarm.

Bry's high, stressed-out voice blared over the trans-comm speaker in the living room, "Unauthorized jumper! Security detail to the operations center, *stat!*"

A designated security force didn't exist as such in the redoubt. All of the personnel were required to become reasonably proficient with firearms, primarily the lightweight "point and shoot" SA-80 subguns. The armed security detail Bry summoned would be anyone who grabbed a gun from the armory and reached the control center under his or her own power.

Kane wriggled into a pair of jeans and snatched a small handblaster from a bedside table drawer. It was a nickel-plated Mustang .380, a memento of his captivity in Area 51. Barefoot and bare chested, he sprinted out into the corridor and into the control complex.

Lakesh, Brigid and Bry stood in the doorway that led into the antechamber. A deep humming tone vibrated from the gateway chamber.

Bright flashes, like strokes of heat lightning, flared on the other side of the brown-tinted armaglass walls. The low-pitched drone climbed to a hurricane wail.

"What the hell is going on?" Kane demanded as he joined them.

Brigid waved to the gateway unit. "We sent the remote probe through to the parallax point on the Moon. The interphaser reactivated just like we programmed it to do—but someone or thing has come back with it!"

Kane noted absently that Brigid was attired in a white bodysuit, so at some point while he slept she had found the time to change clothes.

Lakesh bit out, "Whatever or whoever it is, they're coming into phase."

Gushing lines of energy formed a luminous cloud within the chamber. Almost faster than the eye could perceive, the cloud grew more dense and definite of outline. Through the walls, they vaguely discerned a human figure. The electronic wail from the jump chamber faded, dropping down to silence. The bursts of light behind the translucent slabs disappeared.

Grant ran in, breathing hard, hefting his Sin Eater. He had decided to swing by the armory first. Kane took a step forward into the ready room, fisting his blaster. "Let's see who or what the interphaser brought back."

Kane and Grant cautiously approached the armaglass door of the gateway unit from opposite directions. They took up positions on either side of it, exchanged curt nods, then Grant heaved up on the handle.

The door swung open on its counterbalanced hinges, and tendrils of vapor curled out. Then a lean, faceless banshee howled out of the mist, like a demon flung from a smoldering hell pit. The shriek erupting from the blank, smooth, mouthless face vibrated with a soul-deep terror and murderous rage.

Brigid blurted, "Megaera!"

Chapter 11

Long, stringy hair streamed out like a gray mop from the woman's head. The hem of her ankle-length, sky-blue robe snagged on a riser of the two steps that extended down from the jump platform. She lurched to a stumbling, staggering halt as a torrent of gibberish burst from her featureless face.

After a shocked handful of seconds, all of them realized the woman did indeed have a face but her features were completely concealed by a mask. It bore the contours of a human face and looked like a thin layer of beaten gold. The mask was worked in the likeness of a woman of ethereal beauty, but there were no openings for the eyes, nose or the mouth. The eyes were molded as if closed in sleep.

She waved an odd device in her right hand, a rod of sleek, gleaming black alloy more than two feet long. It was tipped with a spherical knob of a dull, silvery metal, slightly smaller than a fowl's egg. She brandished the rod at Lakesh, Brigid and Bry as she continued to shriek.

Megaera paid no heed to Grant and Kane standing on the gateway platform behind her and was oblivious to the pair of guns trained on her back. More than likely, the mask over her face reduced her field of peripheral vision.

"Freeze, slagger!" both men roared more or less simultaneously, using their Mag voices, a sharp, commanding tone at a volume that intimidated malefactors and broke violent momentum. Megaera didn't so much as turn her head in their direction. She either didn't hear them over her own full-throated screams or didn't understand their language.

Kane shifted the barrel of his blaster downward, preparing to put a bullet in the back of the woman's knee. Alarmed, Lakesh rushed forward, around the long polished table that was the ready room's only furniture. He held out his hands in a conciliatory gesture, showing the woman he was unarmed. "Don't shoot!" he shouted to Grant and Kane.

The gold-masked woman stopped shrieking for a moment, swinging the knobbed end of the wand in her hand toward Lakesh. Brigid bounded forward and body blocked Lakesh to one side, hurling him half atop the table. The rod emitted a small click, as if a piece of wire had broken inside of it.

Light glinted dully from the round object that sprang from the end of the rod. Brigid caught a brief glimpse of spindly silver spider legs unfolding as it flashed over her head. Bry cried out in surprise as it struck the door frame near his shoulder and fell clattering to the floor.

Kane leaped from the elevated platform, landing right behind the woman. She reacted to his presence then, starting to turn, lifting the black tube. Brigid pushed herself away from Lakesh and secured a grip on Megaera's bony wrist, wrenching her arm behind her. The woman struggled, her voice hitting a high-pitched note of pain, mindless terror and frustration.

With the short barrel of the Colt Mustang, Kane knocked the rod from her hand, grabbed her left forearm and jerked up the belled cuff of her sleeve. A metal band studded with what appeared to be opals encircled her bony wrist. Kane groped for the release catch, found it and opened the thick bracelet. As it fell to the floor, Megaera uttered a howl of despondency. He helped Brigid secure a hammerlock. The woman was astonishingly strong, straining against their hands.

Grant joined them, fitting the tips of his fingers beneath the edge of the mask where it tapered down to cover her chin. He pried it away, revealed a seamed, high-boned face and a pair of pale blue eyes that gleamed like ice floating in a polar sea.

DeFore and Farrell pushed past Bry into the ready room, wielding the little SA-80 subguns. Brigid said calmly into Megaera's ear, "I know you can understand me, you demented old bitch. Calm down or we'll calm you down."

Megaera tried to twist her head around, thin lips working as if she wanted to spit in Brigid's face, then she sagged in her arms, head bowed, gray hair screening her face. She muttered a few words. Lakesh cautiously approached her. "We mean you no harm."

In a dull voice hoarse from screaming, Megaera intoned in heavily accented English, "You will all be judged for your sins." She tossed her head backward toward Brigid. "This one escaped my judgment, but the gods have conspired to put her within the reach of my Oubolus again. She will pay."

Brigid cinched up tighter on the woman's arm, dragging a little aspirated cry of pain from her. "Without your Furies to run interference, your reach is very short. "

Lakesh's lips twitched in an effort to repress a smile. To Megaera, he inquired blandly, *"Di-ku?"*

The woman suddenly straightened, looking levelly at Lakesh. Her thin mouth creased in an enigmatic smile. "Yes," she declared pridefully. *"Di-ku."* Then she began shrieking again.

DeFore clapped a hand over the old woman's mouth and looked closely at her, noting the wild blaze in her eyes. "She's nearly hysterical. She could probably benefit from a sedative."

"Put her in detention first," Kane said, handing her off to Farrell, who maintained the hammerlock on her arm.

Domi appeared in the doorway, holding her big Detonics Combat Master autoblaster in a two-fisted grip. "What the hell is going on?"

When she spied the golden mask and black rod lying on the floor, she exclaimed, "Queen of the night-gaunts! How did she get here?"

"She fell down a worm hole," Lakesh replied,

bending to pick up the tube. He sighted along it as if it were a rifle.

To Domi, he said, "Darlingest one, please go with Farrell to Level Three. Make sure our guest doesn't escape."

Grant took a step forward. "I'll go with you."

Domi shook her head. "No need. Got it covered." She backed out of the ready room, her pistol trained on Megaera's seamed face. DeFore trailed along behind them, saying, "I'll stop by the infirmary and see what I have in the way of tranquilizers."

Kane noticed how Domi hadn't so much as glanced in Grant's direction even when she spoke to him, but he figured it wasn't the time or place to remark on it.

Lakesh ran his fingers over the length of black metal and held it up to the light. "There are inscriptions here. Cuneiform markings." He cast an approving look toward Brigid. "Thank you for getting me out of the way of the Oubolus. In the excitement, what you told me about them slipped my mind."

Brigid forced a smile. "I'm glad it didn't mine. And at least we know where Megaera and her Furies came from. It's been bothering me for a long while."

"Me, too," Lakesh murmured, tracing the inscriptions on the rod with a forefinger. "But as we should have learned by now, all things come to he who waits."

THE MYSTERY of Megaera and her shadow-suited Furies was one of many that had been waiting for a solution. Other, more immediate matters had arisen, preventing the Cerberus specialists from performing a full investigation. Now it appeared the answer had arrived right on their doorstep.

A few months before, while following up on yet another mystery—why and who time-trawled Domi at the precise microinstant before she was swallowed by the full lethal fury of a grenade—the Cerberus network sensor indicated activity in the gateway unit in Redoubt Echo. That in itself wasn't unusual. Over the past year and a half, the sensor link had registered an unprecedented volume of mat-trans traffic. Most of it was due to the concerted search for the renegades from Cobaltville, but there had also been the appearance of anomalous activities, signatures of jump lines that could not be traced back to their origin points.

Certainly there were any number of unindexed, mass-produced, modular gateway units of which there were no records. Years ago, when Lakesh had used Baron Cobalt's trust in him to covertly reactivate Cerberus redoubt, he had altered the modulations of the mat-trans gateway so the transmissions were untraceable, at least by conventional means. However, the signal from the gateway in Redoubt Echo wasn't anomalous. The unit was an indexed part of the Cerberus network, and Lakesh believed the activity was connected to Operation Chronos—primarily because Chronos had been headquartered in a subterranean facility in Chicago, at least for a time.

They couldn't open a jump line to the gateway in

Redoubt Echo, so Kane, Brigid, Domi, Grant and DeFore had embarked on a long overland journey to Chicago. There, they encountered the bizarre group of Furies led by Megaera who meted out their own terrible form of justice with the Oubolus rods.

In ancient Greek mythology, Megaera was a Fury, one of three sisters charged by the gods to pursue sinners on Earth. They were inexorable and relentless in their dispensation of justice. A bit of old verse about them claimed that "Not even the sun will transgress his orbit lest the Furies, the ministers of justice, overtake him."

The Oubolus was the collective name for the payment given by souls on their way to the underworld, a form of coin given to Charon, the ferryman for passage across the River Acheron. According to myth, if payment was not made, a soul had to wander the riverbank throughout eternity.

Megaera's version of the Oubolus was a little device that was fired from the hollow baton. When it attached itself to a target, a sinner, it delivered an incapacitating jolt of voltage. Once judgment was levied against the sinner, the wristband control mechanism initiated a horrifying process by which the skeletal structure and internal organs were dissolved, leaving only an empty, carbonized husk in the shape of the sinner.

Megaera and a contingent of Furies had stalked a group of Farers in Chicago, bringing to terrifying life old folk tales about soul-stealing demons called night-gaunts. They never spoke or laughed and never smiled because they had no faces at all to smile with.

Brigid was captured by Megaera, who told her they had been transported from their home "in the mists and the mountains" by a small, smiling god. She believed the god wanted them to continue their work in Chicago.

Brigid managed to escape judgment but not the small, smiling god, who turned out to be Sindri. He took her from Redoubt Echo to the Operation Chronos installation on Thunder Isle. When Grant and Kane followed, they learned Sindri was responsible for not only time-trawling Domi, but also for Megaera and her Furies.

Sindri confessed that while experimenting with the parallax points program, he brought them through, but from where or even when he didn't know. He pretended to be a deity to protect himself from the Oubolus, but when they became too troublesome, he arranged to send them back to wherever they came from.

Since that time, the origin of Megaera had been the latest entry in a long list of unknowns, although DeFore and Brigid had repeated a fairly close approximation of some of the words they heard Megaera speak.

Di-ku was one of them, an ancient Sumerian term that meant "to judge" or "judgment determiner." Lakesh found it very significant, particularly since evidence indicated that the Sumerian civilization was influenced by the root race of the Archons, the Annunaki.

However, there was little evidence to even build a provisional hypothesis about Megaera's connection with Sumeria or the Annunaki. Even Lakesh knew that all the history they knew of the barons, the nukecaust and even the Archons derived from secondhand and dubious sources, with very little supporting empirical evidence. All they really had as a foundation was myth, often distorted and disguised out of all reliable proportion.

Now the opportunity to erase the question mark from the list of unknowns had arrived.

LAKESH HELD UP the little silver spider, gingerly touching the filament-like legs that extended from its oval body. "There are inscriptions on this, too," he observed.

"What do they say?" Kane asked. "If Lost, Please Return To Little Miss Muffet?"

"Very whimsical, friend Kane," Lakesh retorted, deadpan. "Like the markings on the rod, they're in cuneiform script."

"It's a shame you can't read Sumerian," Grant remarked. "But it's nice to know you have some limitations. They'll keep you from getting too big a head."

"I assure you my ego is the proper proportion for a man of my age and accomplishments."

"In which case," Kane put in, "it should properly

be about the size of a pea. Particularly if you factor in a guilty conscience.''

Lakesh took his eyes off the metallic spider long enough to direct a glare at Kane, but he soon returned his attention to examining the little gadget in his hand. He refused to be baited.

Without looking away from the VGA monitor screen, Brigid said, ''Kane, it would be refreshing if you could 'factor' in a new way to get on Lakesh's nerves.''

Kane shrugged. ''Why mess with perfection?''

Lakesh tended to blame himself for many things, and for a long time, Kane gleefully helped him do so. As a project overseer for the Totality Concept, then as an adviser and even something of an architect of the unification program, Lakesh had helped to bring about the tyranny of the barons.

Much later, far too late as far as Kane was concerned, he turned against the hybrids, betraying them and even stealing from them to build his resistance movement. Lakesh found no true sin in betraying betrayers or stealing from thieves. He couldn't think of the hybrid barons in any other way, despite their own preference for the term *new human*.

Lakesh then tried his hand at creating his own new humans. Some forty years before, when he first decided to resist the baronies, he rifled the genetic records on file to find the qualifications he deemed the most desirable. He used the unification program's own fixation with genetic purity against the barons.

By his own confession, he was a physicist cast in the role of an archivist, pretending to be a geneticist, manipulating a political system that was still in a state of flux.

Kane was one such example of that political and genetic manipulation, and when he learned about Lakesh's involvement in his birth, he had very nearly killed him.

From the far end of the operations complex, Bry called from the photo-scanner station, "Almost done."

The Oubolus baton was in the process of being scanned. The inscriptions on its surface would be fed into the main database, where the historical and linguistics banks could hopefully decipher them.

Kane, still bare chested and barefoot, sat in a swivel chair at one of the vacant desks, idling turning around and around on the squeaking gimbal. Brigid sat at the main terminal, chin cupped in one hand, replaying the images recorded by the remote vid probe, doing what she could to augment and enhance them. The quality was exceptionally poor. The tape had apparently been damaged by the electromagnetic pulses emitted by the interphaser. Despite the heavy shielding of the remote, little more than variegated streaks of color and shapeless pixelated images showed up on the screen.

DeFore's voice floated out of the trans-comm. "I've just administered 20 ccs of Seconal to our guest. She should become a little more tractable in a few minutes."

"Will she able to answer questions?" Lakesh asked.

"Maybe." DeFore sounded doubtful. "Maybe not. I could always give her a Sodium Pentothal chaser."

"Let's save that for a last resort," Lakesh replied. "Post Auerbach outside the door so he can keep an eye on her."

"Got it."

Brigid leaned forward over the keyboard, hand on the mouse. "I may have something here."

Grant, Kane and Lakesh stood around her, staring at the streaks and swirls of prismatic color crawling across the four-foot monitor screen. From a pouch on her bodysuit, Brigid withdrew the symbol of her former office as a Cobaltville archivist. She slipped on the pair of rectangular-lensed, wire-framed spectacles and gazed steadily at the screen. Although the eyeglasses were something of a reminder of her past life, they also served as a means to correct an astigmatism.

Still, she squinted at the flashes of color, first leaning very close to the screen, then sitting back. Kane briefly wondered if her vision hadn't been further impaired by the head injury she suffered several months before. The only visible sign of the wound that had laid her scalp open to the bone and put her in a coma for several days was a faintly red horizontal line on her right temple that disappeared into the roots of her hair. Her recovery time had been little short of uncanny. Kane was always impressed by the woman's tensile-spring resiliency.

However, he couldn't help but notice how she needed her glasses more and more in the weeks and months following her release from the redoubt's infirmary.

Pixels flickered over the screen. And slowly images began to form, overlaid by a distracting white glow that strobed like the sputter of dying neon. The fluttering pattern coalesced into a scene that at first they could make little sense of, dimly illuminated and shot through with jagged pixels. They could barely make out a wide chamber filled with dark, unmoving shapes.

Brigid manipulated the mouse and tapped a few keys. The image shuddered and jerked, presumably as the remote probe rolled forward a few feet on its treaded tracks. With a colorful shimmer, the interference faded and the screen showed what at first appeared to be a collection of black statues, all of human beings. She instinctively cringed in her chair, muttering grimly, "Another Hall of the Judged Sinners."

Grant and Kane knew instantly she referred to the chamber in Redoubt Yankee that Megaera and her Furies had filled with the carbonized husks of Farers unfortunate enough to be struck by the Oubolus.

The statues on the screen were as immobile and as jet-black as the victims they had seen in Chicago. Every fold of cloth, every strand of hair was visible. Scattered here and there with no regard for order, they were all distorted in different postures—shielding their heads with up-flung arms, on their knees with their hands clasped together as if they were still pleading for their lives when the calcification process began, others in crouching postures as if they had turned to run. The one common feature was the expression of unendurable terror on the face of each figure.

"What's the light source?" Grant asked.

Brigid shook her head. "I don't know. Whatever it is, it's not direct."

The camera of the remote panned slowly to the left, and for an instant before the view dissolved in a blizzard of pixels, they saw a set of circular metal stairs spiraling up into a square opening. A light-colored, indistinct shape bulked in the shadowy space between the staircase and the wall.

"What's that under the stairs?" Kane wanted to know.

Brigid replayed the short sequence, and when the staircase appeared again Kane directed, "Freeze it there. Can you augment and enhance it?"

"I'll try." By manipulating the mouse and stroking the appropriate sequence of keys, Brigid enlarged the area. Not much could be done about the poor illumination, but the computer program highlighted features and reduced interference. She tapped the keys until, by degrees, the image of a large metal cube swelled on the screen.

"It's a box," Grant stated. "A shipping crate."

"Yeah," Kane agreed, "but there's writing on it. A couple of words."

Brigid leaned forward. Carefully, she spelled it out aloud. "N-A-S-A."

Lakesh's sudden startled intake of breath sounded like steel sliding across wet leather. "It's not just a word—it's the logo of NASA, the National Aeronautics Space Administration."

"That's one issue settled, then," declared Brigid. "The interphaser opened a vortex node on the Moon, apparently inside an old base. It's probably underground."

"There's something else written under it," Grant said, pointing to it. "D-E-V-I. What's Devi?"

"A title held by Indian royalty," Lakesh replied dryly. "I doubt NASA was shipping devis to the Moon."

"Devil, maybe?" Kane ventured.

Lakesh shook his head. "I don't think they were transporting devils to the Moon, either."

The tape began normal forward play again. Two shapes appeared in the doorway and the top of the spiral staircase. Because of the interference, they couldn't quickly be identified as human, animal or mineral. The image continued to break up and clear, and each time it did the shapes had progressed farther down the staircase. Both of them wended their way among the cluster of black statues, apparently intent on investigating both the interphaser and the remote probe.

The closer they drew to the remote, the more their outlines resolved into human figures. Gold flashed dully and Brigid froze the image. ''Megaera,'' she said. ''She moved into the effect radius of the interphaser when it reactivated the node.''

Lakesh bent toward the monitor screen, eyes narrowed. ''Who or what is that behind her?''

Brigid isolated the taller figure and worked on reducing the shadows obscuring it. In slow, fitful jerks the image enlarged until a blurry, pixelated head filled the screen. All of them stared in dumbfounded silence for a moment.

They could see a very tall, lean man-shape wearing a hooded cassock-like garment that appeared to be made of an assortment of rainbow-colored silks. The figure was very tall, towering over the black statues. It looked to be even taller than Grant, but it was excessively slender. It moved with a swaying motion like a reed before a wind. The motion was at once familiar and unnerving.

Although the cowl threw most of the face into shadow, they saw a narrow, elongated skull that held large, almond-shaped eyes with black vertical slits centered in the golden, opalescent irises. They gleamed like molten pools under craggy brow ridges. The leathery skin, stretched tight over a protuberant shelf of cheekbones, held a suggestion of scales and was of a brownish-red hue. Wide nostrils flared above an inhumanly wide, lipless mouth. Although the high-planed face did not hold a definable expression, it seemed to exude a cold intelligence and a perpetual anger.

At length, Grant husked out, "I guess you were right, Lakesh."

"About what?" Lakesh inquired absently, attention still fixed on the face filling the monitor screen.

"NASA didn't need to transport devils to the Moon. There was probably one already there."

Kane uttered the word that had sprang into all of their minds. "Annunaki."

Chapter 12

Horan, Ojaka, McGee and Ormond all silently steeled themselves as the pneumatic-powered elevator hissed to a stop. The four men wore identical bodysuits and held identical file folders in both hands as if they were rare books.

When the doors rolled open, they walked mechanically down the ramp into the entrance foyer to A Level of the Administrative Monolith. Ojaka in particular still thought of it as the baron's level, despite knowing such a habit could earn him anything from a reprimand to a quick trip to E Level and the execution chamber.

A Level was the only one in the Monolith without windows, but a huge gaping cavity had been blown into the wall some months before. It had yet to be repaired, although the maintenance section had covered it with double-strength sheets of Mylar. Ojaka paused briefly to glance out over the city spread below.

Cobaltville was built on the bluffs overlooking a twisting tributary of the Kanab River. Stone walls rose fifty feet high about the hills, and at each intersecting corner protruded a Vulcan-Phalanx gun tower.

Powerful spotlights washed the immediate area outside the walls, leaving nothing hidden from the glare. The bluffs surrounding the walls were kept cleared of vegetation. On the far side of the winding river, tangles of razor wire surrounded cultivated fields.

As in all the fortified villes, a narrow roadbed of crushed gravel led up to the main gate, passing two checkpoint stations. The first, at the mouth of the road, was a small concrete-block cupola, manned only by a single Magistrate. Past the cupola, pyramid-shaped ''dragon's teeth'' obstacles made of reinforced concrete lined both sides of the path. Weighing a thousand pounds each and five feet tall, they were designed to break the tracks or wheels of any assault vehicle trying to cross them.

A dozen yards before the gate, stone blockhouses bracketed the road. Within them were electrically controlled GEC Miniguns, capable of firing 6000 5.56 mm rounds per minute. Past the blockhouses was the main gate itself—twenty feet wide by fifteen high, with a two-foot thickness of rockcrete sheathed by cross-braced iron. The portal was opened by a buried system of huge gears and cables.

One of the official reasons for fortifying the villes was a century-old fear—or paranoid delusion—of a foreign invasion from other nuke-scarred nations. Then there had been the threat of mutie clans, like the vicious stickies, unifying and sweeping across the country. Like the fear of a foreign invasion, such a campaign among the muties had never materialized, but the threat alone burned so brightly in the collective minds of the architects of the Program of Unification, that a major early aspect of the unification program involved wiping out mutie settlements in ville territories.

Inside the walls stretched the complex of spired Enclaves. Each of the four towers was joined to the others by pedestrian bridges. Few of the windows in the towers showed any light, so there was little to indicate that the interconnecting network of stone columns, enclosed walkways, shops and promenades was where nearly four thousand people made their homes.

In the Enclaves, the people who worked for the ville administrators enjoyed lavish apartments, all the bounty of those favored by Baron Cobalt.

Far below the Enclaves, on a sublevel beneath the bluffs, light peeped up from the dark streets of the Tartarus Pits. This sector of Cobaltville was a seething melting pot, where outlanders and slaggers lived. They swarmed with cheap labor, and any movement between the Enclaves and Pits was tightly controlled—only a Magistrate on official business could enter the Pits, and only a Pit-dweller with a legitimate work order could even approach the cellar of an Enclave tower.

Seen from above, the Enclave towers formed a latticework of intersected circles, all connected to the center of the circle, from which rose the Administrative Monolith. The massive round column of white rockcrete jutted three hundred feet into the sky, standing proud and haughty and cold, symbolizing to all and sundry that order had replaced the barbarism of postskydark America.

Every level of the tower was designed to fulfill a specific capacity: E, or Epsilon, Level was a general construction and manufacturing facility. D, or Delta, Level was devoted to the preservation, preparation and distribution of food. C, or Cappa,—an American version of Kappa—Level held the Magistrate Division. On B, or Beta, Level was the Historical Archives, a combination of library, museum and computer center. The archives included almost five hundred thousand books, discovered and restored over the past ninety-five years, not to mention an incredibly varied array of predark artifacts. The work of the administrators was conducted on the highest level, Alpha Level.

Horan, a stocky man with a grizzled crew cut, called to Ojaka in an urgent whisper, "Stop stalling. Let's get this over with."

A shiver shook Ojaka's pudgy body, and he swiftly left the Mylar-covered hole and joined his three companions. Beyond the reception areas, Alpha Level was a labyrinth of concealed chambers and secret corridors. One particular corridor led through a confusing array of rooms and archways, ending finally in a large chamber, illuminated by the sickly gray glow from an unseen light source.

The four men took their places in a formal semicircle in the center of the enormous Persian carpet that covered the floor. They faced an archway draped by a filmy, gauzy curtain. None of the men spoke, since a meeting of the Trust was neither the time nor the place for casual conversation. Every ville had its own version of the Trust. The organization, if it could be called that, was the only face-to-face contact allowed with the barons, and the barons were the only contacts permitted by the Archon Directorate. All of them had been told that secret societies like the Trust had its roots in ancient Egypt, Babylon, Mesopotamia, Greece and even Sumeria. Throughout humankind's history, secret covenants with the entities known as Archons were struck by kings, princes and even presidents.

The Trust's oath revolved around a single theme— the presence of the Directorate must not be revealed to humanity. If the presence of the Archons became known, if the technological marvels they had designed became accessible, if the truth behind the nukecaust filtered down to the people, then humankind would no doubt retaliate with a concerted effort to wipe them out—or the Directorate would be forced to visit another holocaust upon the face of the earth, simply as a measure of self-preservation.

At least, that's what all of them had been told upon their induction into the Trust many years before. Now little of it appeared to be true. All that was left was the ceremony. Of the original eight men comprising Baron Cobalt's Trust, only five remained, including Lakesh who had left the group and had never been replaced. Guende and Abrams were dead, and Salvo's ultimate fate was unknown although it was assumed he was dead. Ojaka reflected bleakly the three men might be the lucky ones.

In the gloom on the other side of the archway, a door slowly opened. Behind the curtain, a golden light suffused in pastel hues slanted down from above. The gong struck thirteen jubilant strokes, and the shaft of muted golden light became a glare. Right before the glare faded to its previous soft hue, a dark figure appeared within it.

Erica van Sloan, the ville Administrator and the imperator's emissary, had arrived.

Erica van Sloan was tall and beautiful with a flawless complexion the hue of fine honey. Her long, straight hair, swept back from a high forehead and pronounced widow's peak, tumbled artlessly about her shoulders. It was so black as to be blue when the light caught it. The large, feline-slanted eyes above high, regal cheekbones looked almost the same color, but glints of violet swam in them. The mark of an aristocrat showed in her delicate features, with the arch of brows and her thin-bridged nose.

A graceful, swanlike neck led to a slender body encased in a strange uniform—high black boots, jodhpurs of a shiny black fabric, with an ebony satin tunic tailored to conform to the thrust of her full breasts. Emblazoned on the left sleeve was a symbol depicting a thick-walled pyramid worked in red thread, enclosing and partially bisected by three elongated but reversed triangles. Small disks topped each one, lending them a resemblance to round-hilted daggers. Once the unifying insignia of the Archon Directorate, the symbol was then adopted by Overproject Excalibur, the Totality Concept's division devoted to genetic engineering. Now it was the insignia of the imperator, as was the black uniform.

In a mild, melodious, beautiful voice, the woman said, "I'm really going to have to do something about that silly gong and light show. I can't find the controls and it's on automatic."

The four men inwardly flinched when Erica van Sloan continued to walk toward them. Instead of remaining half-hidden by the semitransparent curtain and addressing them from the shadows as had Baron Cobalt, she strode boldly up to them. They still connected the audience chamber with the semimystical ritual with which the baron cloaked meetings of the Trust.

"Good evening, gentlemen," she said in a brisk, businesslike tone. "Please give me your reports of the ville's current status. The imperator is very anxious that the rebuilding process be completed as soon as possible."

Horan hesitated, then stepped forward, extending his file folder to the administrator. The other men followed suit, and she accepted each file with a word of thanks.

"You've been very cooperative since I arrived

here,'' she told them with a smile. ''The imperator is very pleased.''

The members of the Trust ducked their heads and murmured, ''We are to serve—''

''It is only our duty—''

''We wish only to please our lord baron—''

Erica's eyes narrowed as they bored in on Ojaka's suddenly stricken face. The man swallowed hard and reflexively raised his mouth as if he were hoping to cram the more incriminating words back into his mouth. The form of address was by rote, something he had said at almost every meeting of the Trust for decades. Sweat sprang to his brow as he stammered, ''For-forgive me, Administrator. I spoke from habit.''

Erica chuckled. ''Don't stress yourself over it, Ojaka. I know more than any of you how hard old habits are to break.''

She didn't clarify her comments for the benefit of the four men but only because vanity kept her from revealing she was at least three times as old as the most senior member of the Trust.

Born in 1974, Dr. Erica van Sloan was of half-Latino and half-British extraction. She had inherited her dark hair and eyes from her Brazilian mother, but she possessed her father's tall frame and long, solid legs. God only knew from which side of her family her 200-point IQ derived, but she knew she received her beautiful singing voice from her mother.

At eighteen years of age, the haughty, beautiful and more than a trifle arrogant Erica earned her Ph.D in cybernetics and computer science. She wanted to pursue a singing career, but within days of her graduation from Cal Tech she went to work for a major Silicon Valley hardware producer as a models and systems analyst.

Eight months later, she left her six-figure salary to accept a position with a government-sponsored ultra-top-secret undertaking known as Overproject Whisper. Only much later did she realize Whisper was a major division of something called the Totality Concept, and she was assigned to one of its subdivisions, Operation Chronos. In the vast installation beneath a mesa in Dulce, New Mexico, she served as the subordinate, lover and occasional victim of a man who made her own officious personality seem mousy and shy by comparison.

Torrence Silas Burr was brilliant, stylish, waspish and nasty. He excelled at using his enormous intellect and equally enormous ego to fuel his cruel sense of humor. He delighted in belittling and degrading not just her, but other scientists assigned to Overproject Whisper. The one scientist he could not deride was Mohandas Lakesh Singh, the genius responsible for the final technological breakthrough of Project Cerberus, which permitted Operation Chronos to finally make some headway.

With the advent of the Cerberus success, the new installations were built and linked by gateway units. Though the COG facilities and the scientific enclaves weren't part of the same program, there was an almost continuous trade-off of design specifications, technology and personnel. Many of the Totality Concept's subdivisions and spin-off researches were relocated to these redoubts. Chronos was moved to Chicago and Cerberus was moved to Montana.

The most ambitious COG facility was code-named the Anthill because of its resemblance in layout to an ant colony. It was a vast complex, with a railway, stores, theaters and even a sports arena. Supplies of foodstuffs, weapons and anything of value was stockpiled, often times in triplicate.

Because of its size, the Anthill was built inside Mount Rushmore, using tunneling and digging machines. The entire mountain was honeycombed with interconnected levels, passageways and chambers.

Erica learned that once construction on the Anthill was completed, the entire Totality Concept program would be moved into it and she was ordered to go along. She couldn't understand why exactly and complained bitterly. When the world blew out on noon of January 20, 2001, she ceased to complain. She would be part of the new world order that would emerge from the radioactive ashes of the old.

The prolonged nuclear winter changed ideas about a new world order. Even if the Anthill personnel managed to outlast skydark, they would still sicken and die, either from radiation sickness or simply old age.

So they embarked on a radical and daring plan. Cybernetic technology had made great leaps in the latter part of the twentieth century, and Erica herself had made some small contributions to those advances. General Kettridge, the self-styled commander of the Anthill, ordered operations to be performed on everyone living in the Anthill, making use of the new techniques in organ transplants and medical technology, as well in cybernetics.

Over a period of years, everyone living inside Mount Rushmore was turned into cyborgs, hybridizations of human and machine. Radiation-burned flesh was replaced by synthetic skin, limbs with cancerous marrows were changed out for ones made of plastic, Dacron and Teflon. With less energy to expend on maintaining the body, the cyborganized subjects ate less and therefore extended the stockpile of foodstuffs by several years.

Since the main difficulty in constructing interfaces between mechanical-electric and organic systems was the wiring, Erica oversaw the implantation of superconducting quantum interface devices—or SQUIDs—directly into the brain. One-hundredth of a micron across, these devices facilitated the subject's control over their new prostheses.

Although Erica herself had designed the implants and oversaw the early operations, she certainly didn't care for the process being performed on her. She knew the SQUIDs could be used to electronically control the personnel, and she wasn't fond of being turned into a biomechanical drone. However, she was even less fond of the alternative—euthanasia.

Of course, the transformations didn't solve all of the Anthill's survival issues. Compensation for the natural aging process of organs and tissues had to be taken into account. The Anthill personnel needed a supply of fresh organs, preferably those of young people, but obviously the supply was severely limited. So General Kettridge, now calling himself the commander in chief, came up with a solution—cryogenics, or a variation thereof.

Kettridge was inspired by the method of keeping organic materials fresh by pumping a hermetically sealed vault full of dry nitrogen gas and lowering the temperature to below freezing. He ordered the internal temperatures inside the installation to be lowered just enough to preserve the tissues but not low enough to damage the organs.

Other scientific disciplines were blended. The interior of the entire facility was permeated with low-level electrostatic fields of the kind hospitals experimented with to maintain the sterility of operating rooms. The form of cryogenesis employed at the installation wasn't the standard freezing process relying on immersing a subject in liquid nitrogen and the removal of blood and organs.

It utilized a technology that employed a stasis screen tied in with the electrostatic sterilizing fields, which for all intents and purposes turned the Anthill complex into an encapsulated deep storage vault. This process created a form of active suspended animation, almost as if the personnel were enclosed by an impenetrable bubble of space and time, slowing to a crawl all metabolic processes. The people achieved a form of immortality, but one completely dependent on technology.

Erica never wondered aloud where the stasis technology came from, but she assumed it derived from the mysterious "they" whom Kettridge accused of betrayal.

However, even those measures were temporary. Erica volunteered to enter a stasis canister for a period of time, to be resurrected at some future date when the sun shone again and the world was secure.

When Erica awakened, more than 122 years had passed. During her long slumber, the Anthill installation suffered near-catastrophic damage. General Kettridge was killed and a number of stasis units malfunctioned, including her canister.

Due to that malfunction, her SQUIDs interface had inflicted neurological damage on her body, and she was resurrected as a cripple. Worse than finding out her long, shapely legs were little more than withered, atrophied sticks was learning the plans made for her while she slept.

Erica was briefed on the unification program, the baronial oligarchy and the true identities of Kettridge's "they." Or at least, they were a given a name. She was told that to be of optimal use to the Archon Directorate and their hybrid plenipotentiaries, she needed to be as fit as it was possible for a human in her physical condition and chronological age. Moreover, Erica was informed she was only one of several preholocaust humans, known as "freezies" in current vernacular, resurrected to serve the baronies and she should consider herself fortunate to be among their number.

In other words, she was not to grieve, mourn, weep

or otherwise feel sorry for herself. She was to concentrate only on what her technological skills could contribute to the furtherance of the Program of Unification. Otherwise, she would be put out of her misery.

Erica was not assigned to a particular ville for any length of time. She was given quarters in Front Royal, and from there she traveled from barony to barony, setting up their computer systems, training personnel in their operation and in troubleshooting procedures. The systems, although in absolutely pristine order, were not state of the art, certainly not by the standards of the first year of the twenty-first century.

None of the mainframes employed the biochip developments that would have been commonplace if the nukecaust had been averted. Most of the software, hardware and support systems were fairly basic, as well, not even approaching the Doomstar program she had helped design when on loan to the Special Cybernetics Operations Unit.

Erica couldn't help but suspect that the truly advanced predark tech was being deliberately suppressed. She could only assume it was done out of fear of the new postnuke society becoming just as dependent on technology as the old one.

Whatever the real reason, she learned quickly not to question. Over the years of Erica's long life, due to her creativity and her intellect, she had undergone many organ transplants so as to extend her value to the united baronies. Despite the pain and suffering that accompanied each successive operation, Erica never regained the use of her legs, and the neurological degeneration grew so acute she became a complete cripple.

Yet Sam had not only put life back into her legs again, he had also restored her youth. Her life was dedicated to his, to building a new, productive society on the framework of the ville system. Since cybernetic principles were applied to management and organizational theory, she always had much to offer in the way of streamlining ville government. Just as everything that occurred in the universe could be analyzed into cause-and-effect chains, the chains themselves could be used to build organizational models.

Now, months after the overthrow of Baron Cobalt, a new model was being constructed.

Erica eyed Ojaka keenly, then the other three men. "But," she said, an edge entering her voice, "your old habits *must* be broken. Your lord baron is gone and will never return. I won't attempt to deceive you by telling you he is dead, but the odds are very high that he is. When he fled Cobaltville at the height of the siege, we kept track of the places to which he could go. He never appeared at any of them."

She took a deep breath, her full bosom straining against the tight tunic. "There is a new order now, a program of reunification. The old baronial system served its purpose, and now it must serve the imperator's vision. If any of you are emotionally disturbed enough to actually miss the old ways, I suggest you resign from your positions immediately."

A cold smile creased her full lips. "Of course, you will resign your ville citizenship in the bargain and

you'll be cast out. I seriously doubt Baron Cobalt
would appreciate such a sacrifice.''

She saw the brief glint of terror in all of the men's
eyes. A ville citizen's reclassification to that of an
outlander was in some ways worse than a death sen-
tence. It was a form of nonexistence. To be recognized as a person with a right to exist, one had to
belong to ville society, even if only in the lowest
caste.

The men hurriedly denied ever considering such a
notion, their words of denial tumbling over one another's in their haste to speak. Erica halted the verbal
groveling by saying sharply, ''Enough. All I expect
from you is efficiency in rebuilding the ville, not how
willing you are to kiss my ass. You're dismissed, all
of you.''

She didn't want to see if the men backed out of the
chamber, bowing and scraping amid a frenzy of fore-
lock tugging. Turning on her heel, Erica marched
through the archway, impatiently thrusting aside the
curtain. She paused for a moment, then gave it a jerk,
yanking it and the crossbar from the wall. She
thought, although she couldn't be sure, she heard a
quickly stifled gasp of horror from the throat of
McGee.

She shook her black-tressed head in contempt. She
knew she shouldn't have been surprised by the sheep-
like obeisance shown by the Trust. All of the barons
in all of the villes, with the exception of Baron
Sharpe, took great pleasure in theatrical trappings, in
presenting a fearsome image to their servants. Part of
the reason was simple protection—physically, they

were fragile, their autoimmune systems at the mercy of infections and diseases that had little effect on the primitive humans they ruled.

Therefore the barons lived insulated, isolated lives, cloaking themselves in melodramatic ceremonies that not only added to their semidivine mystique, but also protected them from contamination—both psychological and physical.

Erica van Sloan entered the suite of rooms that had once served as Baron Cobalt's private quarters. Two members of the Baronial Guard stood impassively in parade-rest postures on either side of the ivory-and-gold-inlaid doors. The two guardsmen had identical Herculean physiques and blue eyes, although one had blond hair and the other black. Both of their faces were subtly sculpted to be the epitome of male beauty.

The red jackets, white trousers and high boots that once comprised their uniforms had been replaced by the satiny jet-black ensemble of the imperator's forces. The pair of men snapped to attention when they saw Erica approach. They didn't speak to her and she didn't address them. The guardsmen didn't have names as far as she knew, so she had christened them Abbott and Costello, in honor of a pair of comedians whose movies she had enjoyed as a child.

Costello opened the door for her and she nodded in acknowledgment. She paused a moment at the threshold, looking from him to Abbott. In a low, throaty voice she said, "Both of you this evening, I think."

Without a flicker of emotion, Abbott and Costello

followed her into the lavishly furnished bedchamber. The four-poster canopied bed was immense and could easily hold all three of them, as Erica knew. The floor was covered by an elaborately embroidered Asian carpet.

Tossing the file folders onto a bedside table, Erica crossed the room and stood before a full-length mirror within an ornately carved oaken frame. Standing before it, she extended her arms and commanded, "Attend to me."

Erica watched her reflection as Abbott and Costello undressed her. She leaned on Abbott as Costello knelt to tug off her jodhpurs. A dew of sweat gathered at Erica's temples, and she felt herself growing moist elsewhere. Her breath came in short, shallow pants.

When she was naked, Erica admired herself in the mirror, once again reminded of marble statues of goddesses she had seen in museums. She noticed how the nipples of her full breasts stood hard and erect and how the flat muscles of her belly quivered, as if in excitement. She kept on her high-heeled boots, liking the effect.

Erica wasn't sure why her sexual energy seemed so enhanced since Sam had restored her youth. She wondered if Lakesh experienced a similar phenomenon. She had toyed with the possibility that Sam had stimulated her metabolism in such a way that her endorphin level was unnaturally high, but she never thought to ask him about it. It wasn't seemly for a mother to ask her son a question of that nature.

The guardsmen slid their hands smoothly over her

flawless skin, fondling her breasts and stroking her in the ways and places she had taught them. While Abbott's and Costello's experience wasn't great, they weren't virgins—at least they weren't after her first night as administrator of Cobaltville. She put her arms around the broad yokes of their shoulders as they caressed her, following her whispered, moaning instructions.

Erica eyed herself in the mirror—and stiffened, catching her breath. Her heart began to pound and the sweat of lust turned cold and clammy on her skin. Oblivious to her sudden change in mood, the two men continued their single-minded touching and fondling.

Impatiently, Erica squirmed away from their hands and stepped closer to the mirror. She clamped her lips tight on the cry of alarm working its way up her throat.

A wide strip of gray ran like a bleached-out ribbon through the left side of her ebony hair.

Chapter 13

It was an axiom of conspiracies that someone or something else always pulled the strings of willing or ignorant puppets. After his revival from cyrosleep, Lakesh expended many years tracing those filaments back through convoluted and manufactured histories to the puppet masters themselves. Even then he realized one man couldn't hope to penetrate a conspiracy of secrecy that had been maintained for twenty thousand years or more.

Lakesh at first believed the puppet strings would terminate with the entities known as Archons, but he was forced to reassess that opinion, particularly when delving into secret government files. The biological studies performed back when the Archons were referred to as Pan Terrestrial Entities were frustratingly incomplete.

At first, the so-called Archons were classified as EBEs, Extraterrestrial Biological Entities, but that designation was later amended, since it may have been premature if not erroneous. When everything known about the Archons was distilled was down to its basic components, all the scientific minds devoted to the subject could agree on only one thing—they knew very little.

Autopsies performed on bodies recovered in the New Mexico desert in the 1940s proved they were composed of the same basic biological matter as humans, although their blood was of the rare Rh type. Although they were erect-standing bipeds, with disproportionately long arms and oversize craniums, forensic and genetic findings indicated they were descended from an unknown reptilian species.

Lakesh had always found that bit of information fascinating and disquieting at the same time. As much of a student of mythology as physics, he knew that for as long as humanity had kept records, there were legends of a mysterious serpent folk descending from the heavens to participate in the creation of humankind. Cultures as widespread as Sumer, Babylonia, China, Japan and even Central America had myth cycles about these reptilian entities. Serpents or dragons signified divine heritage in many Asian countries.

Known in ancient codices and texts as the Serpent Folk, the Sumerians called them the Annunaki. The Judaic *Haggadah* described them as standing upright like humans and in height, "equal to the camel." The document mentioned their superior mental gifts, despite their possession of "a visage like a viper."

The Sumerian records referred to Enki and Enlil as being charged with the task of creating a labor force on Earth to mine ore. This they did by a process that to Lakesh seemed suspiciously like genetic manipulation.

For years Lakesh was vexed by the connection between the Archons and the Annunaki. The possibility the Archons originated on another planet was only that, a possibility. Certainly the Archons had never made such a claim, but they never disputed it, either. Nor did they object to having the "Archon" appellation employed to describe their race.

No clear-cut answers about the Archon Directorate had ever presented themselves. Only its agenda was not open to conjecture. It had been the same for thousands of years. Historically, the Archon Directorate made alliances with certain individuals or governments, who in turn reaped the benefits of power and wealth.

The nuclear apocalypse fit well with Archon strategy. After a century, with the destruction of social structures and severe depopulation, the Archons allied themselves with the nine most powerful barons. They distributed predark technology to them and helped to establish the ville political system, all to consolidate their power over Earth and its disenfranchised, spiritually beaten human inhabitants.

The goal of unifying the world, with all nonessential and nonproductive humans eliminated or hybridized, was so close to completion there was no point in wondering what the Archons actually were.

Lakesh had once hoped the solution to both the riddle of the Archons and the enigma of humanity's mysterious origins lay in ancient religious codices, such as the Mahabharata and the Ramayana, which described the coming of the ''Sons of the Moon and the Sun'' in flying machines called *vimanas*.

The few surviving sacred texts contained only hints, inferences passed down from generation to generation, not actual answers. Millennia-old documents that might have held the truth had crumbled into dust or were deliberately destroyed. It was like trying to assemble a huge jigsaw puzzle with most of the pieces either missing or bent out of shape.

However, with the arrival of Grant, Kane, Brigid and Domi at Cerberus redoubt, the intelligence they gathered on a number of their missions helped Lakesh to make more sense of the puzzle. On a mission to Russia, Brigid, Kane and Grant had learned about the discovery of a creature sealed within a cryogenic stasis canister at the site of the Tunguska disaster. According to their source, he had lain buried for over three decades, until the end of World War II. He was revived, spending several years as a guest of the Soviets before being traded to the West. His name was Balam.

On the British Isles, the self-proclaimed Lord Strongbow confided to them that in the performance of his duties in the twentieth century as a liaison officer between the Totality Concept's Mission Snowbird and Project Sigma, he dealt directly with a representative of the Archons, a creature called Balam. Obviously, Balam had acted as something of a liaison officer himself, an emissary of the Archon Directorate throughout the latter half of the twentieth century. He revealed he knew a great deal about the Archon Directorate, perhaps even more about it than the nine barons.

Strongbow showed them the physical remains of Enlil, the last of the mythical Serpent Kings. The creature wasn't mythical at all, but part of an extraterrestrial race known in Sumeria as the Annunaki, who had arrived on Earth some fifty thousand years before the dawn of recorded history.

Strongbow admitted to using Enlil's genetic code to mutagenically modify himself and his Dragoons. Furthermore, he had created a hybrid mixture of three races—human, Tuatha de Danaan and Annunaki. Enlil died after impregnating a woman with Danaan blood. The woman escaped Strongbow to Ireland and gave birth to an infant having the mixed blood of all three races.

While in Ireland, Brigid experienced a psionic recording embedded in the so-called Speaking Stone of Cascorach. According to what she later reported, she learned that the race known as the Annunaki, the Serpent Kings, arrived on Earth when humankind was still in a protoform of development. They came first in gleaming discs dropping from the sky, and later through glittering archways of fire, portals between far places.

Tall and cold of eye and heart, the Annunaki were a highly developed reptilian race with a natural gift for organization. They viewed Earth as a vast treasure trove of natural resources, upon which their technology depended. As labor was their scarcest commodity, the Annunaki set about redesigning the Earth's primitive inhabitants into models of maximized potentials. The Annunaki remolded the protohumans, grading them at rough intellectual levels and classifying them by physique, agility and dexterity.

Although the early generations of slave labor were only a step above the indigenous hominoid species, the slaves were encouraged to breed so each successive descendant would be superior to the first. The human brain improved and technical skills grew, along with cogent thoughts and the ability to deal with abstract concepts.

After thousands of years, the human slave-race rebelled against the Annunaki, who failed to notice the expansion of cognition on the part of their thralls. Although essentially a peaceful people, the Annunaki arranged for a catastrophe to destroy their labor force, as Earth had become an unprofitable enterprise. The catastrophe was recorded in ancient texts, and even cultural memories, as the Flood.

Millennia after that catastrophe, a new group of visitors arrived on Earth. Humanoid but not human, they were an aristocratic race of scientists, poets and builders, fleeing their own home. This group was mythologically known as the Tuatha de Danaan. This race decided to make fertile, isolated Ireland their home.

They took the tribes living there under their protection and taught them many secrets of art, architecture and mathematics. The essence of Danaan science stemmed from music—the controlled manipulation of sound waves—and this became recorded in legend as the ''music of the spheres.''

Eventually, the Annunaki returned to reclaim their world and their slaves. They were few in number and began to turn humans against the Danaan by filling them with jealousy and fear. Humankind became embroiled in the conflict between the Annunaki and the Danaan, a conflagration that extended even to the outer planets of the solar system, and became immortalized and disguised in human legends as a war in heaven.

Finally, when it appeared that Ireland and even Earth was threatened with annihilation, the war abated under terms. A pact was struck, whereby the two races intermingled to create a new one, which was to serve as a bridge between the two. From this pact sprang the entities later known as the Archons.

Enlil, the last of the Annunaki, and one of the original architects of man, refused to abide by the pact. Determined to use the new hybrid race to spread his beliefs, Enlil made his base in Ireland. Having broken the pact, none of his own race came to his aid, and he was vanquished by Saint Patrick.

Or so Brigid learned, even though she refused to take the tale completely at face value, since it had been colored by folklore and myth.

Months later, on a return trip to New London, Kane and Grant had been perplexed by the disappearance of Enlil's preserved remains. At the time, Lakesh devoted much thought to the disappearance, since it happened at the same time the Imperium Britannia was overthrown. He assumed the invading Celts had found the carcass and destroyed it, although Kane didn't think that was likely.

It wasn't until Lakesh was in the custody of Sam in China that he finally saw Enlil's body for himself. Balam had somehow absconded with the corpse and used its genetic code as the template in the creation of Sam. Or so he was informed, but like Brigid's reaction to the psionic history lesson, Lakesh remained skeptical.

However, he wasn't skeptical about the Annunaki's involvement in human affairs. As far as he was concerned that was a fact. What wasn't so clear was where the race had relocated following the pact with the Tuatha de Danaan. Now it appeared they—or at least one of them—was much closer than he had ever envisioned.

MOST OF THE PEOPLE who lived in Cerberus redoubt acted in the capacity of support personnel. They worked rotating shifts, eight hours a day, seven days a week. For the most part, their work was the routine maintenance and monitoring of the installation's environmental systems, the satellite data feed, the security network.

However, everyone was given at least a superficial understanding of all the redoubt's systems so they could pinch-hit in times of emergency. Fortunately, such a time had never arrived, but still and all, the installation was woefully understaffed. Their small number was a source of constant worry to Lakesh, particularly since he could no longer practice his secret recruitment program, so he felt it was important that everyone have a cursory knowledge of the inner workings that kept the redoubt operational.

Grant and Kane were exempt from this cross training inasmuch as they served as the enforcement arm of Cerberus and undertook far and away the lion's share of the risks. On their downtime between missions they made sure all the ordnance in the armory was in good condition and occasionally tuned up the vehicles in the depot.

Time was measured by the controlled dimming and brightening of lights to simulate sunrise and sunset, and since most of the people there—with the exception of Domi—were ville bred, they didn't mind the artificial changeover from dawn to dusk. Rarely had any of them strayed more than ten miles from the walls of their respective villes.

Kane, however, would frequently complain of suffering from redoubt-fever and borrow one of the vehicles to drive down the treacherous mountain road to the foothills where Sky Dog's band of Sioux and Cheyenne were permanently encamped.

After remaining with the band for a few days, Kane

would return to the redoubt, often dirty and disheveled but always relaxed. Grant wondered if Kane had a willing harem of Indian maidens, but he never inquired about it.

If Brigid Baptiste wondered the same thing, she never put her suspicions into words. When she and Kane were first thrown together, their relationship had been volatile, marked by frequent quarrels, jealousies and resentments. The world in which she came of age was primarily quiet, focused on scholarly pursuits. Kane's was a world wherein he became accustomed to daily violence and supported by a belief system that demanded a ruthless single-mindedness to enforce baronial authority. Despite their differences, or perhaps because of them, the two people managed to forge the chains of partnership that linked them together through mutual respect and trust.

Only once had the links of that chain been stretched to a breaking point. Almost a year before Kane had shot and killed a woman, a distant relative of Brigid's, whom he perceived as a threat to her life. It took her some time to realize that under the confusing circumstances, Kane had had no choice but to make a snap judgment call. Making split-second, life-and-death decisions was part of his conditioning, his training in the Magistrate Division, as deeply ingrained as breathing.

What conflicted her during that time was not the slow process of forgiving him, but coming to terms with what he really was and accepting the reality rather than an illusion. He was a soldier, not an explorer, not an academic, not an intellectual. When she finally understood that about him, she and Kane were able to function as colleagues, not adversaries.

Now, an hour after watching the remote's vid record, Kane and Brigid sat at the table in the ready room and snapped at each other. Grant reflected it was like a return to the old days of bickering and ridiculing of each other's priorities.

He, Kane, Lakesh, Brigid and Domi were there to caucus, trying to reach an agreement of their next course of action. Lakesh hadn't contributed much, busy looking through the stack of printouts provided to him by Bry. The sheets of paper held translations of the cuneiform script inscribed on Megaera's Oubolus rod.

"The Moon my ass," Kane snapped. Before the meeting, he had returned to his quarters to put on a black T-shirt and running shoes.

"You don't know the historical background," Brigid shot back. "This is a discovery of unprecedented importance. Why are you being so obtuse?"

"This is like what—number five in a series of unprecedented discoveries over the past couple of years?" Kane asked sarcastically. "Besides, history has nothing to do with my objections. Going to the goddamn Moon to shake hands—or claws—with a surviving Annunaki doesn't make for sound tactics."

Domi, sitting to the right of Lakesh with her head propped up by a hand, asked idly, "Yeah...why let that thing know about us?'' Her eyelids and lips were painted the same cool shade of aquamarine.

''We'll have to send Megaera back eventually,'' Brigid pointed out testily. ''She'll tell him—or it—about us. She could be very useful to us.''

Grant said mildly, ''This may sound cold-blooded—hell, it *is* cold-blooded—but I don't see why we have to send her back at all.''

Lakesh finally glanced up from the papers spread out before him. He blinked at Grant in bewilderment. ''Why would we want to keep her here? We don't need to strain our resources to support a permanent prisoner—''

Lakesh saw lines deepening around the corners of Grant's eyes and he said simply, ''Oh.''

'''Oh' is right,'' Brigid declared. ''But whether we send her back or not isn't really relevant. We already had a run-in with her in Chicago. It stands to reason she's already talked about me, about all of us once Sindri sent her back.''

''She probably blames us for the disappearance of the small, smiling god,'' said Kane. ''I don't think she'll be very cooperative.''

Brigid took a deep breath, trying to tamp down her rising impatience and annoyance. Linking her fingers on the tabletop, her eyes darted from Kane to Grant, knowing the only way to win them over was to convince them a threat to Cerberus security was pending or that there would be a tangible payoff if they swung their opinions to her side. If the decision had been left up solely to Lakesh, as all decisions had been until recently, they would have reluctantly agreed to the trip—particularly if Brigid insisted that she would go if no one else would.

But making such choices was no longer within Lakesh's exclusive purview. The minicoup staged by Kane, Brigid and Grant nearly a year before had seen to that. Lakesh hadn't been completely unseated from his position of authority, but he was now answerable to a more democratic process. No mission could be assigned or undertaken unless everyone involved was in agreement.

"Can't either of you see how truly important this is?" she asked. "We've got a predark Moonbase apparently still intact, apparently still inhabited by fellow human beings. Among them is an Annunaki, possibly the last of an ancient race that was instrumental in the creation of human civilization. Aren't you the slightest bit curious about how that happened?"

Grant knuckled his chin contemplatively. "Curious, yeah. Willing to take a trip to the Moon to satisfy that curiosity—no."

"And if that creature really is an Annunaki," declared Kane darkly, "then its race was just as instrumental in the destruction of human civilization as its creation. From everything we know about them, they had space flight and hyperdimensional-travel capabilities while Man was still hanging out in trees, right? When they arrived here, they used such brutal tactics on us that ancient depictions of devils were based on early interactions by humanity and Annunaki. That's why serpents came to be symbols of evil."

Lakesh raised his eyes from the scattering of printout. Reprovingly, he said, "That may have some truth to it, but even so we can't allow old superstitions to color our next course of action."

"All right," Grant declared irritably. "Let's not go back to the dawn of time—let's just go back a couple of centuries. Didn't you tell us that in the twentieth century, UFO abduction researchers came across reports of reptilian creatures working in tandem with the Grays, the Archons?"

Lakesh nodded. "I did. But they were reported in a relatively small percentage of abduction cases."

"You also said the witnesses in those cases reported that the Archons showed the reptiles a marked deference," Kane argued. "What does that suggest to you?"

Lakesh said slowly, reluctantly, "It suggests that Balam's people were either working under the command of the Annunaki, their forebears, or simply tolerating their presence, like children who put up with set-in-their-ways grandparents."

Kane expelled a disdainful snort. "Oh, *please.*"

Doggedly, Lakesh went on, "The opportunity to learn where the Annunaki fled after the pact with the Tuatha de Danaan would be an extremely important pieces of data."

"Important to who?" Grant wanted to know.

Domi surprised them all by drawling, "Sam, the

imperator." She glanced questioningly at Lakesh. "Right?"

He favored her with an affectionate smile. "Very, very right, darlingest girl. We would have valuable information that neither the imperator nor Balam possesses."

"We don't know if they have that information or not," Kane retorted. "Or if they even want it."

"Perhaps not," Lakesh replied smoothly. "But to employ a phrase that has been used here a time or two in the past, there's only one sure way to find out."

He picked up a sheet of printout. "If the creature on the tape is indeed an Annunaki, then we—" His words didn't trail away; they simply ended abruptly as if his voice clogged in his throat. He stared fixedly at the columns of symbols and the translations on the paper. His eyes widened.

"Then we what?" Grant demanded impatiently.

Brigid leaned across the table, reaching for the paper in Lakesh's suddenly trembling hand. "What is it?"

Lakesh allowed her to take the printout from his fingers. He coughed and in a strained, hoarse tone he announced, "Apparently, the creature we saw on the tape is not just 'an' Annunaki, but one of the two 'the' Annunaki."

Kane glared at him through slitted eyes. "What?"

"It was Enki, brother and rival to Enlil."

Chapter 14

The bottom level of Cerberus was some 150 feet below solid, shielded rock. It held the nuclear generators, various maintenance and machine rooms and the air-conditioning core. A semidetached wing contained ten detention cubicles, all of them as nicely appointed as the average flat in the Cobaltville Enclaves.

Lakesh tapped in the sec code on the door leading to the detention wing. Followed by Kane, Grant and Brigid, he walked through a dimly lit corridor that had once been bisected by a wire-mesh security checkpoint. He paused before a door, looking through the small ob slit.

"Our guest appears to be awake," Lakesh said quietly. "So we won't rouse her and maybe she won't be so surly when we go in."

Grant and Kane took places on either side of the door. Both men were attired in the black, formfitting shadow suits with dark glasses masking their eyes. Earlier they had agreed that Brigid and Lakesh would be the ones to initially interrogate Megaera, inasmuch as their presence might tend to intimidate her. However, they waited outside just in case intimidation became necessary.

Lakesh tapped in the code on the keypad and unlocked the door. He and Brigid stepped into the cell. The walls and floor were covered by a thick, quilted padding. Water was provided by a soft rubber hose that protruded only half an inch from a socket in the wall. A rimmed depression in the left-hand corner served as a toilet.

Megaera stared up at them from the corner where she sat, arms hugging her knees. Although her eyes were glassy from the sedatives, no fear was visible, only a scornful pride. She made no move to rise.

Brigid met her steady gaze stolidly. "We intend to send you back to where you came from, but we need to ask you a few questions first."

Megaera's mouth twisted in a smirk. "What makes you think I care about your needs?"

Softly, Lakesh said, "You should care very much, madam, since those needs are all that is keeping you alive."

The old woman lifted her chin defiantly. "I do not fear death. I will be rewarded for my lifetime of service in the Abode of Nibiru."

Brigid smiled coldly. "I believe you when you say you don't fear death. But I presume you don't prefer to die."

Uncertainty flickered for an instant in Megaera's eyes, and Brigid pounced on the opportunity. "Where is your home?"

"The land of mist and mountains." Megaera restored her smirk. "But I don't expect that will make any sense to you."

Brigid matched her smirk. "It's up to you to make sense of it. Does your land of mist and mountains have a name?"

Megaera didn't answer so Lakesh ventured, "Do you call it Kingu by any chance? The protector of Nibiru?"

Megaera's eyes widened in surprise. "How can you know that? Those are worship words. You *shouldn't* know that!"

Brigid didn't react to the old woman's outburst. "How did your people come to live on Kingu?"

Megaera licked her lips nervously. "We were brought there to serve."

"Serve what?" Lakesh asked.

"Serve who?" Brigid asked.

"The devil."

Neither Lakesh nor Brigid had expected such a response. Lakesh blinked owlishly at the woman, momentarily at a loss for words. He cast a glance toward Brigid, but she was taken aback, too. Half to herself, she murmured, "Ahriman was the Sumerian god of evil, the archetypal devil." She raised her voice. "Do you mean Ahriman?"

Megaera shook her head impatiently. "The devil, I told you. We serve the devil."

Just as impatiently, Lakesh demanded, "What is your devil's name?"

It was Megaera's turn to blink in confusion as if

she didn't comprehend the question. "It is the devil. D-E-V-I-L."

"'It,'" echoed Brigid. "What does 'it' look like?"

Megaera sighed heavily as if wearied by the questions. "I have never seen it. None of us has. It floats above Kingu, awaiting the time to transform it." She sighed again. "I'm tired of these foolish questions."

Both Lakesh and Brigid Baptiste were historians. Since Brigid's forced exile, she had taken full advantage of Cerberus redoubt's vast database, and as an intellectual omnivore she grazed in all fields, so in many ways her knowledge of an extensive and eclectic number of topics was far more wide-ranging than Lakesh's. Megaera used Sumerian terms, but they didn't seem completely in context with the mythology with which she had familiarized herself.

Based on the translations of the inscriptions on the Oubolus rod, Brigid and Lakesh had earlier conceived a provisional hypothesis before they came to question Megaera. The reference to a devil didn't match up with their theories.

"D-E-V-I," Lakesh suddenly spelled out. "Devi. Those were words we saw stenciled on the NASA crate. We couldn't see the *L*."

"What does that mean?" Brigid asked crossly. "That they have the devil in a box up there on the Moon?"

He shrugged. "Don't ask me." He nodded toward Megaera. "Ask her."

Brigid's lips tightened, and she dropped to one

knee in front of Megaera. Firmly she said, "Old bitch, we can wring what we want to know out of you, but you'd find it exceedingly painful. It might take us a long time to get satisfactory answers, but we have plenty of time. And you'll be in a great deal of pain all during it."

Brigid lowered her voice, packing it with conviction. "After we're done, there won't be much left of you to send back to Kingu. Do you understand?"

Megaera didn't so much as blink or appear to have even heard her. Brigid glared into her seamed face, then called over her shoulder, "Kane!"

The cell door opened and the blacksuited Kane stepped in, his face made grim and ruthless by the set of his jaw and the dark lenses over his eyes. Megaera stiffened at the sight of the man in the garb of her Furies. Brigid extended a hand toward him. "She needs more persuasion."

Reaching behind him, Kane withdrew the Oubolus rod from his belt. Brigid took it from him and peeled back the left sleeve of her bodysuit. The screened, overhead light glittered from the silver, opal-studded circulet around her wrist.

Megaera tried to scoot farther back into the corner, her mouth falling open as if to permit a wail of fright to escape it. She made only a rasping, gargling noise, her eyes bulging in horror.

Brigid's lips stretched in a carefully calculated smile of cruelty. She waved the knobbed end of the baton slowly to and fro before Megaera's face, as if it were the needle of a metronome. The old woman kept her eyes fixed on it in terrified fascination.

"I've been wanting to pay you back in kind," Brigid said in a low, menacing croon, "for what you did to me in Chicago. I almost don't care if you talk or not. Every second you stall is one less second I care whether you cooperate."

Lakesh cleared his throat and said almost apologetically, "Madam, I beseech you to do as she says. I will not be able to intervene. All I will be able to do is listen to you scream."

Megaera lifted her hands in a gesture of defeat, of resignation. "I'll do what you want." Her voice quavered with a tremor of mounting fear. "Just take it away!"

Brigid's smile broadened. "Just like I expected. A classic case of being more than willing to dish it out but not willing to take it." She extended the baton to Kane. "Thank you. I'll let you know if I need this again."

Kane nodded deferentially. "I will be waiting just outside for your command."

He backed out of the cell. Before he closed the door, he caught Lakesh's eye. Kane's face was contorted, suffused with blood as he struggled to repress laughter. Out in the corridor, Kane moved a few feet away from the cell. Grant followed, eyebrows arched at quizzical angles. "Guess it worked."

Kane put a hand to his mouth to muffle a laugh. He lifted the Oubolus. "I'd say so. Megaera was so fused by the very idea of this thing being used on her she didn't look at it closely. If she had—''

He tapped the silver knob with a forefinger. It cracked, collapsing in on itself as if it were no more substantial than an eggshell—which it was. When they couldn't find a way to retract the leg filaments of the little silver spider device, Domi suggested draining an egg, painting the shell and gluing it to the business end of the Oubolus baton.

Kane was skeptical the ruse would work, but Brigid reasoned that Megaera's sedative-fogged senses and fear would keep her from realizing she was being threatened with a fake. And inasmuch as the old woman commanded male Furies, Brigid also figured that a man in a shadow suit with a subservient attitude was a cultural touchstone to which she could relate.

With Lakesh and Brigid employing the time-honored practice of good Mag–bad Mag, Kane assumed the interrogation would proceed smoothly from here on out.

''We don't need to hang around out here anymore,'' Kane continued. ''Brigid has it under control.''

Grant grunted, ''Yeah. You've taught her well.''

Kane started to nod in acknowledgment, then caught himself and cast a suspicious glance toward Grant. As he expected, the big man's expression was inscrutable. Then he turned away, walking toward the checkpoint.

The two men rode up in the elevator in silence.

Grant stared at the wall of the lift car, eyes distant. Unhappiness seemed to drape his big frame like a cloak. Kane didn't know if Domi, Shizuka or the prospect of making a trip to the Moon was responsible, and he didn't ask. Grant was in one of his intractable moods, and there was nothing on Earth more intractable than Grant when he put his mind to it.

The lift doors opened, and Grant stalked out without so much as a muttered ''Later.''

Kane made for his quarters, but some errant impulse turned him down a side passageway. He stopped before a door bearing a keypad rather than a knob.

He hesitated for just a second before tapping in the six-digit code. With a harsh electronic buzz, the lock solenoid slid aside and he pushed the door inward. He stepped into the wide, low-ceilinged room and looked around warily. Despite all of the medical equipment and the computers, Balam's holding facility exuded the atmosphere of a cobwebby attic in an old abandoned house, holding the accumulated brica-brac of lost dreams.

He still remembered with startling clarity the first time Balam had directly addressed him. He'd said, ''Humanity must have a purpose, and only a single vision can give it purpose...we unified you.''

The ''we'' Balam referred to were his forebears, the First Folk who were descended from the crossbreeding program between the Annunaki and the Tuatha de Danaan. The barons were the hybridized issue of the Archons and superior human genetic material.

Kane looked at Balam's empty cell and shook his head in rueful resignation. He knew now that in many ways the entire sequence of events that resulted in the factionalizing of the baronies and the rise of the imperator's forces began when Balam was set free. There were some nights when an insomnia borne of suspicion crowded into his mind and kept him awake all night.

In hindsight, it seemed more and more likely that Balam had manipulated his release, practicing the artful deception his people had directed against the human race for thousands of years. If that was the case, Kane was only a component in a long-range plan Balam had conceived years before. He couldn't help but wonder if Balam had planned his captivity in Area 51 and his own contributions to the hybridization program.

Area 51 was the predark unclassified code name for a training area on Nellis Air Force base. It was also known as Groom Lake, but most predarkers preferred to call it ''Dreamland.''

Contained in the dry lake bed was a vast installation, extending deep into the desert floor. Only a few of the buildings were aboveground. Area 51 was more than just a military installation; it served as an international base operated by a consortium from many countries. Now its operation was overseen by a consortium of barons, which in turn would be overseen by the imperator.

Kane and Domi had penetrated Area 51 and been captured. Domi had been found by a little group of insurgents led by the hybrid female Quavell, while Kane was sentenced by Baron Cobalt to what amounted to stud service.

During his two weeks of captivity, he was fed a steady diet of protein laced with a stimulant of the catecholamine group. It affected the renal blood supply, increasing cardiac output without increasing the need for cardiac oxygen consumption.

Combined with the food loaded with protein to speed sperm production, the stimulant provided Kane with hours of high energy. Since he was forced to achieve erection and ejaculation six times a day every two days, his energy and sperm count had to be preternaturally high, even higher than was normal for him.

Although Kane knew he was supposed to be biologically superior, he also knew the main reason he was chosen to impregnate the female hybrids was simply due to the fact male hybrids were incapable of engaging in conventional acts of procreation, at least physically. Their organs of reproduction were so undeveloped as to be vestigial.

Kane wasn't the first human male to be pressed into service. There had been other men before him, but they had performed unsatisfactorily due to their terror of the hybrids. At first the females selected for the process donned wigs and wore cosmetics in order to appear more human to the trapped sperm donors. The men had to be strapped down and, even after the application of an aphrodisiac gel, had difficulty maintaining an erection.

Such a problem wasn't something a hybrid, baron or no, was likely to ever experience. What made the barons so superior had nothing to do with the physical. The brains of the barons could absorb and process information with exceptional speed, and their cognitive abilities were little short of supernatural.

Almost from the moment the barons emerged from the incubation chambers, they possessed an IQ so far beyond the range of standard tests as to render them meaningless. They mastered language in a matter of weeks, speaking in whole sentences. All of Nature's design faults in the human brain were corrected, modified and improved, specifically the hypothalamus, which regulated the complex biochemical systems of the body.

They could control all autonomous functions of their brains and bodies, even the manufacture and release of chemicals and hormones. They could speed or slow their heartbeats, increase and decrease the amount of adrenaline in their bloodstreams.

They possessed complete control over that mysterious portion of the brain known as the limbic system, a portion that predark scientists had always known possessed great reserves of electromagnetic power and strength.

Physically, the barons were a beautiful people, almost too perfect to be real. Even their expressions were markedly similar to one another—a vast pride, a diffident superiority, authority and even ruthlessness. They were the barons, and as such, they believed themselves to be the avatars of the new humans who would inherit the Earth.

But since they were bred for brilliance, all barons had emotional limitations placed upon their enormous intellects. They were captives of their shared Archon hive-mind heritage, a remorseless mind-set that did not carry with it the simple comprehension of the importance of individual liberty to humans.

Smug in their hybrid arrogance, the baronial oligarchy did not understand the primal beast buried inside the human psyche, the beast that always gave humans a fair chance of winning in the deadly game of survival of the fittest.

Visceral emotions didn't play a large part in the psychologies of the so-called new humans. Even their bursts of passion were of the most rudimentary kind. Although the tissue of their hybridized brains was of the same organic matter as the human brain, the millions of neurons operated a bit differently in the processing of information. Therefore, their thought processes were very structured, extremely linear. When they experienced emotions, they only did so in moments of stress, and then so intensely they were almost consumed by them.

Therefore Kane was surprised when Quavell, during one of their scheduled periods of copulation, confided to him that not every hybrid agreed with the baronial policy toward humanity. He was even more surprised when she helped him and Domi escape. He was forced to reassess everything he thought he knew about the barons, about the hybrids.

With the advent of the imperator and the siege of Cobaltville, everything was different—yet strangely still the same. The imperator was fixated on unification, just as Balam's folk and the barons had been, but with a different objective in mind. His stated intent was to end the tyranny of the barons and unify both hybrid and human and build a new Earth, but Lakesh didn't believe him and Kane had no reason to do so, either. But if it turned out that female hybrids could conceive offspring by human males, then a continued division between the so-called old and new human was pretty much without merit.

Kane had yet to tell either Grant or Brigid about his experiences in Dreamland, and he had sworn Domi to secrecy. So far the albino had kept her word, but it was plain she was confused by his reluctance to tell anyone about it. He wasn't sure why he wanted to keep it a secret, either. He hadn't volunteered for stud service, after all. And it wasn't so much shame that made him mute on the topic—at least, not anymore.

During the first couple of months following his captivity, Kane had successfully managed to keep from dwelling on memories of his forced fornications.

But lately, having gained a certain degree of emotional distance he found himself thinking of Quavell.

Images of the excessively slender and small-statured woman always seemed to insinuate themselves into his mind during the hazy period between wakefulness and sleep. He was never frightened by the images. Long ago Kane had accepted the hybrids' unusual physical appearance, their gracile builds, their inhumanly long fingers, fine-pored skin and small ears set low on the sides of their heads. They were so delicate, so elfin, so self-possessed, he understood why many of them referred to his kind, the old shambling, anarchic humans, as apekin.

When he drowsed, he fancied he could feel the silky blond hair that topped her high, domed head, the texture seeming to be a cross between feathery down and thread. Above prominent cheekbones, huge, up-slanting eyes of a clear crystal blue regarded him silently but gleamed with a flicker of emotion that was uncharacteristic of her kind.

Kane easily recalled other ways in which Quavell was different from the other females he had serviced. Almost all of them mounted him and rode him mechanically, not looking at him at all. It was obvious they would have never engaged in intercourse with any human male but for the baron's orders.

Quavell, he recollected, writhed and moaned a time or two. Although his memories were fragmented, he thought she had orgasmed at least once during their previous couplings.

Her image would waver in his mind, it would change and he would see her with a belly grown large with child, her long fingers clasped protectively over it, her delicate face displaying her determination to keep safe the life growing in her womb.

Kane would jerk awake at that point in the imagery, consumed by a bewildering blizzard of unfamiliar and disturbing emotions. He was never sure if the mental pictures were examples of free association or if Quavell was telepathically transmitting a message when he was the most susceptible. Or, he reflected, everything he had gone through could have been yet another ruse, another control mechanism for humanity.

It certainly wouldn't have been the first time Balam and those of his kind tricked and lied to their human allies—or pawns.

Repressing a shudder, Kane left the room. When it came to Balam and the hybrids, the only thing he could be certain of was that he could be certain of nothing. All he knew for certain was that he and his friends had made the correct choice. When faced with either the bleak acceptance of the reality in which humans were little more than chattel living on the sufferance of the barons or seizing a faint chance of salvaging humanity's future, they chose the faint chance.

They declared war on the dark forces devoted to maintaining the yoke of slavery around the collective necks of humankind. It was a struggle not just for the physical survival of humanity but for the human spirit, the soul of an entire race.

Over the past two years, they scored many victories, defeated many enemies, and solved mysteries of the past that molded the present and the future. More importantly, they began to rekindle the spark of hope within the breasts of the disenfranchised fighting to survive in the Outlands.

Victory, if not within their grasp, at least no longer seemed an unattainable dream. But the war that ended a civilization and began another two centuries later entered a new and far more deadly phase—and it was one that Kane knew he and his friends had unwittingly brought about.

Chapter 15

Megaera's interrogation lasted more than an hour. At the end of it, both Brigid and Lakesh busied themselves on the computer consoles in the operations center. The two people seemed driven, grim, almost like soldiers preparing for battle. After another hour or so, they summoned Kane, Grant and whoever else was interested to attend a formal briefing. DeFore, curious about their guest, volunteered to sit. Domi didn't respond to the invitation at all.

Cerberus redoubt had an officially designated briefing room on the third level. Big and blue walled, with ten rows of theater-type chairs facing a raised speaking dais and a rear-projection screen, it was built to accommodate the majority of the installation's personnel, back before the nukecaust. It was never used now except to watch old movies.

Since the briefings rarely involved more than a handful of people, they were usually convened in the more intimate dining hall. Lakesh, DeFore, Brigid, Grant and Kane sat around a table, sharing a pot of coffee. Access to genuine coffee was one of the inarguable benefits of living as an exile in the redoubt. Real coffee had virtually vanished after skydark, since all of the plantations in South and Central America had been destroyed.

An unsatisfactory synthetic gruel known as "sub" replaced it. Cerberus literally had tons of freeze-dried packages of the authentic article in storage, as well as sugar and powdered milk.

Brigid passed out illustrations, downloaded and printed out from the historical database. Most of them depicted uninteresting lines and symbols with English words beside them.

Without preamble, Lakesh stated, "As we suspected, Megaera apparently lives in a small secret base that had been established on the Moon sometime in the mid-1970s. It was constructed in the Manitius Crater region. We know this site was chosen because of its proximity to artifacts that some scientists speculated were the shattered remains of an incredibly ancient city, once protected by massive geodesic domes."

"And who built these massive domes?" DeFore asked almost challengingly.

"We don't really know. But the best bet is the Annunaki."

DeFore groaned, rolling her eyes. "I told you I hated that ancient-astronaut garbage."

"Whether you hate it or not, dear Doctor," Lakesh said with mock sympathy, "we can't ignore the historical record. You know what I'm talking about, regardless of your discomfort."

DeFore looked away from him, a silent concession

that he was right. A century before the nukecaust, enlightened minds found it fashionable to speculate that Earth's nearest alien neighbors would be found right next door, on the planet Mars.

A hundred years later it was discovered that alien neighbors were a lot closer than nineteenth-century scientific theorists ever dreamed. They were right on Earth and had been for a very, very, *very* long time. So long a time in fact, they felt they had the prior claim.

When humanity dreamed of reaching the stars, speculation about the extraterrestrial life-forms they might encounter inevitably followed. The issue of interaction, of communication with aliens, had consumed a number of government think tanks for many decades.

As Lakesh discovered in the waning years of the twentieth century, all of that hypothesizing was nothing but a diversion, a smoke screen to hide the truth. Humankind's interaction with a nonhuman species had begun at the dawn of Earth's history. That relationship and communication had continued unbroken for thousands of years, cloaked by ritual, religion and mystical traditions.

Brigid stated matter-of-factly, ''Several lengthy reigns of a technologically advanced race who came to be called gods are recorded with great similarity in every culture. They accomplished great feats by most accounts and fought terrible wars in a variety of air, sea and land and space-going craft.

"At least three or four generations of a technologically advanced race are listed in Celtic mythologies with counterparts in other world myths—Greek, Hindu, Chinese. Sumerian legends state our own primitive earthbound race was conquered with ease by the Annunaki. They ruled for many millennia before being torn apart by war.

"At one point, the Annunaki's fear of our potential to rival them caused them to disperse us over the Earth and confuse our speech. They had their own internecine conflicts that embroiled Man long before the Danaan arrived. A war between the Annunaki and the Danaan began perhaps five thousand years ago and extended to our Moon and even Mars."

"We know that already," Grant said, shifting his feet impatiently. "Their war dragged on for centuries, then the Annunaki agreed to make nice and leave Earth alone. So?"

"So," Brigid retorted, "there's a little more to this situation than the Annunaki came, they saw, they conquered, went away, then came back and went away again. But to where they went away was never made clear."

"We always wondered about the location of the home planet of the Annunaki," Lakesh said.

"Some of us did, maybe," DeFore commented dourly.

Brigid ignored her. "A number of Babylonian and Sumerian texts—which predate even the most ancient Egyptian codices—outline the process by which our solar system was created. Most of those records mention twelve worlds, counting the Moon and the Sun.''

"That makes eleven," Kane pointed out.

Brigid regarded him with weary exasperation. "All of us can count, Kane. The twelfth planet was called Nibiru, which translates as 'world of crossing.' The Sumerian symbol for it is on the second line of your handouts."

Kane glanced down, saw a symbol that resembled an asterisk surrounded by a circle and took a sip of coffee.

"The ancient texts," Brigid went on, "assert that the seed of life on Earth was brought to Earth from Nibiru. To quote from the translation, 'He established the station of Nibiru to determine their heavenly bands that none might transgress or fall short.'

"The orbital period of Nibiru around the Sun was 3,600 Earth years. According to the Sumerians, the Annunaki of Nibiru evolved well ahead of hominids on Earth. The word Annunaki literally means 'Those who from Heaven to Earth came.' Sumerian texts repeatedly asserted the Annunaki were all connected, there was no singularity. What one knew, all knew."

Brigid scanned their faces. "I assume all of that has a familiar ring."

No one responded. There was no need. One thing all of them had learned about Balam's people was that they had inherited the Annunaki's interdependent psychic link. They knew Balam was anchored to the hybrid barons through some hyperspatial filaments of their mind energy, akin to the hive mind of certain insect species. When Baron Ragnar was assassinated, Balam had experienced an extreme reaction to the sudden absence of the baron's mind filament. Inasmuch as all of the Archon genetic material had derived from Balam, that connection wasn't particularly surprising.

Lakesh picked up the thread. "We know the Annunaki were a highly developed race with a natural gift for organization. They viewed Earth as a vast treasure trove of natural resources. The Annunaki reached the conclusion that they needed intermediaries between themselves and the masses of humanity. As a bridge between themselves as the 'gods' and humankind, they introduced the concept of the god-king on Earth, appointing human rulers who would assure humanity's service to the gods and channel their teachings and laws to the people. For some reason, they chose Sumeria for this experiment.

"Even at the height of their civilization thousands of years ago, the Sumerians claimed immense antiquity, telling of a golden age governed by the god-kings. Their legends extolled these semidivine rulers, sometimes called the lunar kings. Traditionally, they mated with the daughters of men and helped to build a wondrous and decadent society."

"The gods were the lords to be worshiped and venerated," interposed Brigid. "There was a defined hierarchy, and for millennia the gods oversaw the welfare and fate of humankind all the while remaining clearly apart from the people, approachable only by the high priests and kings on specified dates, communicating with their plenipotentiaries through visions.

"Apparently, there grew a contest for the hearts and minds of people since the gods had come to depend increasingly on human kings and their armies to achieve their ends. When this situation became too unwieldy, the Annunaki chose to create a new dynasty of rulers, known as demigods or god-kings because of their exalted bloodlines."

DeFore, in the process of stirring powdered creamer into her coffee, froze. She squinted toward Lakesh. "That sounds an awful lot like the setup of the baronies."

"Exactly," Brigid replied crisply. "The Program of Unification was little more than the revival of the ancient god-king system. I'm sure Balam was inspired by his forebears."

"Was the Sumerian civilization a reflection of Annunaki society?" Kane asked.

Brigid shook her head. "Who can say? Excavations at Ur show that about 4000 BCE, perhaps even as much a thousand years earlier, the Sumerians had already attained a high level of technology. In the tomb of Queen Shub-ad, archaeologists discovered a rich array of beautifully crafted jewelry, and items that were obviously machined. The metallurgy, craftsmanship and artistry required to fashion treasures of that type suggest many centuries of an advanced, progressive culture.

"The Sumerians also had considerable knowledge of mathematics. They were the first civilization to divide the circle into 360 degrees, said to be the number of days in the year, and the hour into sixty minutes, each with sixty seconds. We accept this legacy from ancient Sumer without full appreciation of the profound philosophical, astronomical and mathematical attainments needed to conceive this division of time."

"Sounds like everything ran smoothly," remarked Grant. "So why did the Annunaki decide humanity needed to be cleansed from Earth?"

Lakesh shrugged. "Sumerian texts state that although the Annunaki retained lordship over the lands and humankind was viewed as little more than a tenant farmer, humanity grew arrogant. Fearing a unified human race, both in culture and purpose, the Annunaki adopted the imperial policy of divide and rule. For while humankind reached higher cultural levels and the populations expanded, the Annunaki themselves were in decline.

"However, with the proliferation of people, states and nations, the Sumerian texts inform us the Annunaki held lengthy councils regarding their future and that of man on Earth."

"We already know what happened next," Grant rumbled. "They tried to flush us away. Or Enlil did."

Lakesh smiled crookedly. "Aptly put, friend Grant. But apparently it wasn't a cut-and-dried decision.

Anu, the ruler of the Annunaki, returned to Nibiru after arranging a division of powers and territories on Earth between his feuding sons, half brothers Enlil and Enki. The first thing Enlil did after Anu departed was to force his brethren to make a decision about what to do about humanity.''

''So we were nerve-racking sons of bitches even back then?'' Kane inquired with a sour smile.

Lakesh didn't respond to the query. ''As humankind procreated and their numbers increased, Enlil grew fearful of us and prevailed on the great council to allow a deluge to wipe humanity off the face of the earth.

''But Enki was not happy about the decision to commit genocide and sought ways to frustrate the plan. Enki summoned a human intermediary to a temple built in his honor and spoke to him from behind a screen. He warned the man, known in various texts as Atra-Hasis, of the impending catastrophe. He provided him instructions on how to build a submersible boat and ordered him to share this information with others.''

Kane felt his eyebrows crawling toward his hairline. ''That sounds suspiciously like the story of Noah.''

''That's because it *is* the story of Noah,'' Brigid retorted. ''Or 'a' Noah, probably one of many. I had no idea you'd become such a student of theology.''

Kane flushed in embarrassment but said, ''I'm full

of surprises, Baptiste. You should know that by now.''

Lakesh ignored the exchange. ''The Annunaki apparently possessed a means by which to control the Earth's environment or wreck it. We know the legends of forty days and nights of rain, but I imagine the process was more complex than that. More than likely, the Annunaki caused tidal waves in the oceans, as well.''

''What kind of weapon could do that?'' DeFore wanted to know.

''It might not have been a weapon at all,'' Brigid replied. ''Or least, it wasn't originally designed as one.''

''Explain,'' said Kane.

Lakesh stated, ''We're getting to it. As the floodwaters slowly receded, the handful of human survivors bred and multiplied. Centuries passed, nations and empires were built and then fell, many sciences passed down from their former masters were practiced and then were forgotten.''

''And then,'' Grant declared, ''the Tuatha de Danaan showed up. Did they come from the same place, this Nibiru?''

Brigid shook her head. ''Doubtful. However, I do think it's probable that the link between the Annunaki and the Danaan may be stronger and far older than the pact they struck to mingle their genetic material. If they were both space-faring races with hyperdimensional technology, they probably came in contact with each other long before the Annunaki planted a colony on Earth.''

Unlike the Annunaki, the human-appearing Tuatha de Danaan took humankind under their protection. They were reported to be an aristocratic race of scientists, warriors and poets, preferring their privacy and able to make themselves invisible but keeping in touch with the human race.

Music was their principal technology, the controlled use of sound waves to lift and move massive objects and often employed as weapons. The megalithic sites in Ireland and Europe served a variety of functions being used for geodetic markers, recorders of mathematical measurements, observatories and in some cases, at least in prehistory, as military strongholds. Everything they had learned about the Tuatha de Danaan was at once simple and complex.

''It's possible the two races were age-old rivals,'' Brigid stated, ''competing with each other for the natural resources of the different planets in the solar system. We know the Danaan established at least an outpost on Mars and were driven from it in the relatively recent past.''

Upon their first encounter with Sindri, he told them that beginning in the 1860s and going to the 1870s, astronomers on Earth reported monstrous explosions occurring on Mars—visible even with the primitive telescopes of the day. The phenomenon ended abruptly in 1872. Sindri theorized the astronomers were witnessing aerial bombardments and missile attacks.

"That's according to Sindri," Grant said darkly. "You can't take anything that crazy little pissant said at face value."

"I don't," shot back Brigid. "But what he told us matched up with the historical record about a conflict that was viewed as a war in heaven. After nearly obliterating their genetically engineered offspring more than once, and coming close to destroying themselves in their own conflicts, both the Annunaki and the Danaan eventually conceded to leave humankind to its own affairs.

"But representatives still interacted with humanity at various times in its history with what seems to be a strong consistency."

Kane nodded. "I suppose we can proceed from the assumption that the snake-faces and the Danaan more or less divided up the solar system between them. But who got what?"

"Apparently," Lakesh answered, "the Annunaki were ceded the Moon. Or at least one Annunaki was. If Megaera is to be believed, it's none other than Enki, Enlil's half brother."

"Why the Moon?" DeFore asked. "That doesn't seem like much of a bargain."

"To us, perhaps not," replied Lakesh. "But the Moon is brimming with natural resources. It has no real atmosphere, though there is some evidence that the solar-wind particles form a thin layer around the

Moon. The lunar surface is covered with craters and mares, the so-called seas of the Moon. There are mountain ranges that literally encircle half its circumference. Most of the lunar rocks are similar to Earth's volcanic rocks but with lower percentages of iron and higher percentages of titanium.

"The Moon is thought to have a thick crust, a thin, partially molten mantle and possibly a core. It is also more active than once thought—seismic instruments left on the Moon by the Apollo missions recorded slight tremors. There may be huge hollow areas within it."

"And what about this devil-in-the-moon thing I heard Megaera mention?" Grant asked. "I have a creepy feeling she wasn't talking about guys with horns and pitchforks."

"She wasn't," Lakesh agreed. "She wasn't quite sure what she was really talking about, either."

"Let me guess," suggested Kane. "She didn't, but the computers did."

Brigid nodded. "They did indeed."

Kane angled a questioning eyebrow. "And?"

"And it seems there's only one possibility connecting the Moon with the concept of a devil. All sorts of tests were conducted on the Manitius base, from the military application of particle-beam lasers to test flights of Trans-Atmospheric Vehicles…not to mention the construction of *Parallax Red*."

"But there was something else?" ventured DeFore.

"A terra-forming project," Lakesh answered. "You're familiar with the term?"

"Only in the way Sindri mentioned it," replied Grant. "It's a process of turning an uninhabitable world into a habitable one, right?"

"Right," Brigid conceded. "There were only two general strategies for colonizing alien worlds—alter humanity to fit the planet through pantropic science as was done with Sindri's people, or alter the planet to fit humanity."

"I thought Sindri said the predark space scientists didn't find it feasible to terra-form Mars," Kane put in.

"Mars was a much more difficult prospect," Lakesh agreed. "Mars has very little atmosphere to work with, whereas Venus had the opposite problem."

"Venus?" DeFore echoed incredulously.

"Venus," Lakesh confirmed. "That world was thought to be suffering from a runaway greenhouse effect, giving it an average surface temperature of around 470 degrees Celsius. Therefore the astroscientists of the day suggested Venus could be terra-formed by the introduction of a planetismal device— essentially a heavy-mass projectile."

"What the hell is that?" growled Grant.

"Devices similar to suborbital nuclear platforms," answered Brigid. "They would be detonated at geo-synchronous points around worlds chosen to be terra-formed. Biocatalytic chemicals such as fluorocarbons, as well as a photon radiation, would blanket the planets and ideally trigger a reaction to positively alter the planetary conditions of Venus.''

''Ideally,'' Kane repeated. ''Something tells me that the ideal wasn't reached.''

Brigid ran her hands through her hair. ''Not according to the data we found. But a device was indeed constructed in geostationary parking orbit above the Manitius base. It was called a Deep Electromotive Valence Induration Lithospherimal process.''

''DEVIL,'' murmured DeFore.

''DEVIL,'' Lakesh stated. ''And it seems as if the people still living on the Moon base are in service to it.''

Grant narrowed his eyes to skeptical slits. ''What do you mean?''

''Trying to piece Megaera's story together to make a coherent whole wasn't easy,'' said Lakesh, ''but apparently she and everyone up there in the Manitius Crater are the descendants of the original base personnel. It also seems as if the DEVIL staff are in control.''

''In service to a satellite?'' DeFore wanted to know.

''DEVIL isn't a satellite, not really,'' said Brigid. ''It was designed to introduce into the atmosphere of Venus certain catalytic chemicals that would create a bioactive matrix. But it could also be a weapon of cataclysmic proportions. If the people in the base are living according to old Sumerian tenets, then something like that hanging over their heads would appeal to their religious beliefs...both a destroyer and a creator hovering above them."

"Do they have a civilization based on ancient Sumeria up there?" Kane asked. "How do Enki and the tech used by Megaera figure into this?"

Lakesh shook his head dolefully. "Even Megaera isn't sure of that. We can only speculate at this juncture."

"The only way to find solid answers is to actually go up there," Brigid declared with a forced breeziness, as if she were suggesting they take a stroll out on the plateau.

"Go there and do what?" demanded Grant, his eyes shadowed by his knitted brows. "Scribble some notes, take some pictures, observe the habits of the natives, then come back so we add some new shit to the database?"

Brigid, much to Kane's surprise, didn't seem to take offense. "Partly, yes. But the most important reason to go is DEVIL. It seems fairly obvious that the Annunaki practiced some type of terra-forming here on Earth hundreds of thousand of years ago. I submit that the means they used to cause the Flood, the deluge of legend, was another application of the same technology."

Lakesh tugged at his nose absently. "It's possible that the technology used to build DEVIL was found there on the Moon, in an ancient Annunaki installation. If so, its destructive potential is far greater than its ability to create.''

''You said it was in parking orbit above the base,'' Kane reminded him. ''Aimed at Venus.''

Brigid gave him an appraising stare. ''He didn't say anything about where it was aimed, Kane. However, judging by what Megaera told us, the DEVIL is not targeted for Venus.''

The faces of Kane and Grant locked into scowls almost at the same time. ''Oh, let me guess,'' Grant said sarcastically. ''It's now aimed for Earth, right?''

Brigid nodded. ''And Enki very well may have his claw on the trigger.''

Chapter 16

They tumbled and plunged through a twisting, writhing tunnel made of raving, shrieking energy. Everyone suffered an assault on their senses—sight, hearing, touch and taste. For a long, terrifying moment,
they felt their bodies dissolve, then re-form.

There was nothing to see but a raging torrent of
light, wild plumes and whorling spindrifts of violet,
of yellow, of blue and green and red. They swirled
like a whirlpool, glowing filaments that congealed and
stretched outward into the black gulfs of space.

Streaks of gray and dark blue became interspersed
with the colorful swirls. Bursts of light flared in garish
displays on the tunnel walls. They felt themselves
plummeting through an alternately brightly lit and
shadow-shrouded abyss, an endless fall into infinity.
They were conscious of a half instant of whirling ver-
tigo as if they hurtled a vast distance at blinding
speed.

Then the sensation of a free fall lessened. Slowly,
as if veils were being drawn away one by one, the
darker colors on the tunnel walls deepened and collected ahead of them into a pool of shimmering radiance.

Brigid, Kane and Grant stepped out of the energy field. Megaera tumbled out of it, falling and rolling awkwardly across a stone floor. She cried out in terror and pain. She remained prone, hanging her head like a dog, face concealed by her hair. She seemed completely disoriented and out of breath.

The cascade of light whirled and spun like a diminishing cyclone, shedding sparks and thread-thin static discharges. As quickly as it appeared, the glowing cone vanished, as if it had been sucked back into the apex of the interphaser.

Kane and Grant automatically dropped into crouches, bringing their Copperheads to bear. The close-assault weapons were stripped-down autoblasters. Gas operated, with a 700-round-per-minute rate of fire, the magazines held 15 rounds of 4.85 mm steel-jacketed bullets. Two feet in length, the weapon featured a grip and trigger unit placed in front of the breech to allow for one-handed use. An optical image intensifier scope was fitted on top, as well as a laser autotargeter.

The two men swung the barrels in short left-to-right arcs, questing for dangers or targets. All they saw were the clusters of black, human-shaped statues frozen in distorted poses. Brigid glanced behind her at the interphaser. The metal exterior of the pyramid was laced with a skein of electricity. It slowly faded and the device emitted a rhythmic ticking as it cycled down.

"Smooth transit," Brigid remarked to no one in particular.

Kane and Grant surveyed the chamber, noting it was much larger than it had appeared on the remote probe's recording. Stalactites hung down like stone draperies from the arched ceiling far above. Feeble light glimmered from the overhead shadows, and to their dismay they saw that the source of the ecto-plasmic illumination came from a small square panel of a glassy substance inset in the ceiling.

All of them had seen the light panels at one time or another. They were of Archon technology, a self-perpetuating light source that appeared to need no bat-teries or recharging. The glow of the light panel showed the outlines of bas-reliefs on the walls, blurred by the merciless hand of time. Otherwise the chamber was empty except for a few unidentifiable fragments of old metal and dust swept into corners.

The crate tucked beneath the spiral staircase was easily visible. The NASA logo was legible, as well as the word DEVIL. The staircase itself was made of some kind of alloy like aluminum. Welds rose like scar tissue on the risers, and all of them knew it was a very late addition to the chamber. The doorway at the head of the stairway was crudely cut, ruining one of the bas-reliefs.

The cold, moist air reeked with a strange, repellent odor, like mildewed clothes mixed in with sour milk. A faint, foul breeze touched their faces. It flowed in from the open door atop the spiral staircase.

As Kane reached down to pick up Megaera, for the first time, it really sank in. He'd lain awake most of the night thinking about it, but the concept hadn't seemed real until that very moment. He and his friends were 238,866 miles from Earth, inside a place that smelled like moldy old clothes and dairy products gone bad. He fought down a choking claustrophobia.

He noticed, however, that his body didn't feel appreciably lighter. In fact, he seemed to weigh actually a little more than he had when he'd stepped into the gateway unit in Cerberus redoubt.

Closing a hand around Megaera's upper arm, he pulled her to her feet. He glanced over at Grant and saw him frowning, hefting his Copperhead in both hands as if he were trying to guess its weight.

Brigid declared, "There's an artificial gravity generator in use. More than likely it's the same kind of grav-stator we found in the Cydonia One compound. For some reason it's notched higher than one g."

She wrinkled her nose. "Mars smelled better than this place."

Grant sniffed the air experimentally but said nothing. His nose had been broken three times in the past, and always poorly reset. Unless an odor was extraordinarily pleasant or virulently repulsive, he was incapable of detecting subtle smells unless they were right under his nostrils. A running joke during his Mag days had been that Grant could eat a hearty dinner with a dead skunk lying on the table next to his plate.

Brigid stepped over to Megaera. ''Remember, you gave us your word to afford us safe passage to your council chambers.''

The old woman nodded. ''I did. We are here.''

Brigid's eyebrows lifted. ''This? *This* place is your—?''

The rest of Brigid's words clogged in her throat as Megaera suddenly threw herself backward against Kane, sidekicking her in the belly in the same motion. Brigid jackknifed at the waist, blurting out a cry of surprise. She staggered back against Grant, who was forced to let his Copperhead dangle by the strap so he could use both hands to keep her from falling.

With wire-taut reflexes astonishing in someone so old, Megaera twisted and wrenched herself free of Kane's grasp. She slammed both hands flat against his chest, shoving him into one of the black statues.

Hairline cracks appeared in the black body, and from them spewed tendrils of equally black smoke. At the same time, an astringent stench filled Kane's nostrils, an odor of hot sulfur mixed with ammonia.

The cracks in the statue's body expanded into deep splits and more of the oily vapor plumed out. The smoke spread quickly, and the figure seemed to unravel at the edges, twists of mist rising like a multitude of loose black threads. Clothing, flesh, bones and hair dissolved into a foul-smelling fog.

Thick, blinding smoke boiled out. As Kane tried to recover his balance, tears streaming from his eyes, he heard Megaera's raucous voice screeching incomprehensible words. Kane stumbled backward as he was showered with foul-smelling ash and blinded by the black mushroom of smoke. He inhaled a mouthful of vapor and succumbed to a coughing fit.

Grant, coughing and sputtering, glimpsed Megaera at the top of the staircase an instant before she lunged through the door. Although he couldn't fully smell the cesspit stink from the destroyed statue, the foul tang of sulfur was sharp on his tongue. He turned his head and spit.

Fanning the air in front of his face, Kane said, "Now what do we—?" He sneezed violently.

Brigid guessed what he was going to ask. "We can't stay here. It'll take the interphaser another few minutes to finish its cycle. Megaera will probably be back here with a squad of Furies in about thirty seconds."

Grant plunged through the settling smoke and ash, eyes narrowed to slits. "Then let's not hang around. We can meet them halfway. Bring the interphaser."

Brigid bent and picked up the machine. "I don't think that's a good idea. What if we're captured and it's taken away from us? Damaged beyond repair? I'll hide it instead."

Kane glanced around the room. Except for the figures of calcified people, the big chamber was essentially featureless. "Hide it where?"

Brigid nibbled her lower lip for a couple of seconds, eyes darting this way and that. Then she smiled and strode among the black statues. She stopped be-

fore one roughly in the center of the cluster. Its arms
were raised as if in fear, crossed over the upper body.
Carefully, Brigid fitted the interphaser into the cradle
formed by the biceps and upper chest.

Kane smiled in approval. The weak, watery illumination in the chamber was so dim and the figure
placed in such a way that someone would have to be
standing literally beside it in order to see the device.
Grant was already scaling the staircase, taking two
steps at a time. "Let's go!" he called over his shoulder.

The stairs led to a dimly lit passageway, looking
as if it had been hacked out of stone and reinforced
with braces of thick, bevel-edged beams of iron. They
paused long enough to put on dark-lensed glasses.
The electrochemical polymer of the lenses gathered
all available light and made the most of it to give
them a limited form of night vision. All three of them
carried Nighthawk microlights, but they were loath to
use them, fearing the glows they produced would pin-
point their position to anyone coming down the dark
passageway ahead of them.

The three people moved swiftly and fairly silently,
the boots of their shadow suits making only faint
rasping sounds. They stepped over irregularities in the
floor and came across branching mouths of other tunnels. They passed a number of the light panels inset
into the walls. They moved steadily ahead, none of
them caring for the cold, damp breeze that wafted
over them from somewhere in the darkness ahead.

From that darkness came odd, faint sounds, very brief but very eerie.

As they strode forward, Kane's imagination could not help but weave visions from the sounds whispering and echoing. Now and then he heard an eerie sobbing cry, then a mechanical clanking and then a distant wail, like the wind through distant pines.

At other times, he thought he sensed presences in the black mouths of the side passages. The skin of Kane's nape prickled. He was conscious of the gaze of unseen eyes. Their ears detected a distant, almost inaudible reverberation. The throbbing drone grew louder the farther they walked, like the murmur of a far-off crowd.

Kane found himself wishing Domi hadn't decided to stand down from the op. Her wilderness-honed senses would have been a great asset at this point. He couldn't blame her, particularly considering how the last recon mission she had undertaken turned out. He was fairly certain, however, that her refusal had more to do with being in Grant's company than shrinking from possible dangers.

The hum grew louder and the tunnel brightened as they approached what appeared to be a large chamber. The three Cerberus exiles moved forward cautiously and found themselves on a balcony. Below them was the source of the throbbing drone—a two-tiered generator.

The sight of the strangely shaped generator was no surprise, considering their location. They had seen identical machines in several places across the world over the past two years. The generator derived from the same source as the light panels—Balam's people.

Brigid stepped to the far side of the balcony, toward a framed portal with metal shutters on the wall. Thin, regularly shaped slits of white light were visible between the metal slats. Brigid slowly began to turn a knob on the frame and the shutters opened, allowing the threads of light to widen. Grant and Kane moved beside her, narrowing their eyes until their vision became accustomed to the brightness.

"Now you can get your bearings, Kane," Brigid announced in a tight voice, breathless with awe.

Dawn was creeping across the outer face of the Moon, the advancing sunlight flowing like a slow orange tide over the stark, peak-ringed craters and bone-white pumice plains. Two lunar peaks towered over them like the calcified finger bones of inestimably huge giants. Cruel, jagged escarpments and buttresses glared blindingly white in the unrelenting brilliance of the unsoftened Sun.

Grant bit back a curse and Kane stiffened. The airless surface of the Moon seemed to meet deep space with its billions of glittering stars. Reflecting back the light of distant suns, the broken surface of the Moon stood out in stark relief. There was no blanket of atmosphere to soften and spread either the light of Sol or the glow from the stars.

Here was either too much sun, if you were on the sun side, or not enough. Looking outward, Kane felt he could actually see the literal meaning of infinity, the vast gulfs of space stretching onward and onward until the mind flinched from trying to measure it.

Brigid reached between the shutters and touched a thick portal made of armaglass. In a muted voice, she said, "Over there is Mare Frigoris, the Sea of Ice. It's called that because the surface is vitrified."

In silence, they watched the dawn tide creep across the face of the Moon. When it touched the fused, glassine surface of Mare Frigoris, it slowly lit up to blinding brilliance. They recoiled and Brigid hastily closed the shutters.

For a long moment none of them spoke, trying to reconcile the concept of traveling to the Moon with the reality of actually being there. Numbly they moved back to the handrail. On the opposite side of the balcony from the shuttered portal, a metal spiral wound down through an opening in the floor.

Kane craned his neck up and back, seeing only a crisscrossing pattern of pipes and conduits. "No way to go up," he murmured. "So I guess it's down."

Grant muttered, "I figured we'd be fighting off an army of night-gaunts by now. But this place seems deserted."

As if on cue, a faint noise emanated from below and commanded all of their attention. They dropped into crouches, peering down between the crossbars of the handrail. A man crept around the base of the generator. He was slightly below average height and was wearing a dark brown coverall. His complexion was of a similar hue, but he was not a Negro. His long black hair hung in lank strands, framing a deeply scarred face.

He slunk along, stooped in a crouch, looking from side to side. The long-barreled pistol grasped in one hand trembled as if he were terrified. When he turned his head slightly, they caught the blaze of wild eyes.

In a whisper, Kane said to Brigid, "He doesn't look like the Fury I unmasked in Chicago."

"Whoever he is," she responded in the same low-pitched tone, "he's scared to death of something."

Grant had overheard the exchange. "But what?"

A shadow suddenly shifted on the other side of the generator, moving smoothly and silently behind the man. It paused for a second at the cube-shaped base and a dark gray bulk rose up from the floor.

"What the hell is that?" Kane demanded, hands tightening on the crossbar. "Some kind of animal?"

In shape, it was almost triangular. A smooth front rose up to an almost comically tiny head, set at the apex of the triangle. The back was a long slope that tapered down to the floor. It appeared to be about six feet long. Four legs were set under it, almost as a kickstand might be set beneath a motorcycle. Two tiny red eyes gleamed above a square snout and a mouth full of needle-tipped, alloy-coated teeth.

Tensely, Brigid breathed, "It's not an animal…it's a droid, a robot."

The mechanoid stood silent for another moment, then its head rose up on a segmented metal neck, turning this way and that, as if it were smelling a breeze. It took one step, halted, took two more and stopped again. The man continued to walk silently, unaware of the machine stalking him. The metal stalk of its neck abruptly lowered, sinking the head between its dull gray shoulders. Then it sprang.

Chapter 17

Brigid acted according to the first impulse of her compassionate nature. She swiftly pulled herself erect and leaned over the rail, shouting stridently, "Look out!"

The man wheeled around instantly before her cry could even begin to echo. He saw the mechanoid vaulting toward him as he fell backward beneath it. The long-barreled pistol in his hand made a noise like the cracking of a monster whip. A puff of smoke bloomed from the machine's underbelly in the split second before it landed directly atop the man. He screamed once.

Brigid rushed to the staircase, evading Kane's restraining hand and ignoring Grant's urgent warning whisper of "Wait!"

She rushed down the three windings of the spiral staircase, hearing Kane and Grant pound the risers directly behind her. Brigid reached man and mechanoid a few seconds before her companions. A high-pitched whine and a castanet-like clicking emanated from within the metal hide of the droid. Acrid smoke curled from seams split open all up and down its length. An odor that smelled somewhat familiar, but one she was unable to identify, wafted out with the smoke.

A thick, yellowish liquid spread out across the floor around the man's body. He lay limply, his head barely visible, his arms spread-eagled. The pistol lay near his right hand.

Grant and Kane spread out, approaching the two bodies from opposite directions, butts of their subguns trained on the robot. The targeting pippers of the laser sights shone like tiny pinheads of blood on its dark gray casing. "Get away from that damn thing, Baptiste," Kane ordered.

She retreated, giving both men clear fields of fire. They came forward cautiously, fingers hovering over the triggers of their Copperheads. Neither man nor machine stirred. The photoreceptors that served as the robot's eyes were dark.

"Some kind of sec droid," Grant grunted, nudging it with a foot. "Never heard of anything like this."

All three of them recalled how Lakesh spoke of military experiments with robotic security forces installed in the Totality Concept redoubts. They ended experimentation in the late 1990s because the robots didn't have the ability to generalize. The sec droids tended to kill any personnel who even slightly matched their programmed enemy profile. Lakesh claimed he witnessed a test where one of the droids killed a congressional aide because he wore a mustache similar to that of a known terrorist.

Kane played the kill-dot of the autotargeter over a

series of small numbers stamped on the machine's dorsal side. Beneath them were the words: Robotek 3000. ''Somebody manufactured this thing.''

Grant touched the widening pool of viscous yellow fluid with the toe of a boot. ''What's this shit? Oil? Some kind of lubricant?''

Brigid knelt at its leading edge and sniffed. ''Doesn't smell like it.''

She dipped the tip of forefinger into it and brought the liquid close to her nose. Her face twisted in first revulsion, then astonishment. ''Oh, my God—''

''What?'' Kane demanded.

In a voice muted by horror, she said, ''This smells like—I think it's *bile*.''

The man beneath the droid suddenly jerked his arms and legs and uttered a deep groan.

Carefully, Kane and Grant wrestled the triangular metal body of the machine up and off of the man. It was heavy, but not less so than they expected. A gaping cavity was punched through its underside. From this leaked the thick fluid, and they glimpsed a glitter of broken circuitry within.

Brigid retrieved the man's pistol and kept it trained on him during the process. She was by no means an expert on firearms, but even she knew the handblaster was very unusual. It held the general configuration of a revolver, but instead of cylinder, a small round ammo drum was fitted into the place where there was normally a trigger guard. There was no real trigger, just a curving switch set into the grip. The barrel was unusually long, nearly ten inches in length. It was made of a lightweight alloy that resembled dulled chrome.

Once the man was freed of the robot's weight, he propped himself up on his elbows and stared at the three people with wild, wide eyes. He moved his lips for several seconds as if he were trying to summon the strength to scream. Kane wondered if the sight of them had unseated his reason.

Finally, he wheezed in English, "Who are you? Where do you come from? You're not of Megaera's brood though you're dressed like them."

Kane smiled in a manner he hoped was reassuring. "These old things? We figured they were the fashion statement of the day up here on the Moon."

The man tried to lever himself into a sitting position, then he grimaced, clutching at the right side of his chest. He coughed rackingly, putting a hand over his mouth. When he brought it away, a glob of pink saliva glistened in the palm. "Broken rib," he said hoarsely. "Punctured my lung, but I don't think it's serious."

He glared with unregenerate, homicidal hatred at the robot and flung the sputum at it. "Fucking carnobot! Too fast for you, wasn't I?"

"Carnobot?" Brigid echoed incredulously.

The man looked toward her, his eyes flicking up and down her lissome, black-clad form in silent appraisal and appreciation. "You were the one who warned me. Thanks."

"Do you have a name?" Grant asked.

He nodded. "Last I heard, yeah. What about you—do you have names?"

Kane made introductions all around. The man nodded to each of them in turn. "Call me Eduardo. It's my name for the moment, but I'm thinking of changing it." He extended a hand toward Brigid. "Can I have my gun back, please?"

"Not yet," said Kane. "Not until we get some answers."

Eduardo made an attempt to rise, but he set his teeth on a groan, kneading his chest. "We can't stay here. They be all around us now."

"Who is 'they'?" inquired Brigid.

"Megaera and her Furies for one." He spit toward the robot. "More of them for another. Our spies told us Megaera disappeared yesterday so we made an incursion. But I saw her not more than ten minutes ago, rallying her troops."

"Rallying her troops for what?" Grant asked.

Teeth gritted against the pain, Eduardo pushed himself to his feet. "This isn't the time. We've got to get to the east life-hutch module." He fetched the carnobot a kick, producing a gonglike chime. "Hate those filthy things!"

He turned and circled the base of the generator. Kane, Brigid and Grant exchanged a quick questioning glance, then fell in at his heels. He led them into a labyrinth of pipes and wheel valves crisscrossing in all directions. Dismantled pieces of machinery lay scattered on the floor. The Cerberus exiles followed Eduardo through the metal maze, Grant bumping his head on low-hanging pipes more than once. When he swore, Eduardo shushed him into silence. He kept turning his head to listen for sounds of pursuit and stared with burning, fearful intensity at every wedge of shadow they passed.

The longer they walked, the more they noticed how light their bodies began to feel. Jumping over a length of tubing in his path, Kane nearly sailed headlong into the ceiling. "What the hell is going on?" he demanded angrily.

Eduardo said tersely, "We're getting farther and farther from the grav-stator field. Don't worry about it, though. Worry about the carnobots that may have caught our scent."

"Droids can't smell," growled Grant.

"These can," Eduardo replied flatly. "They used to be called gastrobots because they operated on E. coli-powered fuel cells."

"A robot that runs on bacteria?" Brigid asked skeptically.

"Not anymore. Now they're powered by meat." Eduardo paused for a moment, panting, hand on his chest. "They derive power through a microbial fuel cell stomach. The stomach breaks down food using Escherichia coli bacteria and then converts the chemical energy from that digestion process into electricity. The microbes from the bacteria decompose the carbohydrates supplied by the food, which releases electrons. The electrons, in turn, supply a charge to the battery through a reduction and oxidation reaction. We call it redox.''

Grant scowled at him fiercely. ''That's crazy.''

Eduardo was in too much pain and too out of breath to reply, but Brigid said musingly, ''No, it makes sense. The system he describes is very similar to how blood supply and respiration works in humans, but the process produces electrons rather than oxygen. So the ideal fuel for powering such a mechanism *is* meat. It has its own digestive system, the synthetic bile.''

''Maybe,'' Kane said dubiously. ''But how can it smell?''

''A lot better than we do,'' Eduardo said, pushing himself away from the wall. ''Nothing more than a sensor chip, like in smoke alarms. Only the carnobots are programmed to detect perspiration and even pheromones.''

''And Megaera controls them?'' Brigid asked, falling into step behind the man again.

''Yeah. And a lot more than droids, too.''

''What's your problem with her?'' Kane asked.

Eduardo uttered a strange sobbing sound. It took a couple of seconds before they interpreted the vocalization as a scornful laugh. ''Any of you ever heard of Charlemagne?''

Only Brigid answered. ''Yes.''

''Emperor Charlemagne passed savage laws against demons and all who held converse with them. For hundreds of years the Catholic Church staged a brutal crusade against demonologists, torturing and executing thousands of people all over Europe with a fanaticism that was demonic itself.''

Grant and Kane looked mystified, but Brigid ventured, ''So Megaera has set herself up as Charlemagne and you're the demon?''

''Something like that.''

Grant muttered, ''You could've said so in the first place.''

Kane whispered into Brigid's ear, ''Looks like you've found a soul mate, Baptiste.''

She ignored him.

Eduardo moved forward in an odd but swift shuffling gait. He led them to an open hatch in the floor and scurried down a wooden ladder. As he descended, he said, ''This is an old drainage system, closed off for years. That's how my people got into this part of the base.''

The four people splashed along a curve-walled conduit, wading ankle deep in seepage, bypassing a dented and rust-streaked pumping station. As they strode along, all of them noticed the temperature was rising. Brigid guessed the Manitius base was in direct sunlight now.

''At the halfway point,'' wheezed Eduardo over his shoulder.

''Halfway point to where?'' Grant asked.

When Eduardo didn't answer, Grant took a long-legged step forward, reaching for the man. Due to the diminished gravity, he ended up slamming into him.

Eduardo nearly went sprawling, but Grant grabbed him by the collar of his coverall and kept him on his feet.

"Where are you taking us?" he demanded, his voice a growl of suspicion.

Eduardo winced, touching his chest, but he didn't try to wrest free. Earnestly he said, "To my people. They're waiting for us. For the love of God, let me go. I'll tell you everything once we get there. Believe me, I'm just as curious about you as you are about me, but this isn't the time!"

Grant glared at him for a silent, menacing second, then released him. The four people moved on again. The narrow conduit opened up on a long, low tunnel stretching away before them, iron I-beams shoring up the sides and ceiling. The ground was earthen, muddy and damp, showing the prints of many feet. The smell of decaying vegetable matter clogged their nostrils.

Eduardo strode swiftly to the end of the tunnel and came to a halt, looking around cautiously. The three Cerberus personnel joined him, gazing in astonishment at the vast bowl-shaped chamber beyond. The walls and domed ceiling were composed of interlocking slabs of a transparent substance all of them recognized as armaglass. Outside the dome, they saw the Manitius base looming around them.

Most of the installation was built into the regolith, the inner walls of the crater. It was a collection of towers and radar dishes and bulldozed flat planes bisected by terraced channels with concrete-paneled sides.

Eduardo pointed, saying, "One of those is our destination, the life-hutch habitat modules."

They saw four smooth cylinders, each with a chute type of tunnel leading to them from a point they couldn't see. Each one was half dug into the side of the crater, presumably for shelter from radiation.

Atop some of the towers were small directional dishes. From others, stairs on elevated girders climbed to pyramidal structures that were part of the solar-cell energy array. The entire expanse was interlaced with thick power cables and conduits stretching along forked pylons.

"Not much to look at it, is it?" Eduardo asked.

"Depends on your perspective," Brigid answered.

Eduardo gave her a jittery smile and moved out from the tunnel. The air was still and hot, thick with veils of steamy mist. "This is a hydroponic farm," Eduardo said. "It grows everything we need to keep us alive. This was the first place Megaera claimed."

Brigid looked out at the walls of the crater looming above them and fanned away steam from her face. "Land of the misty mountains," she muttered. "Now I know what that meant."

They scaled a short ladder leading to a catwalk forming a narrow, elevated bridge between square fields of mossy earth dotted with warm pools of water. Below them were fruit trees, rows of corn, even carrot patches.

At the end of the catwalk, Eduardo turned aside and sidled through a doorway that in turn led to a chamber from which a metal stairway spiraled down into darkness. Eduardo, panting from exertion and pain, pointed into the throat of blackness. "That goes to an accessway below, then to the life-hutch module. Megaera and her Furies and maybe even a carnobot or two might have gotten here ahead of us. But we must take the chance."

All of them quickly descended the winding stair and stepped into a corridor as impenetrably black as the gulfs between the stars. Their dark-vision glasses were useless, and Kane fumbled for his Nighthawk microlight in a belt pouch. He turned it on and the amber beam cast a halo on Eduardo's frightened face. Beads of perspiration glistened on his forehead like polished pearls.

"No!" he barked, clapping both hands around the little flashlight. "I know the way. If an ambush has been laid ahead, we can't let them know we're coming."

Kane hesitated, then clicked off the Nighthawk. "All right," he said in a low voice. "But Grant will keep his blaster on you. Play us false and you'll wish you were dealing with carnobots."

Eduardo was too agitated to react to the threat. "Link hands."

Kane murmured in Brigid's ear, "Let me bring up the rear."

He stepped around her and clasped her right hand

in his left. The four people began a silent march into absolute darkness. Brigid ran her fingertips along the bulkhead as they walked, occasionally feeling a closed doorway.

Kane suddenly heard a faint sound behind them. His flesh crawled as if an army of ants crept along between his skin and the shadow suit. He strained his ears, trying to catch a repetition of the stealthy movement in the corridor. He tried to pierce the blackness with slitted eyes.

He saw nothing and after a moment he was almost ready to attribute the sound to an errant echo and his wire-taut nerves. Then, in the sepia sea two points of red fire appeared, seeming to dance and shift in a weird rhythm. He heard a distant tap-tapping. Between one heartbeat and the next, the tapping rose in volume to a steady clatter and the crimson pinpoints swelled from the size of tiny embers to seething circles of scarlet.

All of them heard the racket, and Eduardo yelped, a note of hysteria in his voice, "Run!"

Grant spit out a curse and Kane pushed Brigid ahead of him, thumbing on the Copperhead's laser autotargeting system. It cut through the darkness like a vermilion thread and touched something that winked metallically.

"Go!" he half snarled, putting a hand between Brigid's shoulder blades and propelling her along.

They sprinted blindly down the corridor as the clatter grew louder and the scarlet spots drew closer.

Their thudding footfalls echoed repeatedly. Kane ran as he'd run few times in his life. The breath seared his lungs and his heart pounded against his ribs. His laboring legs seemed weighted with half-frozen mud. Behind him he heard the scuttle of metal against metal.

Suddenly, Eduardo gasped, "Here it is! It hasn't been opened! Help me—!"

Kane staggered to a halt, bumping into Brigid. Voice raspy, Grant asked, "Help you do what?"

"The hatch!" Eduardo cried out. "Help me open it!"

Grant shouldered Eduardo aside, and his hands groped over a heavy metal door with a wheel lock centered in its rivet-studded mass. Putting both hands on the wheel, he turned it violently. The wheel didn't spin easily; it caught and squeaked during the rotation. He continued spinning until the lock completed its final turn and he heard the metallic snapping of solenoids and latches letting go. Putting his shoulder against it, he pushed the hatch open, hinges squealing in protest.

Eduardo, Brigid and Grant stumbled over the raised lip of the hatchway. Kane shoved Brigid ahead of him and depressed the trigger of the Copperhead. The sub-gun sprayed a steady stream of rounds with a sound like the prolonged ripping of stiff canvas.

The muzzle-flash smeared the darkness with strobing tongues of flame. Little flares sparked in the murk as the rounds struck and ricocheted from metal. He heard a series of staccato clangs, as of a blacksmith hammering on an anvil at an inhumanly fast tempo.

Kane knew that a sustained full-auto burst only wasted ammunition, but his focus was on driving away the carnobot long enough so they could close and dog the hatch. He fired the clip dry and achieved his objective. The monster mechanoid did not advance from the gloom.

Kane threw himself backward, and Grant pulled the hatch closed. Eduardo swiftly dogged it. They heard his hands scraping along the bulkhead and then the snapping of a switch. A wire-encased bulb on the ceiling shed a ghostly illumination. They didn't stand in a room or even a corridor. It was more of a ribbed chute stretching away to a steel-sheathed door about twenty yards away.

Kane gulped air, leaning against the hatch. A heavy weight slammed against it from the outside, causing it to rattle loudly in its frame. He and his friends hastily backed away from it. Eduardo turned and began jogging along the chute, but not with a panicked gait. He seemed more confident. "Come on!"

At the end of the chute, they saw the door panel slide aside and Eduardo called out, "It's me! All clear?"

A vibrant male voice replied, "All clear!"

Brigid, Kane and Grant followed Eduardo down the chute and through the open doorway. They had no time to look before a multitude of gun barrels converged on them from all sides, staring like hollow eyes.

Chapter 18

Neither Grant, Brigid nor Kane raised their hands. The four people in the habitat didn't see Kane and Grant flex the tendons of their right wrists. Nor did they appear to hear the actuators click or the faint, brief drone of tiny electric motors and the solid slap of the butts of the Sin Eaters sliding into the men's palms almost at the same time. But when they saw the handblasters appear almost magically in their hands, they took instinctive steps back.

Eduardo hastily spoke up. "They're friends," he said curtly. "At least, I think they are." He cast a quizzical glance toward Brigid. "Aren't you?"

"For the time being," Brigid answered stiffly. "That all depends on what you tell us."

For a long tick of time, the tense tableau held. The gun-brandishing trio was attired similarly to Eduardo, though their coveralls were all of different colors—red, green and gray.

A woman wearing the red garment stepped around Eduardo, lowering her pistol. "All right, everybody can stand down." Her voice was strong and vibrant and carried a note of command. As gun barrels drooped, she announced, "My name is Mariah."

She wasn't beautiful or young. Her face was pale and angular. Her chestnut hair, threaded here and there with gray, was cut painfully short to the scalp. Deep creases curved out from either side of her nose to the corners of her mouth. Dark-ringed brown eyes gazed at them from beneath long brows that hadn't been plucked in years, if ever. Her teeth, though white, were uneven. "What are your names?" she asked.

After the Cerberus exiles introduced themselves, she identified the other two people. Neukirk was a short, chunky man with weather-beaten features and a white crew cut. He wore the gray coverall.

The man in green was introduced as Philboyd. He was the tallest of the group, a little over six feet, long and lanky of build. Blond-white hair was swept back from a receding hairline. He wore black-rimmed eyeglasses. The right lenses showed a spiderweb pattern of cracks. His cheeks appeared to be pitted with the sort of scars associated with chronic teenage acne.

"Those outfits of yours threw us for a second," Mariah said. "Only the Furies wear them. Where'd you find them?"

"Earth," Kane stated matter-of-factly, expecting all of the people to gape at him in shock or call him a liar. When his one-word response didn't elicit either of those two reactions, he added inanely, "That's where we're from."

Philboyd nodded sagely. "Had to happen eventually, I guess."

"What had to happen?" Brigid inquired.

"That Earth people—what's left of them, any-way—would finally remember we were up here." A bitter, humorless smile twisted his thin lips. "A little too late."

In the moment of awkward silence that followed Philboyd's remark, Brigid glanced around the cylindrical interior of the habitat. She heard oxygen hissing through wall pipes, computer station relays whirred and clicked. Indicator lights on a communications console blinked purposefully. The place seemed in perfect operational order.

In an open cubicle, draped over frameworks, she saw several one-piece suits made of a silver material. Helmets with transparent visors rested on a shelf above them. She recognized the suits and helmets from pix she had seen as environmental suits.

"You seem a little disappointed that we weren't all struck speechless when you said you were from Earth," Mariah said with a dour half smile.

"Not disappointed necessarily," Kane countered, matching her smile. "We're a little surprised, that's all. After all, you people have been up here for a couple of hundred years at least. Or the people you're descended from."

Neukirk grunted. "My parents were farmers in Iowa."

Eduardo gestured to his three companions. "We've been up here since the second of January, 2001. But we slept through most of those two centuries."

Grant drew in a sharp, startled breath. "You're freezies."

Eduardo chuckled, then winced, clutching at his chest. He sank down in a chair. "That's a good one," he commented. "Freezies. Sounds like something you'd buy from an ice-cream truck during the summer."

"If you mean we were in cryostasis," Philboyd stated a little superciliously, "then yes, that's who we are."

"That's who you are, maybe," responded Brigid. "But not what."

"Us?" Mariah inquired with a mocking ingenuousness. "We used to be the project overseers of the DEVIL process. But now we're all that stands between Earth and its obliteration."

She stepped forward, extending a hand toward Brigid. "Pleased to meet you."

GRANT AND KANE RETRACTED their Sin Eaters and Brigid returned Eduardo's pistol to him. Grant asked, "What kind of blasters are those anyway? Never seen anything like them."

Mariah hesitated a moment, then handed her pistol to Grant, butt first. As he examined it, she said, "They fire steel and tungsten carbide pellet loads. A unit of energy inside the grip moves a piston that propels the projectile. They are a sort of dial-a-recoil gas system, to minimize the force with which the shooter would be moved backward in low- or null-gravity fields.''

Brigid nodded. ''Too much recoil out on the surface and the shooter could find himself halfway across the Moon.''

Philboyd said, ''Exactly. There are some three-piece plasma rifles on the base, but the pistol's system proved the best. Radiation- or energy-based weapons can be dangerous to the user.''

Grant turned the gun over in his hands, squinted down its length, then handed it back to Mariah with a word of thanks. The atmosphere in the little hutch became less tense but not particularly relaxed even when everyone took chairs.

Kane cast a wary glance toward the flimsy-looking door. ''What's keeping those carnivorous droids or Furies from breaking in here?''

Neukirk gestured to the consoles. ''We modified one of these stations to triangulate and control the DEVIL platform's position. She doesn't know which hutch has the modifications, so she can't take the chance of damaging any one of them. It's sort of a no-man's-land. She does know that if she happens to break into any of the habitats we occupy, she's taking a big risk.''

Kane raised his eyebrows. ''Just what goes on here, anyhow?''

Mariah said, ''You first. How'd you get here?''

Grant and Kane let Brigid make the explanations. Tersely, without elaboration, she told of their first encounter with Megaera and her Furies in Chicago, where they had embarked on a campaign of sin-cleansing. She related how Sindri apparently brought her there during his experiments with the parallax points program and how they had repeated his mistake. Although she alluded to Cerberus, she didn't go into detail or mention any names.

The four people listened to the story with stolid expressions, occasionally interjecting a question. Kane noticed their questions were strangely free of anything pertaining to current conditions on Earth. For that matter, they didn't seem too surprised by anything Brigid told them.

"What happened to this Sindri fellow?" Neukirk asked.

"We don't know," Brigid answered. "We still don't know why Megaera believed him to be a small, smiling god. I mean, he's small and he smiles a lot, but a deity is the last thing he is."

Eduardo shrugged. "It's all part of Megaera's insane mythography, grafting bits and pieces of old religions into her own, like she's sewing a quilt."

Brigid smiled. "I noted how she had appropriated the Greek myth of the Furies and the Oubolus, even though the rest of her trappings are of Sumerian origin."

"Is there is a small, smiling god in Sumerian myth?" Kane asked. "Somebody she could have mistook Sindri for?"

Eduardo shrugged again as if the matter were of

little importance. ''Adad, a dwarfish cousin of Enlil, is the best candidate.'' He sighed. ''Good thing this Sindri really wasn't who Megaera thought he was. One Sumerian god up here is enough.''

A chill finger stroked the buttons of Kane's spine. ''So there really is an Annunaki here on the Moon.'' He didn't ask a question but made a statement, waiting for either confirmation or denial.

For the first time, the four people displayed a strong reaction. Pitching her voice low to disguise the tremor of fear, Mariah asked, ''You know of the Annunaki?''

Brigid said grimly, ''Yes. Briefly, the Annunaki were intelligent alien beings with space-travel capability. They perfected a method of hyperdimensional travel. They first visited Earth at least three hundred thousand years ago.''

''Enlil,'' Kane prodded laconically.

''I was trying to be brief,'' replied Brigid. ''Enlil was an Annunaki who apparently held lordship over the Earth. He arranged the first catastrophe recorded in ancient texts as the Flood. He didn't want to leave Earth and he died there. We saw his body.''

Mariah sighed heavily, bowing her head and dry-scrubbing her scalp with her fingers. ''Body, you say? He's not alive?''

''As far as we know,'' Grant answered, ''he's most completely thoroughly dead.''

''Thank God,'' Philboyd whispered fervently. ''Thank God for that at least. We were terrified that he was here and we just couldn't find him. We found the rest of the pantheon, but—'' He broke off suddenly, his eyes widening as if he realized he had said too much.

''What do you mean by pantheon?'' Kane demanded.

When no reply was forthcoming from Eduardo, Brigid said, ''Do you mean the royal family?''

''What?'' Grant half growled the word. ''You found other Annunaki on the Moon?''

Eduardo pointed to himself and his companions. ''Not us, exactly.'' He stopped talking again.

In a low, measured tone, Kane asked, ''You expect us to believe you found a nest of Sumerian gods up here?''

Philboyd's eyes flashed with sudden sparks of anger. ''Hey, back off, man. We're scientists.''

''You're not sounding like it,'' Brigid pointed out.

None of the four people said anything. They just looked at one another in discomfort, all but squirming in their chairs.

''Time for your contribution to the story hour,'' Kane declared firmly.

''You want it from the beginning?'' Mariah asked peevishly.

''That would help,'' rumbled Grant.

''All right,'' the woman said smoothly. ''The effort to colonize the Moon started with the landing of Apollo 11 in the summer of 1969. Other landings were scheduled from mid-1969 to 1972. The second, Apollo 12, aimed for the maria on the western side of the Moon. The third targeted a highland formation like the Fra Mauro Crater in the western highland region. The fourth was aimed at the eastern cratered highlands near Censorinus. The fifth explored the region of the Littrow craters east of the Mare Serenititatis—the sixth, the great crater, Tycho. The seventh landed on the volcanic domes of the marius Hills, the eighth was aimed at Schroter's Valley, where luminous gas emissions had been reported by Earth observers for more than a century. The ninth landing was in the Hyginus Rille, one of the most prominent faultlike structures on the Moon, and the tenth was in Copernicus, where it was hoped that material blown out of the interior would be found. Apollo 17 was the end of the line. Officially.''

She tapped her chest with a forefinger, "I was part of the twenty-first manned landing here in the Manitius Crater region…one the American public knew nothing about.''

Neukirk said, "I was on that flight, too.''

"I was on the twenty-sixth,'' Eduardo put in.

"I'm the latecomer,'' Philboyd said. "I didn't get here until after the mat-trans unit was installed. I think that was the thirtieth manned landing.''

Kane arched an eyebrow but said nothing. Mariah caught the brow motion. "Please don't expect us to explain the mat-trans gateways. I barely understood it even after it was explained to me. I refused to use it. I preferred the eight-day flight back to Earth.''

"Yeah,'' agreed Neukirk. "I was a quantum physicist, and it was almost beyond me how the damn things worked. You'd have to ask the boy genius about it...and for that you'd need a medium—or a swami, since he was Indian.''

Kane saw that Brigid did her best to repress a smile. ''We know what the mat-trans units are. But the question begs to be asked—''

''Why didn't we use the one here to gate ourselves off this rock?'' Philboyd broke in. ''First off, after the nuke, we figured we were safer here.''

''So you know about the nukecaust,'' rumbled Grant. ''I wasn't sure.''

Mariah made a gesture toward the door and the chute beyond. ''We watched it from where the hydroponic farm is now. Hell of a light show.'' She smiled, but it didn't reach her eyes.

''You don't seem too broken up about it,'' Kane observed dryly.

''It's been two hundred years,'' said Eduardo flatly. ''Little late for a wake, don't you think?''

Mariah sighed, shifting in her chair. ''To be honest with you, a number of the base personnel went completely off the deep end. Some committed suicide, some simply took long walks outside...without wearing space suits. After a few years, a group of us, the main DEVIL crew, decided to go into cryostasis to keep from straining the base's resources.''

''How long has the base been here?'' Brigid wanted to know.

''Construction began in the late 1970s,'' answered

Neukirk, "after the shuttle-craft program kicked into gear. This site was chosen because the early Apollo missions reported a base had already existed here. There were chambers and tunnels dug into the regolith—the crater walls—that extended for miles."

"At the time," Eduardo offered, "God only knew how many thousands of years old the base was or who built it."

Grimly, Mariah said, "We found out later."

As Mariah described it, the objective of the Manitius base was twofold—to establish a self-sufficient colony and to provide a jumping-off point to ferry materials and personnel to build a space station on the Moon's dark side. There were also agricultural and mining ventures. Construction of the base was an ongoing process, expanding it, improving it, modifying it. By the mid-1990s, there were over three hundred more or less permanent residents. Around that time, another mission was attached to the base.

"The Deep Electromotive Valence Induration Lithospherimal process?" Brigid inquired.

"Almost right," Philboyd retorted glumly. "But the E doesn't stand for 'electromotive.'"

"No?"

Mariah shook her head. "It did on paper, when it was sold to Congress as an experimental terraforming project. In its first incarnation, DEVIL involved the covert assembly in low Moon orbit of a planetismal projectile, if you know the term."

"I do," Brigid answered crisply.

"It was designed to make the atmosphere of Venus habitable for colonization," Philboyd went on. "But it…" He paused, groping for the proper term. "Mutated."

"Mutated?" echoed Grant.

Mariah, expression bleak, declared, "Mutated into not just a travesty of the original project but into a genocidal monster. It was a 'black project.' There was no way Congress would have approved funding for a device that turned the workings of the universe inside out."

Brigid's face creased in a frown. "How could that happen?"

Eduardo tried to force a grin. "When you change the E from 'electromotive' to 'entropic.'"

Kane exchanged a puzzled glance with Brigid, then stated, "You're going to have to explain yourself."

Mariah arose from her chair and stepped over to the communications console. She flicked a pair of toggle switches and a screen blurred with an image. For a long moment, Kane, Brigid and Grant had no idea what they were looking at. It resembled nothing so much as a spherical mass made of rusting plates of metal. They could barely distinguish little directional antennas bristling from its surface.

"It looks like junk," Brigid said quietly.

"It was supposed to," Neukirk said. "A bunch of space junk in parking orbit. Nobody would get suspicious."

"Define 'nobody,'" Grant suggested.

"The Russians, for one," Eduardo replied. "Investigators from our own government, for another."

Mariah manipulated a dial and magnified the image. "The real problem was launching the components from the base and assembling them in space without attracting attention."

Inset between the plates of rusted metal they saw long sleek, rocket-shaped assemblies and a complexity of machinery. Mariah touched the various components. "Nuke drivers, stabilizers and calibration equipment."

With a sour smile, Philboyd commented, "Put them all together and it spells DEVIL. As in taking the hindmost or, in extreme cases, in a blue dress."

Kane cast the man an annoyed glance, but he didn't appear to notice.

Mariah sighed heavily, unhappily. "The true meaning of the DEVIL acronym was always Deep Entropic Valence Induration Lithospherimal. Only the designers and the operations team knew that. Essentially, DEVIL was built as an encapsulated, speeded-up manifestation of the second law of thermodynamics—the law of increasing entropy."

Seeing the scowls settle on the faces of Kane and Grant, Neukirk declared, "Entropy describes a process by which the universe is slowly running down, so slowly that it can only be measured in terms of centuries. Every particle of matter is losing energy, and this energy in the form of heat and light gradually accumulates throughout the universe. The rate at which bodies lose their energy is the entropic gradient. It appears that this process is also part of the process that we call the passage of time, or our perception of its passage. The entropic gradient is steady and inexorable.''

Mariah said, ''All transfers of energy in our universe are controlled by the laws of thermodynamics. The first law states that mass/energy cannot be created or destroyed. The second law adds that the disorganization or entropy of the universe increases with every energy transfer. Some energy is always degraded to useless heat dissipation.''

''And?'' Grant asked, a dangerous edge to his voice.

''And,'' Brigid said smoothly, ''the beginning of the universe, or the Big Bang, displayed a jolt of antientropy, resulting in increased complexity of mass. After the Big Bang, expansion of mass began to slow and reverse itself. When the mass catches up with the slowing expansion, the law of entropy applies.''

Mariah smiled at her approvingly. ''Theoretically, entropy would cause the dimming of stars for lack of fuel. They would become black dwarfs, neutron stars or black holes. Multiple collisions between these neutron stars will form supermassive black holes whose gravity will suck in everything until there is no matter, no radiation, nothing. Entropy at its maximum is nonexistence. But the holes decay faster than they shrink. Their lifetime is only about a second. The phenomenon depends not just on density but on total mass, so there is not a singularity at the center.''

Brigid's shoulders stiffened as she straightened swiftly in her chair. Kane and Grant could easily assess her sudden fear from her body language, even though her face remained calm and her tone uninflected when she said, "Please tell me that does *not* mean what I think it does.''

As if they were performers in a stage act, Philboyd, Neukirk, Mariah and Eduardo all nodded at the same time. Their expressions were all of a type, as well—grim. Eduardo was the first to answer her. "I'm afraid it does.''

"What are you talking about?'' Kane demanded. "It makes everything slow down?''

"It makes everything slow down and decay.'' Philboyd snapped his fingers. "Just like that.''

"The Sun could conceivably age billions of years in a second.'' Mariah's voice was a flat, unemotional monotone, a direct counterpoint to the fright gleaming in her eyes. "It would not be able to support life on Earth.''

"Transliteration is one term for it,'' Eduardo interjected. "Spacial discontinuity is another. But whatever you call it, total annihilation is the end result.''

Grant stood so suddenly his chair rolled backward on squealing casters, bumping into a console. He looked frightened and angry because of it. He raked the four scientists with furious eyes. "Goddamn white-coats,'' he spit contemptuously. ''Why would you build something like that?''

Eduardo, Mariah, Neukirk and Philboyd all looked at one another nervously. For a long moment none of them spoke. Finally, in a subdued half whisper, Mariah said, ''We didn't. Enki did.''

Chapter 19

Philboyd called the little plane a flitter-gig, even though its official designation was a TAV, a Transatmospheric Vehicle. It was well over two hundred years old, but he was obviously proud of it, despite the fact that one turboramjet repellor didn't work, causing the small, six-meter-long craft to list dangerously to port. At some time in the past, Philboyd had removed the control console and replaced it with a jury-rigged tangle of raggedly spliced wires and naked circuit boards.

The astrophysicist explained that three of the TAVs out of a fleet of ten survived on the base. All the others had been damaged in accidents over the years, and his flitter-gig was one of them. It was little more than a wedge with curves, a javelin equipped with two different kinds of engines—a ramjet and rocket engines that worked in tandem to enable the craft to fly in a vacuum.

Philboyd steered the flitter-gig with a joystick-type contrivance, and he leaned forward in the uncomfortable bucket seat to peer through the sand-scoured and cracked canopy. "Found this in the salvage yard about two years ago," he declared. He was shouting in order to be heard over the straining whine of the thrusters. He voice echoed within the confines of the helmets Brigid, Kane and Grant wore.

"A real classic, one of the secret prototypes made by Hiflite Industries back in the 1990s. Course I don't expect the postnuke generations to appreciate something like this. You've got to really love seat-of-the-pants flying to park your ass in one of these babies."

Kane wondered briefly how Grant, an experienced Deathbird jockey, would respond to such a challenge, or what swearword Wegmann would evoke upon first spying the craft. From the rear, he heard Brigid murmuring something about "function without form."

Or was that "form without function"? Before Kane could turn in his seat to ask Brigid for a clarification, Philboyd announced, "Look over there." He pointed to the south. "We call it the Wild Lands."

They saw a tumbled, rocky wilderness of the great southwest crater region. In the naked glow of starlight, the tightly clustered craters presented a forbidding spectacle. Everywhere the lunar plains and deserts were cracked by deep fissures.

"That's where most of the mining operations were conducted," Philboyd continued. "See that? One the greatest wonders of the Moon."

Brigid, Kane and Grant craned their necks, peering to see through the canopy. In the distance, a great slash curved through the barren lunar plain, wide and cut in clean like a surgical incision. It was an enormous, yawning chasm that stretched out of sight from east to west. Its sheer rock sides dropped into an impenetrable darkness of inestimable depth.

"The Great Chasm," Philboyd announced as if he were proud of it. "Eight hundred miles long, nearly fifty miles wide. It makes the Grand Canyon look like a pothole. God only knows how deep it is, but it's honeycombed by tunnels and hollows shaped by unequal cooling aeons ago."

"Cooling?" Grant asked uneasily. "Cooling down from what?"

Brigid said, "There are numerous theories about the origin of the Moon. One is the fission theory in which part of the rapidly spinning Earth was flung off to create the Moon. Another version of the fission theory stated that the Moon originated from the Pacific Ocean."

Philboyd nodded inside his helmet. His lips were creased in an approving smile. "And here I'd pretty much convinced myself that the descendants of the war were going to be as well-read as your average heavy-metal fan. I'm glad to be proved wrong. Anyway, if the fission theory is correct, then there would have been a lot of volcanic activity here."

Philboyd turned the craft a few degrees to starboard. "Look over there, to the left of the chasm. There's your evidence of volcanism."

Kane looked and saw nothing at first. Then light flashed, white and bright. It was like sunlight reflecting from an immense, highly polished surface.

"Mare Frigoris," Philboyd declared. "The Sea of

Ice. Pumice fused into glass. In a couple of hours, it'll be like a giant mirror.''

The flitter-gig returned to its original course, arrowing between a pair of conical peaks. On the other side lay the grounds of the mine. Huge, dirty ore-processing structures shouldered the open sky, skeletal frameworks stretched this way and that between gargantuan storage bins. In the starlight, the mine looked oddly unfinished, like the foundations of a city someone might get around to building one day.

Philboyd slowed their speed and went into a vertical descent. He set the flitter-gig down on a flat concrete pad opposite a flat-roofed building marked Operations. There were no windows, only an exterior air lock bearing the warning Authorized Space Command Personnel Only.

In a tense voice, Brigid asked, ''You expect us to moon-walk over there?''

''Why not?'' Philboyd asked as he throttled down the engines. ''The flitter-gig wasn't pressurized and you survived the flight, didn't you? Besides, it's only one-sixth of a g. You won't go floating out into space.''

Inside his helmet, Kane heard an almost imperceptible grunt from Grant, even over the whisper of oxygen feeding from the twin tanks on his back. During the flight from Manitius he had heard the soft clicking of an apparatus that cleared out the toxic residues in the recycled air.

All four people wore EVA suits, routinely known

in old NASA vernacular as extravehicular activity
suits. At least Mariah referred to it as vernacular, referring to a time when tramping around in the hard
vacuum of the Moon's surface was something not
lightly done.

In actuality, the one-piece garments were not too
different from the environmental suits found in Cerberus redoubt. They weighed about thirty pounds
apiece and consisted of ten layers of aluminized Mylar insulation interlaced with six layers of Dacron and
tough outer facings of Kevlar to absorb micromete-
orites.

The EVA suits had been designed to create micro-
environments, pressuring the skin so the pressure of
the body would not rupture blood vessels. They even
came equipped with a sealed water dispenser and sip-
ping tube attached to the inner wall of the helmet.
Their heads moved freely within them. The Plexiglas
visors instantly adjusted to different light levels, and
all four people communicated over UTEL radio systems.

Philboyd slid open the canopy and he, Grant, Kane
and Brigid climbed out. Kane looked toward the
looming storage bins and repressed a shiver. Seemingly perched atop a lunar peak like a ball was the
blue-white globe of the Earth.

A couple of years before he had seen a satellite
view of Earth. Now as then he was filled with awe
and a sense of despair. Earth seemed shadowy, dim,
with a lost look to it as though the universe had for-

gotten about it long ago. He saw large areas of the planet lying under an impenetrable belt of dust and debris. In some places, the belt looked like a dense blanket of boiling, red-tinged fog. The clouds were the last vestige of skydark, the generation-long nuclear winter.

The four people trekked the fifty yards to the air lock. Kane kept stifling the impulse to take Brigid's gloved hand as they walked over the open lunar terrain, and his steps kept lifting him into ungainly hops. He and Grant had left their Copperheads in the flitter-gig, but their Sin Eaters were strapped around their forearms. Their weight provided a degree of ballast, though the actuators weren't as sensitive through the layers of their EVA suits.

The lock system wasn't particularly complex—Philboyd punched in a series of digits on the keypad beside it, and two gasketed irises slid open. They stepped inside a narrow cubicle as the lock closed behind them. They faced a metal disk surrounded by a thick collar gleaming like copper. A light fixture above it flashed green and the metal disk rolled to the left, into a slot inside the collar.

Philboyd announced, ''It's safe to take off your helmets.''

They all stepped out of the cubicle, disengaging the seals and lifting the helmets off their heads. They looked around the room, which once had served as the main operations center for the aluminum mine. The air smelled stale and sour. At the far edges of audibility, they heard the steady drone of a grav-stator.

There were a dozen desks, most of them covered with computer microtapes, notebooks and printouts. Brigid moved to a computer terminal and pressed the activation tab. The monitor screen juiced up with a whine and a soft chime. After a moment she announced, "The main database is still accessible. The rest of you might as well make yourselves comfortable. This is going to take a little while."

Philboyd, Grant and Kane found chairs and sat down. In Earth-normal gravity, the suits had become uncomfortably heavy. Kane glanced over at Philboyd and suggested, "You can finish up your history lesson as long as we've got the time."

Philboyd sighed. "Like Mariah said, most of it is speculation. We really don't know all the details."

"Tell us anyway," Grant rumbled, rotating his helmet between his big gauntleted hands.

Philboyd shrugged. The four astrophysicists had provided a fragmented back story, a tapestry wherein scientific principle was threaded with superstition and interwoven with insanity. "Like I said, after the war, what you call the nukecaust, all of us here tried to come to terms with being marooned...that there would be no rescue missions. Most of us had spent years on the Moon anyway, so it wasn't that big of a stretch. But for some of us here—well, there's that old saying. If you can't adapt, you die."

Even before the nukecaust forever separated 330

human beings 238,866 miles from the world of their birth, Manitius base was divided into two castes—the support personnel with the military among them, and the scientists.

Unsurprisingly, the scientists composed the elite of the new society, and for a few years following the nukecaust, the two groups dwelt in peace, practicing a form of democracy. But the physicists who had labored for years on the DEVIL project to the exclusion of all else became obsessed with deactivating it. The rest of the base's inhabitants had no idea that the focus of the project had changed from terra-forming, and they couldn't understand why the device wasn't put to use in restoring health to the nuke-ravaged Earth.

The disagreements boiled over into dissension. The military and support people reached the conclusion that since scientists had brought on the holocaust and scientists were withholding the means to reverse its effects, scientists should have no part of the new lunar society.

Philboyd's lips pursed as if he were about to spit. "Once those assholes got around to building one, that is."

"Apparently," Brigid said from the computer station, "they did."

"They were more interested in destroying the old from what I remember," Philboyd retorted sharply. "Already, even in the days when everybody more or less got along, the base was divided between the two factions. My group withdrew into a quarter of the installation where we worked on trying to figure out a way to either deactivate DEVIL or bring it down. We were getting close—and then everything turned to shit.''

"How so?" Kane asked.

Face set in a grim mask, Philboyd told how all their efforts were undone by one of their own fellow scientists, a woman named Seramis. In the years preceding the nukecaust, she served as Manitius's chief geologist and historian. She had made the initial discoveries that a highly developed race had, in ages past, planted a colony on the Moon. She continued her work even after the nukecaust. She had already uncovered the clues that indicated the existence of a hidden city.

Seramis and a group of followers performed excavations in the so-called Wild Lands and she discovered secrets about the Moon she never told anyone. She found tunnels and passages that led to the crypts of the Serpent Kings, the Annunaki. She plundered the tombs of their dead and stole much of their technology. Seramis claimed that a vast lost knowledge was hidden in those catacombs, that on the Moon were secrets that were old when Sumeria was new, that were ancient when the pyramids were built in Egypt. She lost herself completely in the ancient culture of the Annunaki.

"Seramis found one of the great science centers of ancient days, apparently a citadel of some kind,''

Philboyd said brusquely. "She and her crew would come back here for supplies, eat and drink and wouldn't answer questions. She'd just stare at us when we asked what she was doing, then go back out there. This went on for weeks, for months. Then one day, she went out and didn't come back."

"You never saw her again?" Grant asked.

Philboyd hesitated, then in a slow, painful tone said, "Not as Seramis. But we saw her as Megaera."

Startled, Brigid half turned in her chair. "Megaera is a freezie like you?"

Philboyd shook his head. "Would you believe me if I tell you that I don't know if this particular Megaera is the same as the original?"

"No," Kane said coldly. "That's a convenient bit of ignorance if you ask me."

Philboyd sighed heavily, wearily. Clasping his hands together, he slouched in his chair, hanging his head. "I don't know what to tell you, then. All I know is that a woman calling herself Megaera, complete with a contingent of Furies wearing the black outfits you call shadow suits, invaded our part of the base. Those of us who resisted were killed, calcified by the Oubolus rods. The rest of us were pursued like deer all over the base."

In a rustling whisper, Philboyd told of terrifying pursuits, of ambushes on staircases, of his friends dying one by one, judged and turned to stone by Megaera and her Furies.

"Obviously, the Oubolus and the shadow suits had

been found in the citadel," Philboyd stated. "But none of us knew where it was. But we do know Seramis used this old mining center as her base of operations."

"Who were the Furies?" Kane asked.

Philboyd looked at him in surprise, as if he hadn't expected the question. "I presume people she swung to her cause."

"You never saw their faces?"

"No…not then or now. They always wore those masks. Why do you ask?"

Kane only shook his head. He remembered the dead Fury he had unmasked in Chicago, recalling its long-jawed, narrow-chinned, high-cheekboned face. He'd recognized the facial type—he had seen it often enough over the past couple of years, particularly during his captivity in Area 51.

The man was a hybrid. If not a full-fledged one, then certainly some traces of Balam's genetic material were buried in his familial woodpile. He had been much taller than the average hybrid, and his eyes hadn't possessed the prominent supraorbital ridge arches, either. Lakesh had learned that the DNA of Balam's folk was infinitely adaptable, malleable, its segments able to achieve a near seamless sequencing pattern with whatever biological material was spliced to it. In some ways, it acted like a virus, overwriting other genetic codes, picking and choosing the best human qualities to enhance. Their DNA could be tinkered with to create endless variations, adjusted and fine-tuned.

Strongbow had led them all to believe that Enlil's DNA possessed the same qualities, so it was possible the Furies were some mixture of human and Annunaki.

"Anyhow," went on Philboyd, "after a couple of months only me, Mariah, Eduardo and Neukirk were left. They captured us but they didn't kill us. They put us into cryostasis."

Grant's eyebrows knitted in confusion. "Why? Why didn't you get the same treatment as all the others?"

"Like I said, we four were the main DEVIL project team. Megaera needed us—or she figured she would need us at some future date, so were put into storage."

"And that date arrived?" Kane inquired.

Philboyd nodded. "We were revived a little over a year ago. The DEVIL platform's positioning system had malfunctioned, and we were expected to fix it." His lips twitched in a mirthless smile. "We did, but we did more than that. We downloaded all the secondary analogues from our mainframes and changed all the access codes, targeting and trajectory programs, recognition signals and launch commands. All the primary codes have been rewritten, and any attempts to delete the new program results in an immediate lockout."

"Nobody figured it out?" Brigid asked.

Philboyd's eyes narrowed. "Most of the old technical knowledge was lost during our 193 years in stasis. The descendants of the original base personnel know enough to keep certain important systems functioning, but that's about it."

"How many people on the base now?" inquired Kane.

"I never did get an accurate idea. Megaera kept us isolated from the main population. It was only after she and her Furies disappeared for a while that we had the run of the place. Even then, those goddamn carnobots kept us from going to a lot of the different sections."

"Who made those things, anyway?" Grant demanded.

"They were manufactured back before the holocaust," Philboyd answered. "They were field-tested up here. Sometime during our period in stasis, their programming was altered. I don't know what they were thinking when they did that."

"'They'?" echoed Grant.

"The new society that arose here." His tone became bleak and bitter. "A kind of insane mixture of Sumerian mythology and old paganism, with a little nature worship thrown in. How something like that took hold is beyond me."

Thinking of the Valley of the Divinely Inspired, Kane smiled crookedly. "You'd be surprised how easy it is to create new and crazy societies."

"That's true," agreed Brigid. "The first step is to

destroy the old one and old mind-sets. The nukecaust did that for you. A completely new system of thinking, of believing, of dealing with everyday life was forced on the people up here. Their old mind-sets were totally unsuitable to function within that new system. For a time the changeover was held in check through force of habit, but in the long run nothing short of a complete transformation of the way people perceived and processed reality would do. That appears to have happened while you were sleeping.''

The computer emitted a soft beep and Brigid announced, ''All right. I think I've found what we were looking for.''

Kane and Philboyd joined her at the machine. Words and numbers scrolled across the screen with a dizzying rapidity. Philboyd demanded, ''How the hell can you read anything at that speed?''

''This *is* a pretty old model,'' Brigid replied agreeably. ''If I had the opportunity, I could upgrade the access and scroll time.''

It took a couple of seconds for the meaning of Brigid's response to register with the man. When it did, Philboyd scowled and opened his mouth to speak, but Brigid brought the data stream to an abrupt halt.

She tapped a series of numbers glowing the screen with a forefinger. ''Seramis or the original Megaera kept a log of her excavations and explorations at least in the beginning. Here we have a set of coordinates that correspond to the location of the Great Chasm. It was there she found the passageway that led to the

catacombs and then later to the citadel of the Annunaki.''

"And that's where she found all the technology she
used to become Megaera." Kane was not asking a
question; he was making a statement. "And, apparently, where she found the Annunaki themselves. Or
at least one of them.''

"Enki," confirmed Philboyd, lips compressing in
a tight line. "Or so Seramis would have had us believe. She claimed she found a god.''

"She must have been a hell of a scientist," Kane
observed snidely, "to assume an alien that looks like
a lizard is a god.''

Philboyd shrugged. "The ruling council of the Annunaki, according to myths, had locked Enki into a
hidden tomb. She said she found it and released
him.''

"You never saw him yourself?" Grant asked.

He repressed a shudder. "Only from a distance.
Megaera spoke for him, saying Enki wanted the
power of the DEVIL returned to him.''

Brigid pushed back her chair from the computer
terminal. "If the hidden citadel of the Annunaki actually exists here on the Moon, Seramis noted its coordinates. So that's where we'll go.''

"You know Megaera and her people are looking
for you," Philboyd pointed out. "They know we took
my flitter-gig and TAV patrols will be scouring the
region. And I'll bet she has carnobots stationed
around the chasm.''

"You don't have to go with us," Kane said.

"I wasn't intending to," retorted Philboyd.

"You're that scared of her?" Brigid challenged.

The man's eyes flashed with sudden anger behind the lenses of his glasses. "Yes, but that doesn't have anything to do with my decision. As long as I'm alive, the DEVIL platform can be permanently deactivated. If I'm killed—" Philboyd clapped his gauntleted hands together. "Goodbye and thanks for all the fish."

None of the three people knew the meaning of his bromide and they weren't inclined to ask. Philboyd took his chair again. "I'll just sit here and wait. That is if you can find your way out of the chasm. Getting in is no big deal."

Brigid, Grant and Kane exchanged long glances, then Grant said, "How do you propose we get to the chasm?"

Philboyd smiled a little mockingly. "You know how to fly, don't you?"

Chapter 20

Grant quickly worked out the intricacies of the flitter-gig. It wasn't difficult, since Philboyd had removed most of the electronics from the space plane. It wasn't all that much different than driving a wag.

But Grant's piloting was less cautious than Philboyd's. He kept the craft's altitude low, skirting rock formations and sometimes passing between outcroppings.

Philboyd had warned them that Megaera's patrols would be out and since the stealth capacity of the TAV was exactly nil, Grant was making it as difficult as possible for heat-tracking devices to lock on to their burn emissions.

Kane looked down at the rugged terrain flashing by beneath them, then cast a glance at Brigid. He half expected to see her eyes screwed up tight, with a white-knuckled grip on the edge of her seat. She had reacted in such a fashion during a flight from Russia to Mongolia nearly two years ago. But now she watched as the canyons and rocky crags blurred by so quickly they became mere ripples of contrasting texture and color. One crater replaced another so fast it became almost impossible to distinguish one from another.

Grant turned the joystick and the flitter-gig declined farther toward the Moon's horizon. "Kane," he said.

Kane leaned forward and looked over his shoulder. Far ahead, dark mountains rose against the dark, star-speckled sky. The highest peak looked like an impossibly huge church spire. "Yeah," he said. "Impressive."

"Not the mountains," Grant said impatiently. "This side of them, at about twelve o'clock."

Kane peered through his visor and the scratched canopy and saw the small black speck against the gray-white furrows of the mountains. It rapidly grew bigger.

"Another TAV," he said dismally.

"Worse," Grant commented. "It's bigger than this one, and I'll bet it's armed."

Kane settled back in the seat and said to Brigid, "Hang on. I think we're in for a little rough water."

"With Grant at the controls, I figured as much," she retorted dryly.

The TAV came swooping at them. As Grant said, it was larger than their flitter-gig, having twice their beam and breadth. Its general configurations reminded Kane of a manta ray.

Grant pulled at the joystick and the flitter-gig stood on its tail. A dark object with a flaming tail flashed by.

"Missiles," Grant commented calmly as he straightened their craft. "Pretty damn close, too."

He performed a swift loop and sent the little space plane arrowing forward again, lancing beneath the TAV. It veered around in a fast curve, another missile flaring from its port wing. It streaked beneath the flitter-gig and impacted against a pillar of stone with a yellow-orange fireball.

Grant pulled back on the joystick controls again, went up over the TAV, veered off in the opposite direction, then dived again. He opened full throttle and went skittering beneath the larger aircraft in a whipping spiral. They were slapped back against their seats, but the g-force assault lasted only a second. The pilot of the TAV seemed momentarily bewildered by the unexpected maneuver.

The flitter-gig banked, and through the canopy it appeared the horizon was wheeling crazily around them. Under Grant's guidance, the aircraft performed barrel rolls, loop-de-loops and wide, swinging yaws. Kane wondered if he wasn't showing off for the pilot of the pursuit craft, since he obviously had little experience beyond rudimentary up and down, forward and backward.

Grant put the flitter-gig into a sharp dive, pulled up equally sharply, reversing an old Deathbird maneuver he called the peel up, pop down. He threw the plane from side to side, trying to confuse the TAV's missile targeter. Another projectile smoked from the craft's launcher, streaking well below them and disappearing into a crater.

Twisting in his seat, Kane watched the TAV tilting to starboard, curving back toward them in a wide, flat turn. Suddenly, Grant snarled, "Son of a bitch!"

"What?" Kane and Brigid demanded almost in unison.

Deceleration jumped on their chests, slamming the air from their lungs in uncontrollable exhalations. Then just as suddenly, the pressure was gone. Kane could feel the vibrations of the overstressed stabilizers rattling through the deck at his feet. A queasy, liquid sensation began in his stomach, and the shuddering that racked the flitter-gig from stem to stern didn't help it any.

"Losing power," snapped Grant, working at the joystick frantically. "She's not responding."

The turbojets chose that moment to stop working, the blue flames disappearing from the vents with the suddenness of candles being snuffed out. For a long time—it couldn't really have been more than a handful of seconds—the flitter-gig seemed to hang suspended between the airless sky and the lunar terrain. Then it plunged.

As the flitter-gig dropped, it turned and struck at an angle. It seemed to crash with the force of a battering ram. Kane's body strained against the recoil harness and then slammed back violently. All the air exploded from his lungs as he was engulfed in a thundering wave of shock, followed by pain. For an instant, all he heard were his own strangulated gasps as he fought for air and struggled against the cloak of darkness settling over his mind.

He fought back to consciousness with the sound of the wind keening in his ears. A moment later he realized it was the hissing of oxygen filtering into his helmet. With throbbing muscles and dazed senses, he fumbled with the release catch of his safety harness. He managed to free himself and heard, with relief, Grant mumbling a curse and Brigid biting back a groan. He looked up just as the silent shape of the TAV zipped over the little craft it had just crashed.

They had landed among a forest of monolithic rock formations at the base of a ridge. The outcroppings thrust up all around from the soil like skeletal fingers. The flitter-gig had skated between two of them but crashed into a third, the impact causing it to topple over, so there was little room for the TAV to make a vertical descent in the immediate area.

"Is everybody all right?" Brigid asked in a breathless voice, tight with the effort to control pain.

Kane's right hip was throbbing, but as far as he could tell no bones had been broken. "I think so. You?"

"A little bruised and battered, but nothing broken. Grant?"

Grant pushed himself away from the shambles of the control console and slid open the canopy. "I can move, if that's any consolation. Sorry about the landing. This damn thing was too fragile to take the kind of jockeying I'm used to.''

''I'm sure Philboyd will understand,'' Brigid muttered, levering herself out of her seat. ''If he doesn't—'' She didn't finish the thought.

They collected their weapons and disembarked. Luckily, the flitter-gig was on reasonably level ground so they were able to jump out without falling or stumbling. A hundred or so yards away, they saw the TAV slowly descending, its landing thrusters causing lunar dust to billow out in clouds.

Kane, Grant and Brigid ran at top speed in long, dangerously high strides. They slipped and stumbled on loose rock before they managed to reach the ridgeline and plunge over it. They lay prone and peered down.

''We just made it,'' wheezed Grant. ''I don't think they spotted us.''

At least ten helmeted men in environmental suits carrying heavy blasters milled around the crashed flitter-gig. They looked at the footprints leading away from it and up the face of the ridge.

''Those weapons don't look like the ones Philboyd and his bunch had,'' Grant murmured. ''Maybe they're the plasma rifles we were told about.''

Kane nodded inside his helmet, realized his companions couldn't see his head movement and said, ''Let's get out of range, then.''

The three people quickly slid down the slope on their backsides to the floor of a valley cut between the curving outer walls of two craters. Kane led the way quickly to the spot where the valley became a tumbled wilderness of lunar peaks. They struck out through a pass. Before them, the white desert stretched northward toward the glaring, glassy brilliance of Mare Frigoris.

They paused at the edge and looked behind them. There was no sign of pursuit, but that didn't mean much. "We really don't have much choice," Brigid stated grimly. "We have to go across it and fast."

They quickened their pace as they slogged out across the pumice plain. The ground was as yielding underfoot as beach sand. The heat it contained was easily felt even through their insulated environmental suits. They had covered but a few miles when Kane called a sharp warning. The TAV was swinging out from the peaks on the far side of the sand sea.

"Goddammit!" snarled Grant. "They've nailed us. There's no place to hide."

"Down on the ground," Brigid said sharply. "Throw it over ourselves."

Kane and Grant flung themselves down immediately, covering themselves with handfuls of the powdery white pumice. Brigid swiftly followed suit, burrowing beneath the surface. Kane kept part of his visor clear so he could watch the sky.

The space plane swung past at a low altitude, a half mile to the west. Heaving himself up, he said, "I think they're gone for the time being."

The three people scrambled to their feet, brushed

off one another and continued on their laborious way. The foothill peaks of the Montes Carpatas Range soon dropped behind them. The small size of the Moon made its horizons always unsettlingly close.

A thin line of intolerably white, bright line glimmered on the horizon ahead of them. It grew into a seething glow like a lake of molten metal, stretching across their path. It was so bright they couldn't look directly at it, even with the polarized visors of their helmets. They would have to cross an outlying corner of the Mare Frigoris in order to reach the Great Chasm.

Brigid checked their oxygen tanks and said, "We've all got about two hours of air left. If the chasm was the site for a mine, we might be able to find extra tanks there. We don't have enough oxygen to make it back to the processing center."

They steeled themselves for the ordeal as they approached. Mare Frigoris was anything but frigid. It was a sprawling, roughly circular region in which the lunar rock had somehow been fused and vitrified to the composition of glass or ice. Whatever had caused the phenomenon, the Sea of Ice was a vast, glittering sheet that reflected the Sun's radiant light like a lake-sized, polished mirror.

"Keep your eyes shut as much as possible," Brigid warned her companions as they approached the demarcation point between the pumice plain and the fused glass.

"Hell," said Grant, "I've had my eyes shut for the last half hour anyway."

Linking their hands, the three people inched out onto the glassy, slick surface of the great sheet. The fierce reflection forced itself through their polarized visors and even between their tightly closed eyelids. The heat was also so intense that even through the insulation of their EVA suits the thermal regulator controls of their shadow suits were overwhelmed. Within seconds, all of them were perspiring profusely.

Their feet slipped constantly on the smooth surface, their boot treads having difficulty finding traction. They dared open their eyes only a fraction every few minutes, trying to keep the northwestward course. But their eyes were soon so blurred and seared by the unremitting glare they could see nothing. They stumbled blindly on, Brigid trusting her eidetic memory and Grant and Kane relying on their instincts to keep them on course. They spoke little, hearing only the labored rasp of one another's breathing in their helmets.

It felt like a furnace inside their environmental suits. Their skin dried out and seemed to flinch every time it came in contact with the inner lining of the garments. The moisture in their mouths evaporated, and their tongues felt like strips of shoe leather. They drank but sparingly from their internal water supply. It was tepid anyway, tasting like bathwater.

Kane, Brigid and Grant were aware only of the slippery glass surface underfoot and the touch of their hands as they clung blindly together. Time became meaningless and none of them could even hazard a guess how long they traversed the inferno.

Grant spoke suddenly, causing both Brigid and Kane to jump. Matter-of-factly he stated, "I just opened my eyes and I can't see a thing. I'm completely blind."

For a long moment, no one responded to his comment; they just kept trudging onward. Finally, Brigid panted, "I'm sure it's just temporary...your rods and cones are probably overstressed." She tried to sound reassuring, but her voice was a croak.

"There should only be a few miles more," Kane said. "Let's keep moving."

His head pounding from the heat, Kane stumbled on, fearing that he was blind himself. Blinded, sweating and half suffocated, they fought their way onward, struggling to gain a foot, then a yard. No sight of anything was possible in the inferno. The fused sand underfoot crunched and collapsed in places, throwing all of them off balance.

The ache of the injuries they had sustained in the crash throbbed in cadence with their heartbeats. They kept walking, focused on a single necessity—to survive, they had to keep moving. So they plodded onward, linked together, ears filled only with the labored rasp of their respiration, eyes seeing nothing but a never-ending hellish glare. Their feet dragged, and they kept themselves from falling only by savage efforts of will.

Their bodies lost all feeling, numb to every sensation except putting one foot in front of the other. One minute, the temperature was dropping, and in the next, it seemed to increase like a wind out of a furnace.

Suddenly, Brigid came to a halt, and they stumbled on rubbery legs.

"We're through," she declared.

"I still can't see anything," said Grant hoarsely.

"Me, either," Brigid admitted. "I'm blind myself."

All Kane could see were vague, indistinct shapes overlaid by swimming fiery globes, but he didn't mention it. A few yards ahead of him he barely made out a overhang of rock, so he led his companions beneath it. "Let's rest a few minutes."

It took more than a few minutes for Brigid's and Grant's vision to return and Kane's eyes to clear. They discovered themselves on a white pumice plain again.

Kane took their bearings again from the sunken desert of Mare Frigoris, then they trudged on, moving through the narrowing strait between the Montes Carpatus. They were not more than a mile south from the Great Chasm. Their eyes constantly scanned the horizon for an opening into the gorge. Finally, he spied one, like a dark, irregular line bisecting the horizon.

"There it is," he said, his heart lurching with relief.

"I don't know why you sound so damn happy,"

Grant observed sourly. ''God knows what we'll find in there.''

''Being inside the Moon can't be any worse than being outside of it,'' Brigid commented. She paused a moment, then added quietly, ''I hope.''

Chapter 21

The gorge was so deep that the blazing sunlight didn't penetrate to its bottom, which was little more than a channel filled with house-sized boulders. Shadowed, yawning fissures bisected the sheer walls. Bright streaks of metallic ores and mineral deposits gleamed under the helmet lights of Kane, Brigid and Grant.

The opening by which they entered the chasm was a mine shaft quarried out of the rock. Exposed wiring and fluorescent light fixtures stretched along the ceiling as far as the eye could see. Girders of punched steel shored up the ceiling, and from these hung cabling. Motorized gurney tracks disappeared down the tunnel where no light could reach.

They clambered down into the gloomy bottom of the gorge and began walking between the jagged masses of boulders toward the distant west end, occasionally confused by the writhing shadows cast by their lights. They hadn't gone far when Kane lurched to a halt, biting back a startled exclamation.

Grinning up at them from the hard-packed soil was a yellow-white skull. The sight of it raised the nape hairs on all of them. "Where's the rest of the body?"

Grant murmured. "And if there's no atmosphere, how could it rot?"

Kane bent over it, his helmet light casting the deep indentations scored in the bone into shadow. "Those look like teeth marks. Carnobots, maybe?"

Nobody answered. They resumed their tense, silent progress through the tunnel. Kane tried to keep other thoughts, other worries and fears from intruding into his single-minded march, but a few penetrated the mental wall he constructed. Grant's questions about the skull had been particularly salient, and he suspected there was only one answer.

The passageway narrowed, and the three people were forced to crab-walk sideways. It crept downward at a gradual forty-five-degree angle. Finally, the tunnel widened and they were able to walk normally again. Irregularly shaped stalactites stretched down from above, and they wended their way around stalagmites thrusting up from the floor.

Gesturing to the ceiling, Brigid declared, "That proves the Moon once had water."

"Fascinating," Grant grunted. "I'm more interested in finding those spare oxygen tanks."

As they walked, they felt the occasional jarring of the ground at uneven intervals, causing little showers of pebbles and dirt to patter down from above.

"What the hell is causing that?" Grant asked, looking around uneasily.

"Seismic disturbances probably," Brigid answered, but she didn't sound as if she believed it, either.

The labyrinth they followed now was a split in the rock walls, so narrow they moved in a single file. Ponderous masses of rock hung precariously over them, needing very little to dislodge them. The three people moved with extreme caution, fearing that even the vibration of their footsteps would cause an avalanche.

They saw no more light fixtures. The darkness around them became complete, as if they were moving through a sea of black ink alleviated only a little by lights cast by their helmets. The crevasse debouched into a gloomy gallery with vaulted walls of black lunar basalt. A half-dozen fissures branched out from the cavern.

"According to the log of Seramis," Brigid announced, "the citadel is in that general direction." She gestured to the fissure.

They entered the opening and again began squeezing through narrow passageways and clambering over fallen slabs of stone. The signs of excavation became less and less frequent. The fissure slanted upward after a few hundred yards.

For the next hour, Brigid, Grant and Kane moved deeper into the maze of branching tunnels and galleries that rifted the Moon's under crust. Brigid tried to steer a course, but many times they walked into dead ends and were forced to backtrack.

The darkness and utter absence of anything resembling life were unrelievedly oppressive. The oxygen in their tanks ran lower, and they had to stop several times and turn down the intake valves in order to conserve it.

The unspoken grim understanding that they had to reach the citadel in order to replenish their air was the spur that drove the three people onward. Still, all of them began to feel frustration, then a touch of despair when after following a long channel for nearly half an hour, they found it led only to a dead end.

Growling a curse, Grant struck the rock wall angrily with a fist. Wearily, Brigid leaned her helmeted head on the wall. She started to speak, then closed her mouth, her eyes narrowing. When Grant began a profane diatribe, she silenced him with a fierce "Hush!" and a sharp gesture.

"Listen!" Brigid exclaimed.

"To what?" Kane demanded impatiently.

"Do what I'm doing," she retorted.

Skeptically, Kane and Grant pressed the foreports of their helmets against the wall. The rock transmitted through the material of their helmets a distant, rhythmic throb.

"That sounds like a generator," Grant said.

"There's a hollow space behind this," Brigid declared. "Another tunnel or cavern." She poked at the rock with her fingers, and flakes crumbled beneath the pressure. "We might be able to dig our way through."

Their only tools for digging were Grant's and Kane's combat knives. The two men applied the tungsten-steel blades to the rock, chipping and hacking, prying loose masses of the dark stone. Brigid cleared away the debris collecting at their feet. Their lungs burned and their temples throbbed.

It was slow and painful labor, as well as dangerous. A network of black cracks spread through the wall, an ominous warning that the entire mass of rock might collapse onto them. After twenty minutes, when the knives opened a small opening, the three of them pulled at the edges, quickly enlarging it. Kane squeezed through first, helped by a shove from Grant. He shone his light around, illuminating a cavern so huge that the beam couldn't reach the ceiling.

Grant and Brigid entered uncertainly, the glow of their helmet lights splashing onto a broad path on the cavern floor that led into the unrelieved darkness. The steady drone was faint, though audible, which was disquieting. Dust and grit sifted down from above like intermittent snow flurries.

"You hear that, right?" Kane asked his friends.

Both people nodded their heads inside their helmets, and Brigid commented, "But I don't know how unless there's some sort of atmosphere down here to conduct the sound. I suppose the rocks might be conductors."

They pressed their helmeted heads against the black rock wall, and the metal transmitted the steady reverberations clearly. The regularity of the rhythm gave them instantly the key to its source.

"That's a machine," Grant bit out. "Definitely a generator."

Brigid let out her breath in a relieved sigh. "We may be right under the citadel, then."

They started moving again. The gallery curved, turning almost at right angles. As they walked around the bend, the tunnel curved again even more sharply, then turned once more, adding to three people's growing bewilderment and apprehension. As they made another turn, they were startled to see a patch of light far ahead. Vaguely rectangular in shape and of an unearthly greenish hue, the light wavered and flickered eerily, at times almost disappearing, at times flaring to a lurid, momentary brilliance shot through with flashes of red and even blue.

To their astonishment, they saw the ceiling of the gallery formed a perfect triangle, an inverted V like of the roof of an A-framed house. It was useless to speculate about whether the shape was natural or crafted by intelligent hands. They continued forward. As they drew closer to the light, they were relieved to find that the lunar crust sifted down less frequently and the illumination down the passageway grew more steady and distinct.

The gallery ended as if on the brink of a precipice. The three people stared down, through an abyss glowing a sickly yellow-green and into a chasm as wide and as deep as the drop-off on the plateau of Cerberus redoubt. But the walls of the cliff face were sheer, straight and smooth. At the bottom, more than a thousand feet blew, spread the bare, level floor of a cavern that stretched out beyond their ability to see.

There was such an atmosphere of unreality about it all that only by degrees could Kane absorb the details. On the gentle curve of the ceiling, which arched a few hundred feet above them, there were fantastic sculptures, vaguely man-shaped and standing out sharply in cameo. A multitude of greenish-yellow elongated rods hung from the ceiling like glowing stalactites. Small round openings, like ob ports, perforated the opposite wall.

At least a minute passed in silence while he, Grant and Brigid stood there spellbound. "What the hell is this place?" Kane asked, voice hushed by equal parts of awe and dread.

"I don't know," Brigid answered. "Some kind of memorial, maybe. A work of art. I really don't know."

A narrow ledge followed the line of the right-hand wall, pitching toward the cavern floor at an ever steepening slant. "We can go down there, or we can go back," Grant said.

The three people looked at one another expectantly. At length, Kane said curtly, "The longer we stand around here waiting for one of us to make the decision, the more air we use."

Smiling wanly, Brigid inched out onto the narrow parapet, flattening herself against the rock wall, digging her fingers into the fissures and crevices. After a moment of hard swallowing, Kane stepped out after her. Grant followed.

The ledge made a turn to the right after a few steps, and its pitch descended at an increasingly sharper angle. Grant, Kane and Brigid were forced to edge along it with their hands gripping the wall tightly.

It was a slow, perilous journey because the lip of the ledge crumbled beneath their combined weight.

All of them feared the entire walkway might give way altogether.

The ledge gradually widened into a true path. The three people breathed easier when they no longer had to inch sideways. The parapet met and joined with an unnaturally smooth floor. It led to a blank wall, featureless except for a man-size cavity that had been punched through it. A heap of debris lay beneath it. Black scorch marks around the jagged edges indicated the hole had been made with a high explosive.

They inspected the area around the wall and Kane saw a dark shape humped up in a corner. He stepped over to it, lifting away a square sheet of canvas that was draped over a number of bulky objects. He found metal rakes, a collection of picks and shovels and the metal cylinders of a dozen oxygen tanks. ''Seramis's excavations reached this far at least,'' he declared.

His first surge of relief was replaced by dread when he picked up an oxygen tank and saw the gauge's needle was frozen at zero. Brigid and Grant joined him. While Grant opened the crates, Brigid helped Kane examine the tanks.

''We've got some demolition charges here,'' Grant announced, holding a pair of flat disks the size and shape of saucers. Red buttons protruded from the tops and suction cups extended from the undersides.

''Wonderful,'' commented Kane dourly. ''We can blow ourselves up instead of suffocating.''

Brigid uttered a short, wordless exclamation. She hefted a tank in her hands. ''This one is full.''

Kane eyed the cylinder critically. Even by dividing its contents equally between them they were only buying time, not saving themselves. But since it was the only option available, it was the best option.

Brigid went to work detaching the feed lines from their back tanks and replenishing them. When she was done, they all had another hour of relatively easy respiration. After that, it would become decidedly uncomfortable.

As the fresh air filled his helmet, Kane inhaled gratefully. The painful throbbing in his temples slowly ebbed. Turning toward the hole in the cavern wall, he said, "Let's get moving."

He stepped through the cavity first, noting that Brigid carried the oxygen tank and Grant had slipped two of the demolition charges into pouches on the outside of his EVA suit. He didn't ask his companions about it, assuming both people had their reasons.

They found themselves in a short tunnel that became a doorway into a vastly wider space. Kane looked around, casting his helmet light into the shadows. A little farther along the passageway on either side of an archway loomed a pair of strange statues of a brassy metal, both about twelve feet tall. They represented creatures almost exactly like the corpse of Enlil, inhuman but with strangely noble features. The figures stood, each with a slender arm raised, as though to warn Kane, Grant and Brigid back. Upon the pedestal of each statue was a lengthy inscription in cuneiform characters.

"The Annunaki?" Grant asked wonderingly as they passed between the statues. He came to a sudden stop and Brigid nearly trod on his heels. She started to speak, then fell silent, her face a mask of shock in the glow.

Kane murmured, ''Their tomb.''

All around them dark shapes loomed up. Blurred as they were by the dense shadows, they looked like hideous travesties of humanity. Taller than Grant, leaner by far than Kane, double rows of lizard-things sat upright on thrones, their bowed, powerful legs tucked beneath them. Brigid, Grant and Kane stared wide-eyed, stunned, shocked and awed. And terrified.

The Serpent Kings had been buried royally, each one carefully embalmed and positioned upright on a funerary throne, wearing all the trappings of the godhood they had assumed upon Earth. The beautifully polished stone of the ceilings and walls had been carved in reliefs showing events in the lives of the various Annunaki who sat stiffly all down the length of the great hall.

Grant, Kane and Brigid could easily imagine carpets on the cold floor and a great deal of ornate furnishings. But all of that ancient splendor was long gone. The excavations of the human explorers had caved in the rock-cut chambers and the explorers themselves had taken all the funeral finery. Only the thrones and the Serpent Kings remained, shriveled corpses staring into nothingness. The three humans gazed at the cadavers, their flesh crawling and their minds reeling with conjectures.

''The pantheon of Sumerian gods,'' Brigid half whispered. ''This is what Philboyd meant when he said they found them.''

In a harsh, gravelly voice, Grant said, "Let's get the hell out of here."

The hall of the dead led straight ahead. The three of them moved as fast they dared, watching for cracks and splits in the floor. There seemed to be nothing but shadows behind them, and ahead of them only murk.

The tomb opened suddenly into a vault-walled chamber of huge proportions, so vast that its nether end was lost in the shadows. The floor was so flat and smooth they knew it had been leveled artificially. A broken ring of cyclopean blocks stood alone.

Silently, they wended their way around them. Kane glanced up, trying to see the ceiling. Instead he saw a wedge of starlight far above. Beneath it a shelf of stone jutted out, allowing access to the opening. He gusted out a relieved sigh. "I think we're almost out of here."

The three people quickened their pace. As they came around the base of one looming mass of stone, they were suddenly confronted by three carnobots.

Chapter 22

The lights shining from atop their helmets gleamed dully against gray alloyed flesh. Red, multifaceted eyes stared expressionlessly at the three people. Then they sprang, their needlelike incisors glittering briefly in the glow of the lights.

Grant and Kane immediately squeezed off shots with their Copperheads, though they knew the rounds would only bounce off the dense coatings of the mechanoid creatures. They kept the rate-of-fire selector switch on single shot, for fear of being driven backward by the continuous recoil. Sparks jumped from the droid's surfaces as the bullets ricocheted away.

The trio of carnobots didn't move for a moment, their immobility puzzling. Then Kane saw a pack of the unearthly gray automatons come racing out the shadows from behind the three. The uncanny silence in which the creatures advanced was more blood-chilling than if they'd howled like wolves.

Their fangs gleamed brightly against the murk. Kane, Grant and Brigid knew if they were bowled off their feet by the horde, the vicious talons and teeth would rip the Kevlar weave of their environmental suits and all of them would die, either by asphyxiation, freezing or decompression.

''Make for the ledge!'' Grant shouted.

The three people lunged forward, sprinting through the shadows and boulders toward the shelflike projection of rock. Kane didn't look behind him toward the droids, but he doubted they could reach the ledge before the mechanoids overtook them.

The carnobots closed in on them by leaps and bounds, and the ledge was still a hundred feet ahead. Kane felt certain they could never reach it before they were overwhelmed. Then Brigid made a diversion.

She whirled, opening the valve of the oxygen tank, flinging a plume of frozen atmosphere. The creatures in the lead recoiled in momentary confusion, their vision sensors coated by frost. The respite gave Grant and Kane time to reach the ledge and bound atop it. The top was nearly ten feet above the cavern, but the diminished gravity allowed the powerful leg muscles of the two men to propel them to safety in a single jump. Brigid's leg muscles weren't as powerful. She managed to throw her upper body over the edge, but she began slipping backward almost immediately. Grabbing Brigid by the forearms, Kane hauled her up onto the flat slab of stone an instant before a droid's jaws would have snapped shut on an ankle.

The pack reached the base of the ledge and slammed into one another in their eagerness to get at the three humans above them. Grant used his Copperhead as a bludgeon, knocking them backward.

The eight carnobots retreated hastily from the ledge, regrouped and charged again. Kane joined Grant at the edge of the shelf, and for a few seconds they pounded and clubbed at metal skulls. The creatures backed away again, then crouched below the ledge to wait.

"What do we do now?" Grant wheezed. "If we try to climb out, the bastards will pull us down. And they can just sit there until we run out of oxygen."

"I think we have a more immediate problem," Brigid said grimly. "I don't think those things are just allowed to wander loose down here. They'd run out of fuel eventually. Somebody let the hounds out, and I'm sure they'll be along."

Kane bit back a curse, fighting the impulse to trigger a long burst at the mechanoids with his subgun, but he doubted the bullets would penetrate their metal sheathings. He looked beyond the pack of carnobots, toward the way they had come. For an instant he saw a glimmer of light against the tapestry of black shadows. "I believe they're on their way now."

Grant growled deep in his throat, glaring in frustrated fury first at the carnobots, then at the distant glimmer of light. He gripped his subgun as if he were seriously considering leaping down about the droids and doing as much damage as he could before they dragged him down.

"Don't get any crazy ideas," Brigid said, a note of alarm in her voice.

"Yeah," Kane agreed in a studiedly neutral tone. "That's my department."

Grant swiveled his head to look at him. "Then come up with one fast."

Kane eyes followed the line of the ledge to where it melded with the cavern wall, then looked up at the cleft fifteen or so feet above him. On its other side he saw rock walls looming against the starlit sky.

"That hole leads back up to the gorge," he said.

"So?" Brigid inquired anxiously.

"Even if we managed to get up there without being eaten, we'd still have those damn things on our trail."

"Unless," Grant declared, "we get them off our trail and get out of here at the same time." From the pouch on his EVA suit, he removed one of the demolition disks.

"My thoughts exactly," Kane said approvingly.

Brigid looked toward the lights again. They were no longer so distant and had resolved themselves into several bobbing balls of yellow-white luminescence. They were obviously attached to helmets, and she counted at least ten of them.

Grant placed the disk in a narrow gouge that ran like a fault line across the breadth of the ledge. "I don't know if there's a timing sequence after the button is pushed. I don't know if it works at all."

"What do you suggest?" Brigid asked.

Grant gestured to the deeply fissured wall. "You two go first. I'll keep the droids back. Once you're up there, I'll make the climb and you can keep those damn hounds from snacking on my ass. When I get to the top, I'll shoot the detonator.''

Neither Brigid nor Kane felt inclined to question his confidence about making such a difficult shot. The man's marksmanship was uncanny, as they both had reason to know.

"A sound plan," said Brigid.

"Not quite as crazy as I'd like," Kane commented with a wry grin, "but it'll do."

Without hesitation, Brigid began clambering up the rock face, her gloved fingers seizing handholds. Aided by the lighter gravity, she literally swarmed up the stone wall.

Slinging his subgun over his back, Kane climbed after her. Some of the handholds were mere cracks in the porous stone, but he wedged his fingers in and pulled himself along, the top of his helmet only inches from the soles of Brigid's boots. Encumbered by his helmet, he couldn't turn his head to see if the car-nobots were making an attempt to scale the ledge after them. He guessed not, since Grant's respiration hadn't changed. Still, he asked, "Anything going on?"

"The droids are just sitting there, watching you," Grant replied flatly. "They're not moving." He paused and a moment later said, "Something I can't say about that patrol. They see us, too. They're spreading out. Maybe you two ought to speed up your progress."

Kane straightened swiftly, planting the top of his

helmet firmly against Brigid's backside. She started to voice a protest but he said sharply, "Just go in the direction I'm pushing, Baptiste."

"Where have I heard that before?" she muttered, but she did as he said.

Working in tandem, the two people heaved and scrabbled their way upward. The pressure on top of Kane's helmet disappeared, and he dragged himself over the rough edges of the opening. He glanced quickly around at their surroundings, seeing the walls of the gorge rising steeply on either side, then he hitched around. Panting, he lay on his stomach, peering through the hole back into the cavern.

Grant was backing slowly toward the rock wall, his attention fixed on the figures flitting like shifting shadows through the gloom. "Come on," Kane urged.

Wheeling, Grant suddenly kicked himself up from the shelf of rock and began scaling the wall with almost frantic haste. As if his movement had been a signal, a carnobot lunged up from the cavern floor, pulling itself atop the ledge. Kane squeezed off a shot with his Copperhead, the round striking the mechanoid with a flare of sparks. The creature kept coming. Another droid appeared.

"Hurry!" Brigid cried, panic thick in her voice.

Grant snarled wordlessly, twisting so he faced the cavern. He held onto the wall with one hand while he pointed the subgun down at the demolition disk.

"No!" Kane shouted. "You're too close!"

He threw the upper half of his body into the hole, groping for Grant's hand just as the man fired a single shot. The demolition charge erupted in a flash of orange flame and white smoke. Although he heard nothing, the concussion shoved Kane backward out of the opening and against Brigid. Ugly black cracks spread out in a spiderweb pattern around the cleft. Then the entire cliff face appeared to be in motion, collapsing in on itself.

Brigid and Kane kicked themselves backward as a seething avalanche of rock slabs and lunar dust cascaded down the steep face of the gorge wall. Their surroundings gave a convulsive lurch like a ship's deck during a gale at sea. Kane heard Grant's sharp, startled shout. It was drowned by the crunching, grinding and groaning of rock, and a low rumbling from the sublunar depths. Then he was pitched headlong to the gorge floor and the ground heaved beneath them. He heard the rasp of panic in Brigid's respiration as she tried to clutch a spike of rock. She struggled to her feet, only to be hurled down again.

As Kane reached for her, his ears rang with the clangor of rock striking his helmet. A huge slab of stone crashed down from above, and from beneath it spread a pattern of cracks in the gallery floor. A broad black fissure opened, and desperately, like mountain climbers on a crumbling precipice, they tried to hold their balance. In silent horror they watched the fissure widening and spreading out, and then the ground collapsed beneath their feet. Kane heard Brigid's cry and he felt himself falling.

He didn't fall far or for very long. The wall of the fissure sloped at an angle of thirty degrees so that while rolling over and over in the lighter gravity, he was spared a direct perpendicular drop. He didn't grope for very long. A breath-robbing crash numbed his body, and he was only dimly aware of tumbling head over heels down the slope.

The vibrations of tumbling, rolling rock slowly faded as the avalanche bled itself out. Settling stone continued to click and grate. Lowering his arms, peering through the thick pall of dust, he saw a vast heap of broken earth, shale and titanic boulders completely filling the cleft.

Brigid pushed herself up from beside him, brushing at the dust occluding her visor. She cried out shrilly, *"Grant!"*

She rose to her feet, lunging for the rock slide, but Kane grabbed her by the arm, pulling her arm. "It's no use," he said grimly. "We can't dig through that."

Brigid struggled to free herself from his grasp. "He may be hurt."

"He may be dead," Kane snapped.

She stopped trying to free herself, turning to face him. Her eyes glittered like wet emeralds within the shadows cast by her helmet. "I don't believe that."

"I don't, either." Kane pitched his voice to a low, unemotional level. "But whether he is or isn't, we can't help him from here. We won't be able to dig through a fraction of that mess before our oxygen runs out.''

Brigid gazed steadily into his face for a moment, then nodded, her shoulders sagging in resignation. ''You're right.''

Kane turned toward the gorge stretching away before them and eyed the sheer walls curving overhead. He estimated they towered at least a thousand feet. ''It'll take too long to climb out of here.''

Brigid gestured to the gorge floor stretching away in front of them. ''That's the only way we can go.''

Kane took the first step and sank knee-deep in loose lunar dust. He reached out for Brigid's hand, and she grasped it tightly. ''Whatever you do,'' he said, ''don't let go.''

''Funny,'' she said, ''I was about to say the very same thing.''

They exchanged quick smiles, then began walking. The dust lay in the gorge like snow. It was up to Kane's neck in most places, and in long stretches it was completely over his head. The path had to be broken, not walked. Even in the lighter gravity, it was like trying to stride through a corridor composed of spun sugar.

The ancient gorge became deeper as they moved southward. They marched beneath the surface of the white, crystalline powder. There was nothing for either of them to see but the blank white dust around and above them. At any rate, they were invisible to any patrol craft that might cross the gorge overhead. They lost track of time as they trooped on through the passageway forced by their bodies. Kane surreptitiously turned the valve of his air tanks, reducing the flow of oxygen.

Brigid turned down her own oxygen outfeed so they had to stop frequently to rest. During their fourth stop, Brigid said, ''Lift me up so I can see how close we are.''

Kane heaved Brigid up so she stood in a stirrup he made of his linked hands. Almost instantly, she recoiled and said, ''We're almost inside the city!''

''Do you see anybody?'' he asked tensely.

Brigid raised her helmeted head more carefully until her eyes were just above the surface of the cindery dust. She looked around, her heart beating fast with a mixture of fascination and fear. ''Only a wall. Let me down.''

Kane complied. Their nerves were stretched taut as they moved on through the white blanket. At Brigid's direction, they veered to the northern side of the channel. A few minutes later their advance through the cinders was stopped by a solid stone wall of dark stone. ''This is it,'' Brigid quietly announced.

They pulled themselves up by the wide cracks between the huge stone blocks, thrusting their heads out of the dust. Black, square structures loomed on both sides of the channel.

The collection of buildings looked eerie in the eternal twilight. The city was in ruins. Great blocks of basalt and granite had fallen from the buildings, and broken statues lay in the lunar dust. Less than a quarter of a mile away towered the citadel of the Serpent Kings, a titanic black bulk dominating the buildings like a thundercloud.

Kane looked at it, feeling fear and hate-filled loathing rising within him. He knew without really knowing that the citadel had looked the same for countless centuries. On Earth, the attrition caused by the elements, the friction of moving wind and blowing sand, eventually crumbled even the strongest structures. Here, no atmosphere had ever carried water vapor to condense as rain and snow that would eventually erode away even mountains.

The tower rose arrogantly, the stonework tapering in close at the top, and on its highest point was a glinting of a reflective object, like a captive star.

"Are we going in or not?" Kane inquired.

"Unless you'd rather suffocate out here," said Brigid, "I think we'd better go in. We know Seramis got this far. We can only hope we can find another air tank or two."

Kane cleared out a small cavity in the dust to give them room for maneuvering. They pulled themselves to the top of the wall and saw it was an outer barrier with another wall a few yards beyond it. The inner and outer walls were joined at regular intervals by load-bearing trusses of metal. Although spaced several feet apart, they formed a latticework that could be climbed like a ladder. They proceeded to climb

down between the walls, their helmet lights illuminating the way.

The went downward between the walls, cramped
by the narrow space until Kane judged they were
level with the main courtyard. They edged their way
along the outer wall until they came to an open archway. They stepped out among cyclopean masses of
crumbled black masonry towering solemnly out of the
lunar dust.

There had once been paved streets and courtyards,
Kane saw, but they were broken and covered by pumice. There had been curving colonnades, but of them
there remained nothing but a few broken, lonely black
pillars.

Brigid and Kane had looked upon dead cities before. They had seen Kharo-Khoto, the lost city of the
Black Gobi, and even the mysterious monuments of
Mars. But they had never looked upon a place more
somber and darkly poignant than this ruined and forgotten metropolis that brooded beneath the naked
stars. The spirit of an inconceivably ancient past
reached from it to lay cold fingers on their hearts.

A causeway of black stone led up toward the citadel.

"You scared?" Brigid asked.

"Hell, yes," he retorted. "What about you?"

"Terrified."

"Then the situation is normal. Let's go."

Kane and Brigid set their feet resolutely upon the
black causeway.

Chapter 23

Grant realized, as the explosion of the demolition charge caught him in the back blast, he couldn't escape the approaching rock slide. He glimpsed Kane staring at him through the tinted faceplate of his helmet, then a shower of shattered dark rock poured down from above.

Grant flung himself aside, leaping clear of the ledge. As he fell onto the cavern floor, he reflexively turned his fall into a roll.

He sprang to his feet, shielding his head with his arms as he ran toward a fissure in the wall to avoid being crushed by larger chunks of rock.

He lay, pinned down by the weight of the fallen stone, the slide vibrating deafeningly through his helmet. Finally, after what seemed like an interlocking chain of eternities, the reverberations of falling rock ceased.

Grant strained against the stone, trying to lever himself free, but it was a useless effort. His legs were pinned down, and though he felt no distinct pressure at any one point, an ache seemed to penetrate his entire body. He couldn't see or hear anything except the rasp of his respiration. He could only hope that

Brigid and Kane weren't caught in the slide and buried like him.

By craning his neck within his helmet, he glimpsed a glimmer of light through cracks in the stone. Within a few minutes he felt faint vibrations through the mass of rock. He guessed the patrol of men was working to clear away the rock slide. At least, he hoped it was the patrol and not the carnobots trying to dig him out like a piece of offal buried by a dog.

Grant felt the broken rock being removed from his legs even though his upper body was still trapped by a slab of stone. Even through the tough fabric of his boots, he felt a length of cable encircle his ankles then cinch tight. He swore as he realized they were binding him as they uncovered him. They were taking no chances.

Methodically, he felt knees pressing into his thighs and his arms were bent back and secured in a painful hammerlock. By the time the last chunk of rock had been removed from Grant's body, his wrists were bound at the small of his back and he was dragged ignominiously by his feet away from the heap of shattered stone. He made a couple of attempts to kick free, but the bindings were too tight.

The whole cavern was brightly illuminated by powerful halogen lamps on small, collapsible tripods. Ten men in EVA suits identical to his milled about him uncertainly. They looked down at him as if surprised by what they had caught. They were all tall, lean men of the same body type of the night-gaunts, the Furies he had fought in Chicago. Even through their face-plates, he saw the unnatural pallor of their flesh. He saw no sign of the carnobots, and he fervently hoped their metal carcasses lay somewhere beneath the tons of stone.

Grant carefully strained at the bindings around his wrists and explored with his fingertips. His Sin Eater was still secured to his forearm. Apparently his captors hadn't recognized it as a weapon and simply wrapped the cable around the end of the holster. Surreptitiously, he worked at it, trying to free it.

He had lost his Copperhead during the rock slide, and he swept his gaze over the armament of the men standing around him. Two of them carried spidery, riflelike blasters in their arms. The sectionalized barrels terminated in long cylinders, reminiscent of oversize sound suppressors. He guessed they were the three-piece plasma rifles Philboyd had mentioned.

The men walked around him, their expressions slightly troubled. He saw their lips moving but he heard nothing. Either his UTEL unit was damaged or they communicated on a completely different radio frequency. He assumed his helmet comm was inoperable, since he hadn't heard anything from either Kane or Brigid.

A tall man with a rifle gestured to him with the barrel, indicating that he should get up. Grant stared up at him blankly, uncomprehendingly. The man repeated the motion, then nudged him with a foot. Grant nodded, then made an elaborate show of struggling to rise. He rocked back and forth, as if trying to get his feet underneath him. He pretended his bound ankles hampered his efforts to rise.

The rifleman's face contorted in a grimace of annoyance, and he spoke a couple of words. A pair of men slid their arms through Grant's crooked elbows and heaved him upright—or they tried to. He deliberately let his body go slack without visibly appearing to do so. Despite the lighter gravity, his 235 pounds of dead, uncooperative weight took the men by surprise. When they finally managed to hoist him erect, he swayed, lost his balance and fell down on his left side.

Grant repressed a grin, imagining the kind of profanity filling his captors' helmets. They roughly pushed him onto his back, and a man knelt to untie the cables around his ankles—the hoped-for result of his subterfuge.

Once his legs were freed, the rifleman gestured for him to rise again. Grant placed the palms of his hands flat against the floor and pushed himself up. In the same motion, he flexed his wrist tendons, squeezing tightly so the actuators would be triggered even through the padding of the EVA suit. The Sin Eater slid from the holster, snagging for a second on the cable, then slapped comfortingly into his palm. As Grant rose, he twisted slightly and pressed the trigger stud. He felt the pistol buck in his hand, the recoil traveling up his arm. On the periphery of his vision, he saw a man clutch at his chest and kick backward from the floor, as though performing an acrobatic trick. The round hadn't penetrated the multilayered EVA suit, but the kinetic shock drove the man a score of feet backward.

While his companions gaped at him in goggle-eyed shock, Grant made a lunging rush toward the rifleman. His shoulder clipped the man and sent him spinning completely around. Raw blue energy blazed out of the extended barrel in a wide arc, engulfing the three members of the patrol.

Their bodies flamed up like torches. The visors of their helmets shattered as they fell. Grant stared at the sputtering, charred husks that had been men only seconds before and swallowed down bile.

One of the men reached for him and he dived low behind him, kicking him at ankle level. The man fell, the blaster jarred from his hands and Grant moved in, stamping in the visor of his helmet. Three stomps broke the glass, escaped atmosphere plumed up in a cloud, blinding everyone in the immediate vicinity.

Then Grant ran deep into the cavern, jerking at the cables pinning his wrists together. Bolts of blue stabbed through the darkness after him. He snapped off a shot behind him but he knew he didn't hit anything, and more than likely the patrol wasn't even aware he had fired.

Grant cursed, realizing his helmet light acted as a beacon. A stream of plasma streaked toward him. He bounded headlong into a wedge of shadow, feeling heat sear his back. He turned his leap into a somersault, dragging his bound wrists down along the backs of his legs. After a moment or two of skin-chafing, muscle-wrenching gyrations, he managed to pull his bound hands over the soles of his boots and put them in front of him.

Struggling dizzily to his feet, he set off at a shambling run, heedless of where he was going. His throat constricted, his lungs labored. Hammers of pain pounded at the walls of his skull. He didn't need to consult his oxygen gauge to know he was fast running out of air. However, he was fairly certain the patrol would find him before he asphyxiated.

He had moved in a perfect stealth pattern, circling outward between rocks, stalactites and searching men so that motion detectors would have difficulty differentiating him from their own.

He moved instinctively from cover to cover, from shadow patch to shadow patch, automatically placing his feet so they raised a minimum of dust and didn't dislodge loose stones. He studied places where sentries and blastermen might be lurking.

After a few minutes of cat and mousing without seeing so much as a flicker from the patrol's helmet lights, he hunkered down behind an outcropping and worked frantically on freeing his hands. It wasn't easy, but he managed to slip the loops of cable from his wrists. Although the prospect of being plunged into impenetrable blackness made his flesh crawl, he reached up and disconnected the light attached to the forepart of his helmet.

Once it went out, he was pleasantly surprised to realize he could still see, at least after a fashion. Light was coming from somewhere. Hazy and uncertain, it was just bright enough to permit him to see a few feet in front of him but too dim to make out shapes clearly.

With one hand on the rock wall, he moved through the cavern. The wall curved gradually to the left, and he saw the source of the light. A misty blue glow permeated a gallery, seeming to emanate from the walls like fog. He entered cautiously, noting the glow was a kind of phosphorescence.

As he walked deeper into the gallery, he saw drops of condensation beading his helmet's faceplate. It took his oxygen-starved brain a moment to understand the implications, and he came to a sudden halt.

He gazed around, seeing the gleam of moisture on stone and vaporous steam arising from points all over the Blue Gallery, as he named it. The steam wafted up from what appeared to be a peat bog at the far end of the gallery, and the sight rooted him in his tracks. Grant recalled what Philboyd had said about volcanism in the Moon, and he wondered if he had stumbled into a little pocket of such activity, like a hot springs.

Grant realized if there was steam then there was some sort of atmosphere. After a few seconds of trying to ponder the pros and cons, he undid the seals on his helmet and tentatively lifted it off. He sniffed the air experimentally, and despite an impaired sense of smell, a stench like a thousand open cesspits assaulted his nostrils. The air was thick, clammy and fetid but it was breathable. However, the stench was so repulsive he wasn't sure if he didn't prefer suffocating inside his helmet.

Nevertheless he stood there and inhaled slowly through his mouth, enriching his lungs. By degrees, his fierce headache ebbed, even though a sulfurous taste coated his tongue. He had no idea how there could be an atmosphere of any sort within the Moon, but he wasn't inclined to investigate the mystery. He would leave that up to Brigid. A muted, stealthy sound reached his ears. A breathable atmosphere also conducted sound, and he tried to quiet his breathing.

Dim shapes came into view, moving out through the haze from the right. Dropping onto his hands and knees, Grant crawled headlong into the peat bog, algae occluding his vision. He struck out for the far side, moving through the muck as quietly as he could. His boots struck solid footing, and he pushed himself across the pond. The bottom rose beneath him, slanting upward, and he lifted his head onto the bank.

The patrol was behind him, and it was also turned away. Grant crawled up onto the cavern floor and kept to the shadows as much as possible. Stealthily, he slipped through the haze-shrouded gallery. Keeping always within the shadows of the outcroppings, he crept soundlessly over the cavern floor. He breathed more easily when he couldn't see so much as an outline of the patrol.

He stood—just as the carnobot sprang at him. Grant had no time to bring his Sin Eater to bear. The torrent of flame that washed over its alloyed hide seemed to come from nowhere. The robot rose on its hind legs, wrapped in a wreath of fire, then its body exploded outward. Seams split, spewing sparks and smoke. Bits of metal pattered down around him.

Grant, too numbed to do more than gape at the wreckage clattering over the rock floor, didn't immediately respond to the male voice saying, "Come on! We don't have much time!"

Turning slightly, he saw a medium-sized man stepping out of a fissure in the gallery wall, brandishing a plasma rifle. His hair was cut short like Neukirk's, only it was black. He wore a one-piece zippered coverall like the people he had met at the base. "Who the hell are you?" Grant demanded.

The man said with an angry impatience, "It doesn't matter right now. We both have limited time to reach the citadel."

Grant stepped closer to him. A small circular body, gleaming like brushed aluminum, was attached to his mastoid bone. From it stretched ten tiny wires, like spider legs made of jointed alloy, each one tipped with a curving claw. Each of the claws appeared deeply embedded in the man's flesh.

His belly turned a cold flip-flop. "You've been tagged by the Furies."

The man nodded grimly. "That's why my time is limited. Once she—"

The man jerked convulsively, dropping the plasma rifle. He clawed at the silver spider on the side of his neck. A halo of pale blue light sprang up and shimmered around it.

The man's body swayed, and the sway became a tremble, then the tremble turned into a spasm. His eyes remained open, but they didn't see. His mouth gaped open, but no words came out. He croaked a sound of pain and terror and agony.

Grant took a hasty step back, horror filling his mind.

With a faint crackling sound similar to that of burning wood, a gray pallor suddenly swept over the man's body, spreading out from the device attached to his neck. Before Grant's eyes, his flesh and clothes were transmuted to an ash-gray substance. It swiftly darkened, becoming like a layer of anthracite between one eye blink and another.

The man's back arched violently, as if he had received a heavy blow between the shoulders. His arms contorted and drew up like the gnarled branches of a leafless tree as the blanket of dark gray petrifaction crept over his torso and down his legs.

A ghastly dry gargling came from his mouth, then the gray tide covered his lips, smothering his voice. Within another pair of eye blinks, a coal-black calcified statue knelt before the podium. The silver spider seemed to have dissolved, absorbed by the same process that turned flesh to carbon.

A ghostly voice caressed his ears. "He thought to

escape my judgment. Like so many others, he was deluded.''

He recognized the voice as belonging to Megaera. She stepped out of the fissure and around the black statue. Grant's finger touched the trigger stud of his Sin Eater, then he became aware of movement in the fog around him.

Half a dozen tall, lean men, as gaunt as cadavers, closed in on him, moving with measured deliberation. From throat to fingertip to heel they were clad in one-piece black garments that fitted as tightly as doeskin gloves. Even their heads were hooded in tight black cowls. They bore Oubolus rods in their hands. Beneath the cowls their visages were smooth, featureless ovals.

Megaera lovingly caressed the gems on the band encircling her right wrist. ''But as for you,'' she said in a low croon, ''the great god Enki himself will pass judgment.''

BRIGID'S HELMET LIGHT flashed its bright beam along the gloomy passage. It disclosed a maze of squared chambers and galleries that long, long ago had been hewed out of the citadel's base. The first chamber they looked into held the wreckage of an ancient chemical laboratory. There had been racks of instruments and receptacles, but they were smashed and scattered.

Kane and Brigid moved on from one great chamber to another. They saw a battery of what seemed to have once been a series of generators. Another chamber held the ruins of a pump apparatus that she guessed had been used for oxygenation. Other, smaller chambers seemed to have been living quarters.

"This is the place of the Annunaki," Brigid breathed in a hushed voice.

They moved on along the passageway and saw the vague outlines of towering metal shapes rising out of the dimness ahead. They were big mechanisms of such an unfamiliar design their purpose was unfathomable. One was a complexity of cogged wheels of silver metal, geared to a sliding hollow cylinder that suggested the barrel of an artillery piece. Another was a massive upright metal bulb that suggested nothing. Upon the base of each machine was a lengthy inscription in Sumerian.

"If I could only read those," Brigid said in angry frustration.

Kane knew she was feeling the strain of apprehension. The knowledge that somewhere ahead of them waited the last of the Serpent Kings and behind them Grant's unknown fate was like a lit match on the tender flesh of her mind.

Suddenly, a high-pitched whine reverberated through his helmet. He came to a sudden halt, lifting his Sin Eater. "Do you hear that?" he demanded.

Brigid stopped and looked around. "I hear something," she admitted at length. "Like the vibrations of machinery we heard before."

"How can we hear it through our helmets?"

"Maybe we're passing through a sonic field of some sort."

Standing motionless, listening intently, he cast his eyes quickly around. He could see nothing but the mysterious, sinisterly silent machines towering about him in the red-lit murk. They crept forward, both people moving soundlessly. Kane took the point, walking heel to toe as he always did in a potential killzone.

"There's a legend associated with Enki," Brigid said quietly, almost reluctantly. "Something about his command of the thunder. It was so powerful, it crushed his enemies."

Kane said dismissively, "Whatever we're hearing, it isn't thunder, Baptiste."

"Not yet, anyway," she retorted.

The whine seemed to rise in pitch with every step they took, straining to hit an ultrahigh frequency and put it out of the range of audibility. He almost wished it would happen. A cry of pain from Brigid galvanized him, caused him to skip around, heart pounding.

She clutched futilely at the sides of her helmet. Through clenched teeth, she said, "Whatever the sound is, it's feeding through our helmet comms, turning them into receivers."

Kane said, "Maybe we can disconnect them."

A white-hot wire seemed to lance through his head, passing into one ear and out the other. He was only dimly aware of crying out. Over the humming sleet storm of agony in his head, he heard Brigid blurt, "The Thunder of Enki!"

Sound could grow too deep, too high or simply too loud for the human ear to record. But the Thunder of Enki had an unbearable depth, an intolerable volume, yet the ear and the mind were keenly responsive to its resonance and did not grow numb or dulled.

Its terrible sweetness was beyond human endurance. It suffocated them in a shivering blanket of vibration that was edged with fangs. Kane gasped and struggled. He was aware that Brigid held her hands over the sides of her helmet, but he didn't realize he was writhing on the floor, too consumed with agony even to scream.

Epilogue

Domi returned the red-eyed glare of the slavering three-headed hound on the wall. She wondered briefly if they were baring their fangs in snarls or grins. At the moment, she felt like doing both.

Grasping the green lever inset into the wall beside the illustration of Cerberus, she pulled it to a midpoint position. With a rumble and whine of buried hydraulics and gears, the massive sec door began folding aside, opening like an accordion. It was so heavy, it took nearly half a minute for it to open just enough to allow her to step out onto the mountain plateau. Sunrise flooded the broad plateau with a golden radiance, striking highlights from the scraps of the chain link enclosing the perimeter. The air smelled fresh, rich with the hint of spring growth wafting up from the foothills far below. It still carried a chill and she shivered.

Domi turned at the sound of a footfall behind her. Lakesh stepped through the opening in the sec door, smoothing down his hair, still disheveled from sleep. He gazed reproachfully at her with bleary eyes.

"Darlingest one," he said severely, "you could have waited for me. I'm not my best this early in the morning. Besides, what can be so important that you rouse me literally at the crack of dawn and tell me to follow you out here?''

Quietly, as if she feared waking the other residents of the redoubt, she said, ''We have guests arriving.''

Lakesh's eyes went wide in surprise, then narrowed with a wary skepticism. ''How can you possibly know that?''

''A trans-comm call came in a little while ago,'' she replied. ''Farrell received it. He woke me up to tell me he couldn't find you.''

''A trans-comm call?'' Lakesh echoed incredulously. ''From whom?''

''Sky Dog.''

Lakesh nodded in understanding. Sky Dog's band of Sioux and Cheyenne were the Cerberus redoubt's nearest neighbors—its only neighbors, for that matter. Not so much a chief as a shaman, a warrior priest, Sky Dog was Cobaltville-bred like they were. Unlike them, he had been exiled from the ville while still a youth due to his Lakota ancestry. He joined a band of Cheyenne and Sioux living in the foothills of the Bitterroot Range and eventually earned a position of high authority and respect among them.

Kane, on one of his visits, had entrusted the man with one of the trans-comm units. Though its range was limited to a couple of miles, it was better than no means of communication at all.

''So when Sky Dog made the call,'' Lakesh said, ''he was already in sight of our front door.''

"Yeah."

"Why is he coming here at such an ungodly hour?"

"He's bringing…" Domi paused as if groping for the proper term. "Something that belongs to Kane."

Lakesh frowned, becoming annoyed at the vague information Domi was supplying. "Something he left in the village during one of his trips down there? That makes no sense. Whatever it was, it couldn't have been that important."

Domi turned to favor him with an intense stare he found discomfiting. "No, Lakesh," she said softly. "It's not something he left in the village. It's something Kane never talked about with anybody here. He never talked about it with me, either, but that's because I already knew about it. Or I knew the possibility this day might come."

A chill caused Lakesh to shiver, but it wasn't due to the temperature. Fingers of dread knotted in his stomach. "This involves your captivity in Area 51, doesn't it?"

She nodded once, a short jerk of her white-haired head, and she fell silent. Lakesh waited for her to say more, and when she didn't he was on the verge of demanding further explanation when the steady clop-clop of hooves on asphalt reached his ears.

Domi tensed, watching the point where the plateau narrowed down into the road. The sound grew louder and Lakesh realized two horses were approaching, coming up the incline. Silhouetted against the rising sun, two figures mounted on horseback appeared at the edge of the plateau.

"Sky Dog," Domi murmured.

Lakesh had never met the shaman, permitting Kane to act as both ambassador and liaison. He squinted at the second figure astride a pony. Even in the uncertain light, he could see the figure was very slight of build, almost childlike. A blanket lay draped over the head and shoulders.

"Who is that other one?" Lakesh asked.

Domi didn't answer. She strode quickly forward to meet them. Sky Dog reined his horse to a halt and gestured to her. "*Hou, mita cola,* Domi. It's been a while."

Domi acknowledged the comment with a jittery smile. She moved swiftly to the other mounted person and spoke in such low murmurs, Lakesh couldn't catch a single word. He glanced up at Sky Dog. The man's face was lean and sharply planed with wide cheekbones and narrow eyes the color of obsidian. Shiny black hair plaited in two braids fell almost to his waist. Behind his right ear, a single white eagle feather dangled.

"I'm Sky Dog," he said pleasantly. "I don't believe I've had the pleasure."

Lakesh stepped forward, extending a hand. "My name is Lakesh. I've heard a lot about you, sir."

Sky Dog's eyes flashed with surprise. "Same here, Lakesh. I have to confess you don't look anything like the man I expected."

He clasped Lakesh's hand tightly. Lakesh winced a bit at the strength of the man's grip and replied, "I've had what used to be called a makeover. What brings you here?"

Sky Dog's face registered surprise a second time. "You mean you don't know?"

He jerked his head toward the blanket-swathed figure who Domi was helping dismount. "She showed up in my village two days ago, begging to be brought here. She claimed she knew all of you, particularly Kane. She said it was a matter of life and death."

Lakesh gazed suspiciously at the figure. "Whose life?"

When the blanket dropped, his suspicious gaze become a gape of goggle-eyed shock. The hybrid female was small, smaller even than Domi. Her huge, up-slanting eyes of a clear crystal blue gave Lakesh a silent appraisal. They looked haunted. White hair the texture of silk threads fell from her domed-skull and curled inward at her slender shoulders.

Her compact, tiny-breasted form was encased in a silvery-gray, skintight bodysuit. It only accentuated the distended condition of her belly. Lakesh's experience with pregnant women was exceptionally slight, but he guessed she was at least six months along.

Holding her belly with both long-fingered hands, she said in a high, almost childlike voice, "*This* life. My name is Quavell, and I have traveled a very long way in order to save it."

A state-of-the-art conspiracy opens the gates of
Hell in the Middle East....

PRELUDE
TO WAR

A team of brilliant computer specialists and stategists
and a field force of battle-hardened commandos make
rapid-deployment repsonses to world crises. But now even
Stony Man has met its match: a techno-genius whose cyber
army has lit the fuse of war in the Middle East. Stony Man's
Phoenix Force hits the ground running at the scene, racing
against time to stop an all-out conflagration that promises
to trap America in the flames.

*Available in
June 2002
at your favorite
retail outlet.*

Stony Man is deployed against an armed invastion
on American soil....

DEFENSIVE ACTION

A conspiracy to cripple a sophisticated antimissle system—and
the United States itself—is under way, fueled by the twisted
ideology of a domestic militia group. Their campaign against the
government has gone global, their terrorist agenda refinanced
and expanded by a cabal of America's enemies: North Korea,
Russia and China. Crisscrossing the North American continent,
Stony Man enters a desperate race against time to halt this act of
attrition…before America pays the price in blood.

STONY MAN

*Available in
August 2002
at your favorite
retail outlet.*

OUTLANDERS®

FROM THE CREATOR OF

DEATH LANDS®

AMERICA'S POST-HOLOCAUST HISTORY CONTINUES....